THE
INDIGO
PRESS

OGADINMA
Or,
EVERYTHING
WILL BE ALL RIGHT

OGADINMA
Or,
EVERYTHING WILL BE ALL RIGHT

UKAMAKA OLISAKWE

THE
INDIGO
PRESS

THE INDIGO PRESS
50 Albemarle Street
London W1S 4BD
www.theindigopress.com

The Indigo Press Publishing Limited Reg. No. 10995574
Registered Office: Wellesley House, Duke of Wellington Avenue
Royal Arsenal, London SE18 6SS

First published in Great Britain in 2020 by The Indigo Press
A CIP catalogue record for this book is available from the British Library

ISBN: 978-1-911648-16-1
eBook ISBN: 978-1-911648-17-8

Design by www.salu.io
Typeset in Goudy Old Style by Tetragon, London
Printed and bound in Great Britain by TJ International, Padstow

For my children,
Chidinma, Chisom, and Chukwubuikem,
umu chi m jili gozie m.

PART 1

1

It was the early eighties, around the time a group of senior army officers overthrew the democratically elected government, when Austrian lace and aso-oke were trendy and church services were fashion shows – an endless, shameless carnival of women in colourful blouses blended with expensive ichafu which they tied in layers and pleats until the scarves were piled atop their heads like large plants, obstructing the view of everyone seated behind them. Everyone looked forward to Sundays, to going to church. Those who could not afford these processions snuck in very early for the children's service, because that was the graceful thing to do – to worship with children in their simple clothes of cheap blouses over Nigerian wax, and okrika shoes whose heels had worn out and made *koi-koi-koi* sounds on the tiled floor.

It was on a Monday after one of those Sundays that Ogadinma walked into Barrister Chima's office for the first time.

The room was empty. The fan whirled, scattering the papers on the cluttered desk. They floated to the floor, slid under the table, under the chair, by the door and by her feet. She wondered if it would be awkward to walk in uninvited and pick them up. She knocked again, louder this time. 'Hello!' she called out, her voice echoing. There was a click of heels. A girl emerged from the connecting door, her blue skirt so short she would not be comfortable if she were to bend over to get the papers. The name tag pinned to her white blouse said she was 'Amara'.

'What do you want?' she asked, her gaze piercing.

'Your papers,' Ogadinma pointed at the floor, but Amara wrinkled her nose, ignoring the scattered sheets, arching an eyebrow. 'I am looking for Barrister Chima,' Ogadinma said, bringing out the business card her father gave her, holding it up for Amara to see.

'Come in,' Amara said, waving her into the waiting room, and only after Ogadinma had gone in did Amara crouch carefully – not bend, because she could never bend without exposing her underwear – to pick up the scattered papers.

When her father described the address, Ogadinma had expected a proper workplace, or at least, a hall split into cubicles. She had never been in a barrister's office and so did not know what the place would look like. But this was anything but an office. It was a typical two- or three-bedroom flat, the same model many houses around the area replicated. Without being told, she knew that the 'waiting room' was originally designed to be a parlour, that the connecting door led to Barrister Chima's office, which most likely had a master toilet. A small TV, half the size of her family's Philips black-and-white TV, was locked away in a metal cage knocked into the wall. She resisted the urge to laugh, because who on God's earth would want anything to do with that toy?

Amara returned but headed straight for the barrister's office. 'Barrister Chima will see you after he is done attending to the client inside,' she said when she re-emerged, an exaggerated air of importance about her.

Ogadinma began to say 'thank you', but Amara was already koi-koi-ing away. She looked no more than seventeen or eighteen, perhaps a secondary school leaver like Ogadinma, who was passing time as a receptionist while waiting for a university admission letter.

A short bespectacled man walked in and took the seat opposite. Ogadinma greeted him but the man did not respond. Soon other visitors arrived, some wearing long faces, others tapping their feet impatiently after a few minutes. Ogadinma wondered what cases they were battling, or if they had also come to seek Barrister Chima's help with things like getting an admission into a university. She opened her bag and brought out her JAMB result: 240. Good enough to get her an admission into the state university. But her father wanted her to study in the east, so she had chosen the University of Nigeria in Nsukka. Nsukka was a place they barely knew: plus, often, the number of students that passed the exam exceeded the capacity a school could admit, so it was customary to go through people who knew powerful staff in a university. Why they needed Barrister Chima's help.

She folded the test result into her handbag. The room had filled to bursting. Visitors were sitting, standing, hanging by the door. A man came out of Barrister Chima's office, dragging a walking stick. He adjusted his glasses and made for the reception.

Amara went into the office and returned seconds later. 'Barrister Chima will see you now,' she told Ogadinma. Her skirt had ridden higher up her thighs.

The barrister was seated behind his desk, his head bent over a sheaf of paper, the room chilled to freezing point, the shelves cluttered with law books.

'Good morning, sir,' Ogadinma said, and stood waiting for the invitation to sit. He lifted his head, a man not much older than her father, but with features so striking it was as though his face was chiselled out of fine wood, his skin the colour of roasted groundnut husk. He waved her over to the only chair across from his desk and held her gaze with eyes that made her forget how to speak, how to move. She became conscious of her outfit, the loose skirt that stopped at her ankles, her cornrows that were old and fuzzy. Her heart was scudding hard.

'Good morning, sir,' she said again, folding her hands on her lap. She could not hold his gaze, and so she stared at a spot on his chest.

'How old are you?' he said.

'I am seventeen.'

'You don't look seventeen at all.'

She waited for him to say how old she looked. He didn't. Instead he went on to ask questions about her visit: who sent her, who her father was. 'I have never met him,' he said, his tone dismissive. 'I don't know how he got my card.'

He was speaking too fast. Ogadinma wanted to explain that her father got the contact through a customer who spoke highly of Barrister Chima. But the words were clogged in her throat; he was talking too fast. He was in a haste to send her on her way, or he was orchestrating this to make her miserable. She moved closer to the edge of her chair, her hands held out, and when she spoke, she could barely hear herself.

'Help me, please. I don't want to stay at home for one year doing nothing,' she said, her hands still bunched together. 'Please, help me, sir.'

He was looking at her, his eyes unblinking. Ogadinma lowered her eyes, dug her fingernails into her palms. There was a knock and then the door opened. Amara looked in, passed a curious glance at her before turning to her boss. 'Madam Afuecheta is here. I have told her to wait. She is crying,' she said.

Barrister Chima nodded, and Amara left. When he spoke again, his words were slower. 'I am going to attend to a desperate client. Will you come back by three, so we can talk about this admission you seek?'

She was bobbing her head even before he was done speaking. 'Yes, sir, I will come back by three. Thank you so much, sir.'

But he had returned to the sheaf of papers. Her cue to leave. She thanked him again, furiously. When she walked into the hot waiting room, she was so giddy she almost stumbled. She was able to breathe again.

Her father wanted to know how the trip went. 'I phoned my customer and he said he spoke with Barrister Chima this morning, before you left to see him. He said Barrister Chima was eager to meet you. So, how did it go?'

She swallowed her surprise. 'He has agreed to help me, Papa,' she told him. She would not share details of the awkward first meeting. 'He said I should return by three to start the process.'

Her father was ecstatic. Ogadinma counted the seconds until afternoon came. When she walked into Barrister Chima's office, the place was empty and Amara had kicked off her heels and was walking around in flip-flops which made *slap-slap-slap* sounds under her feet. Barrister Chima asked her to wait for a minute and then she waited for thirty. Then he emerged from his office, carrying his bag.

'Come with me,' he told her, and she followed. He gave her the bag to hold as they went down the flight of stairs. And she held it, happiness fluttering in her heart. This was progress. He was no longer as stuck-up as before. Everything would work out fine.

Outside, he led the way to a Mercedes parked by the side of the road. 'I am so hungry. Have you eaten yet?' he asked as he fished for his key in his pocket.

She had snacked on meat pie and Coca-Cola, so she bobbed her head. 'Yes sir, I have eaten.'

'Now you will watch me do as you have done. Get in the car,' he said, laughter in his voice. It unsettled and tickled her. She got into the car. He folded his long frame into the small compartment, revved the engine and turned to her. 'Choose the music: hip-hop or R&B?'

'R&B.'

He pulled the car off the pavement, his gaze half on the road and half on her face as he worked the stereo. 'Who is your favourite?'

'Diana Ross,' she said.

'Great! You have passed your first test.' He looked like a boy when he laughed. Diana Ross and Lionel Richie's voices floated into the car. He sang along to 'Endless Love'. Ogadinma watched him, cautiously. When he glanced at her, still miming to the music, she offered a small smile.

'Come on! Sing with me, I thought you loved her.'

Music, laughter: the perfect way to spend an afternoon with someone else, someone like Mary, her childhood friend. Mary was wild and fearless. She would definitely sing along with Barrister Chima. But Barrister Chima made Ogadinma uncomfortable and she did not want to sing with him. And so she imagined she was alone in her room, or with a friend, maybe Emeka from her secondary school. Emeka loved Lionel Richie and Marvin Gaye. Ogadinma had always liked Emeka. Back in school, they trekked home together, had lunch together, were almost boyfriend and girlfriend, until that day when he invited her to his home on Aitken Road and she refused to join him. He had been hurt by that rejection. For many days, he would not speak to her or look at her. She still liked him, still longed for the moments they shared together. She shut her eyes and imagined she was in the car with Emeka. And soon her voice, tiny and melodious, pierced the air.

Barrister Chima drove past her street, and all the way to the quiet, residential area of Nomansland, the street on the fringes of the safe haven Sabon Gari provided during the religious riots. She had only been to Nomansland once in her entire life. Barrister Chima rolled the car to a stop in front of a white bungalow. 'We are home,' he said, and headed for the gate. He did not stop to see the confusion on her face.

'I thought we were going to a restaurant,' she said.

He whipped around. Frowned. 'I cook my own food,' he said.

She wanted to ask why he didn't tell her that he was bringing her to his house, but she didn't need to. She only looked at him, at the criss-crossed lines crumpling his forehead, each one thickened with tension, and knew that this was what he wanted and she must either abide by his rules or forget about the university. He unlocked the gate and walked inside the compound, and she hurried behind him. He paused for her to catch up, then he threw a hand over her shoulder.

He unlocked the door, ushered her into the dark room and flipped the light switch. The fluorescent lamp flooded light into the parlour, which was cramped with brown leatherette sofas, a glass centre table and a large TV with two antennae sticking out from behind it. He disappeared into a connecting room. She walked over to stare at the TV and spread her hands to measure its width.

He returned, clutching a bottle of Maltex. 'Do you want me to switch that on for you?' He set the drink on a side table.

She sat. 'Yes. Thank you.' She refrained from adding 'sir'.

He was barefoot, and he had untucked his shirt and folded the cuffs to his elbows. His arms rippled with muscles.

He switched on the TV and stood, gazing, as NTA belted out news. The United States had taken sides with the pro-Jumayyil Christian brigades of the Lebanese Army in the Mountain War, killing any hope of reuniting the Lebanese Christians and the Muslims.

'Have you been following the US involvement in the Lebanese Civil War?' His gaze was still on the news.

'No.'

'The United States is not helping matters at all. They have just shelled the centres populated by the Druze people and the Shia Muslims, proving everyone's suspicion all along that they didn't get involved in the war to broker peace, but to side with the Lebanese Christians! This is not good at all.' He whipped around, his features tense. 'Do you know what that means, how this will trigger reprisal attacks against the American properties and citizens in Lebanon? How this can even affect Nigeria? You know how our Muslim neighbours think. Ronald Reagan must step aside and stop pouring more fuel on a burning fire!'

Ogadinma glanced at the screen and back at him. Her palms had grown wet. The last thing in the world she needed was to be in Barrister Chima's house, to be in the house of a man who was not her father. People would find out. Sabon Gari was such a small place; neighbours always bumped into each other on the streets. They would see her leaving Barrister Chima's house and they would whisper. The rumour would spread in the neighbourhood. To the church. Into her father's ears. And she would be in trouble. She rubbed her palms on her skirt.

'Do you follow world news at all?'

She took a deep breath. 'I watch the news, but not all the time,' she said.

'What course do you want to study at university?'

'Literature.'

He frowned. 'Interesting. And how are you going to succeed in commenting on books if you don't know what is happening in the world? Do you read newspapers?'

She sat straighter, her knees pressed together. Why was he asking all these questions? What had they to do with helping her get admission into the university? 'I read *Punch* and *Tribune*. My father brings them home every day.'

'And beyond Diana Ross and reading newspapers, what other things do you love to do?'

'I write.'

'What do you write?'

'Stories.'

He arched his brows.

'I make diary entries. I writes short stories when I am bored. I read a lot of books, too.'

He looked dubious. 'Who do you read?'

'Frederick Forsyth. Sydney Sheldon. James Hadley Chase. Chinua Achebe—'

'Please don't mention Chinua Achebe. He's a compulsory read in schools, right? Whether you like him or not.'

'Yes. But I have read his other books which aren't on the curriculum. I also read other books, mostly everything in the library on Okonkwo Avenue, all the African Writers Series. Ngugi wa Thiong'o, Ama Ata Aidoo. Bessie Head, Nadine Gordimer.' She was out of breath. He had made her uncomfortable with his questions, with his gaze, and how he hovered above her. Her heart thudded too fast. She tried to breathe calmly, but she knew he enjoyed making her uncomfortable. It was in the way he smiled, the way he towered over her. He made her feel so small.

'Does that library still function? The one on Okonkwo Avenue,' he said.

She swallowed and said, 'They have closed down now. There are no more libraries around here.'

He regarded her for a minute. 'I will get you some books when I visit Lagos next week.'

'Thank you.' She smiled cautiously.

'I like the way you smile,' he said. 'Come here.'

A pause. He urged her with a lift of his brow.

What was he trying to do? As she went to him, her heart pushing painfully against her chest, she thought of what it was he wanted to do. Hug her? Kiss her? What? She glanced fleetingly at the door; there was a small part of her that told her to race to the door, but she didn't. She wanted to go to school. When she got that admission, she would never speak to this man again. She would never have to visit him ever again. She stood before him, glanced at his face and lowered her eyes immediately.

'Are you afraid of me?' He touched her cheek.

Her hands trembled violently. 'No.'

'So why are you staring at your feet?'

'Sorry,' she whispered.

He pulled her closer, left his hand to rest against her cheek. 'Are you afraid of me?'

She nodded. 'Yes.'

'You don't have to be.' He cupped her face, rubbed the sides of her lips with his fingers. Bent down and pressed his mouth against hers. She steeled herself, pinched her lips shut, but he prodded and they slackened. His erection rubbed against her stomach. She averted her face and he grabbed her buttocks.

'Come.' He pulled her through the connecting door. She was walking in a daze. The passageway melted into the room where white light flooded in from the tall windows. She was falling, and he was crushing her on the soft bed, his smell of muted perfume and sweat filling her nose.

'I have never done this before,' she said. 'Please.'

'Then I promise I will go slowly. I won't hurt you.' He started to tug at her underwear, her skirt. 'You have my word.'

There was a moment when a scream came to her throat, but she clamped her lips shut. She would be going to the university. She would get into the best university. She would study Literature, and all of this would no longer matter. She spoke these words to herself, even when her body stretched and a sharp pain travelled swiftly to her waist. He arched above her, his thrusts feverish, his face contorted into an ugly mask. Dollops of sweat from his face and neck spattered on her chest, her breasts. The room was so bright; outside the window the sun shone with passionate intensity. A lone bird flew past, and she thought how wonderful it would be to wing into the sky and fly away, far away from here.

He made a sound, an animal choking. And then he collapsed on her body and rolled off to his side of the bed.

'Are you crying?'

She swiped at her face. 'No.'

She sat up. There was blood on the sheet between her legs. She did not even begin to think where this came from, what this meant. She only concentrated on pacing her breathing and blinking fast to hold back her tears. He was looking at the stain too. He inspected his flaccid penis, confusion and satisfaction on his face at the sight of the blotch of blood on the tip.

He pulled her to his chest, held her for a second, left her. 'Go to the bathroom and wash. I will change the sheets and make us some spaghetti and fish. You eat spaghetti? That's my favourite food in the whole world.'

She came to hate spaghetti after she had shat a tapeworm when she was seven or eight. The worm was the length and colour of a cooked spaghetti strand.

In the bathroom, she climbed into the white tub and turned on the tap to fill up the red bucket sitting under it. She scooped water and splashed between her legs, then rust-coloured goo slid down her legs and rushed down the drain.

When she returned, Barrister Chima had changed the sheet, and her dress was folded neatly on the bed. He was whistling a tune in the kitchen, banging pots and spoons. She put on her clothes and returned to the parlour. She looked down at the stool before her, where the sweating bottle of Maltex still sat waiting for her. And she knew that this bottle would always trigger sad memories, that she would never ever drink this brand of malt again. She pushed the stool away, further from her line of sight, and then returned her gaze to the TV. But she could no longer hear what was being said because she was busy pushing the memories of today away from her mind, folding them into careful sizes and chucking them into her mental loft, so that even if she ever looked back, she would never again know the horror she had experienced.

He emerged half an hour later with a bowl of spaghetti and fish. They ate, sitting side by side on the sofa, their eyes fixed on the TV.

'Do you like it?' he asked.

She nodded.

'I cook everything I eat. These restaurants are all dirty. Two years ago at Tropicana Restaurant, I saw a cockroach in the bowl of vegetable soup they served me. And that did it for me.' He chewed on a piece of fish. 'Do you cook?'

'I cook everything we eat.'

'Your mother doesn't help?'

She put her plate down. 'She left us.'

'Oh, baby. So sorry.' He touched her shoulder, her cheek. 'When did she die?'

'She is not dead!' she said curtly. 'My mother is not dead.' As if repeating the words would mean keeping her mother alive, wherever she was.

Barrister Chima was staring at her, his brows furrowed with what seemed like irritation.

She looked down at the blue ceramic plate with the gold trimming. She was too scared to look up again. She had behaved badly, had shouted at the man that was supposed to help her. She wished she could take her words back. And when he put his hand on her shoulder and rubbed it, she did not resist. All she did was stare at her plate and listen to his heavy breathing as he rubbed her cheek. Then he lifted her chin to meet his gaze.

'I am sorry I shouted,' she said.

'One day you will tell me about her?'

She lowered her eyes, and put the plate on the table.

'You didn't finish your food.'

'I am okay.'

'I should have asked the quantity you could finish.' He picked up her plate and headed to the kitchen.

'Thank you for the food,' she said, but he had already left. She grabbed her bag and placed it on her lap. When he returned, he looked at the bag and her face.

'We haven't talked about your admission yet.' He stood by the telephone, lifted the handset, stubbed a finger into the wheel and began to dial a number. He cradled the handset by his neck. 'So, tell me: what's your JAMB score?'

'Two hundred and forty.'

'That's a good score. And you chose Literature?'

'Yes.'

He held a hand over the mouthpiece and said, 'I am calling my brother at the university. He hasn't picked up the phone yet.'

Fear jumped in her throat. She sat forward, willed the man at the other end to pick up the phone. But Barrister Chima put the phone down.

'I will call him again at night.' He returned to her side, kissed her on the cheek. 'Everything is going to be all right, just like your name – or don't you think so?' He kissed her again. 'Your name is so apt. Ogadinma. *Everything is going to be all right.*'

'Yes,' she said.

'You want to watch a movie? I just bought this rare VHS player and some tapes. I have really good movies here.' His cheeks were dotted with pimples that had begun to ripen, the tips filled with pus.

'I have to go.' But she wanted to stay so that if his brother at the university called back she could listen to their conversation, and she would respond to his questions if he needed more details about her. The chair sucked her in. The clock on the wall behind the TV chimed. It was five already; her father would be home in an hour. She stood up. 'I really have to go home. My father will be home by six.'

'Oh, my poor baby.' He pulled her on to his lap, her back to him. He groped her breasts. She tried to slide off his lap but he pinned her with the other hand. She began to count; it was easier this way, counting, because she would not have to remember how she felt. She only had to remember how long she had counted. When he was done, she pulled on her clothes. She did not look at him. She grabbed her bag and headed for the door.

'Come by the office tomorrow and I will let you know what my brother thinks.'

She nodded, and stepped outside into the sun.

Her father had not yet returned when she got home. In the bathroom, she scrubbed herself vigorously, every inch of skin, everywhere Barrister Chima's hands had touched.

In her room, she brought out her JAMB result and stared at the part that said: FIRST CHOICE: UNIVERSITY OF NIGERIA, NSUKKA.

Only a year ago, she used to sit hunched in the school library that smelled of rotting wood, studying for her final senior secondary school exams. Afterwards, she would trek to her father's shop twenty minutes away, where she would have a late lunch. On one such occasion she had just settled into her father's chair and dug into a plate of jollof rice, while her father sat outside chatting with a neighbour, when they heard cries.

At first she did not understand what was happening, until her father rushed in and yelled *Hide under the table!* as he drew the metal doors shut. A blanket of darkness fell over them. Her father was crouched beside her, panting. They could hear the scuttle of feet outside, the screech of machete on tarred road, the smash of bottles, the piercing cries and chants of rioters. People ran up and down.

Someone slammed a metal club against their doors, again and again. Ogadinma peed on herself. Metal warred with metal. The doors did not yield, and he gave up. The air soon grew hot; things had been set on fire. And she was crippled with fear. Had they set the shop on fire? But then the chaos retreated slowly. The rioters carried their mayhem out of hearing range.

Her father opened the doors an hour later. His Peugeot pickup he had parked by the roadside was on fire. The same devastation was strewn all around Burma Road. Shopfronts were smashed in. The air was thick with the smell of something burning, like the familiar smell that hung heavy during Christmas, when her father slaughtered a goat and roasted off its hair and hooves on a tripod. But this was not the smell of a burning goat. She stepped outside. In the middle of the road were the charred remains of a man.

Later, they would learn that the riot started because their Muslim neighbours were angry with the Christians in nearby Fagge who were reconstructing a church situated too close to a mosque.

If the riot had not happened – if the boys had not burned down properties belonging to Christians, including her father – he would not have insisted that she choose a university in the east. She might just have been admitted in the north because that was much easier.

If she hadn't chosen the eastern university, they might not have needed Barrister Chima's help.

Months had passed since she filled out the form, and she wanted to reach back and choose another university. She could have chosen the University of Lagos. She would not have crossed paths with Barrister Chima. Things would have been as they used to be. But she had made that choice, and now she could not imagine retaking JAMB. She could not waste away at home for another year.

And so she returned to Barrister Chima the following day. He spoke with someone who requested her details. After he ended the call, he led her to his car again. They went home again, her heart thumping each time. Though disgust rose from her stomach and stained her tongue bitter, and she returned home to wash and scrub her body, she still went back to him again and again.

January came. It was time for the new academic session and students who had gotten admission letters were leaving home. Ogadinma's name had yet to appear on the admissions list. She continued to submit to Barrister Chima, and at home, she began to sleep too much.

'Your name will be on the last list,' he said one Monday afternoon, when she was so tired to the bones that she rested her head on his desk. 'Are you feeling ill? You look so dull,' he said, his voice heavy with concern.

'I think I have malaria.' She was dizzy.

He glanced at her dubiously and then he got out his wallet, brought out some cash, much more than she had ever received, and folded the notes into her palm. 'Here, go and take care of yourself,' he said.

She did not remember how she got home, but she slept all through the evening and until the next morning. When she opened her eyes again, her father was staring down at her, worry wrinkling his brow.

'We are going to the hospital,' he said. 'You don't look well at all.'

'But Papa, I have to go to Barrister Chima. The third list will be out today. My name will be on that list.'

He sank down on the space beside her. 'Your name is not on the list. Barrister Chima told my friend to tell you.'

She sat up. 'How, Papa?'

'You didn't meet the cut-off mark. The university set it at two hundred and fifty. We will try again next year.'

She opened and closed her mouth, and then a whimper left her lips. She held onto her father and wept until her stomach felt as though everything in it had been dug out. Later, he insisted they were going to the hospital still.

'I am fine, Papa. I am just tired,' she said, reassuring him and herself: perhaps if she did it convincingly everything would be all right, as it used to be.

It had always been the two of them since her mother left during the Biafran War, when their town fell. Though her father had never told her about it, how he returned from fighting the enemies, worn out and dried up, to learn that her mother had left. Ogadinma had gathered bits and pieces of the retellings of the story, fitting and stitching them together until she constructed a logical narrative: the war had tired her mother; the burden of caring for a constantly hungry baby tired her, and one morning, the day after their town fell to the Nigerian soldiers, she thrust Ogadinma into her mother-in-law's arms and walked out of the compound. She did not stop walking, not even when her grandmother gave chase, thrusting Ogadinma back into her hands. She did not hold Ogadinma and she did not stop walking.

If her father minded being unmarried all these years, he hadn't shown it. He didn't show it when he brought his sister, Aunty Okwy, from the village to live with them in Kano. He didn't show it those times his mother begged him to take another wife. He didn't show it when they travelled for Christmas and the wives of the umunna brought their daughters for him to choose from. Instead, he stripped the flat of her mother's memories. There were no pictures of her mother lying around, nothing for Ogadinma to hold onto as the years went by.

After her father left for his shop, Ogadinma checked the Michelin calendar hanging on her wall. The date was 18 January. She had been so obsessed with getting admission into the university that she had forgotten to check the dates; a month had passed since she last saw her period. Her knees weakened and she collapsed on the floor. Sweat beaded her forehead. From her position, she could see outside her window. A child was standing on the veranda of the opposite flat. Mary's flat. Mary was holidaying in Benin. Mary would know what to do with a pregnancy. Mary, who taught her how to roll papers into cigarettes, who dug up bugs and squashed them on their nipples when their breasts had yet to bud. The thought of Mary, of Mary's wildness and bravery, changed something in her, returned strength to her knees.

She stood and walked into the kitchen, opened the fridge and stared at the contents for a minute, before she reached for the limes in a compartment. She cut four of the limes and squeezed them into a cup, then she picked out the seeds and gulped down the juice in one swig. Her teeth rattled. Her stomach churned. She boiled water and drank it hastily, her mouth burning. Tears leaked out of her eyes.

Afterwards, she stepped onto the veranda and made for the stairs. Then she ran up and down the stairs, pausing only to catch her breath. Up and down, she went – ten, fifteen, twenty times. Her knees buckled and she limped to her room and wept.

'Is anything wrong with your legs? Why are you walking like that?' her father asked that evening, after she served him dinner, casting a worried glance at her face. 'You are walking somehow.'

'I bumped my foot against a stone, Papa. I am fine now.'

He looked at her, unconvinced. 'Ndo, go and rest. I will wash the plates later.'

In her room, she squeezed more limes into a cup and drank. Her stomach hurt. She balled her hands into fists, raised and brought them hard against her stomach, again and again, until she buckled under intense pain.

That night, she woke frequently to check her underwear for blood spotting, but only found her clean panty lining staring back.

She continued the routine: running up and down the stairs, drinking warm water, drinking lime juice. The torture changed nothing. At the end of the month, vomit began to rise to her throat. Sour-smelling spittle filled her mouth. She hated the smell of fried onions; she developed strong aversions. And she slept too much.

One morning, an idea crept into her mind and grew root: she would go to the hospital, the massive three-storey building one street away from their home. She would take care of herself. Wasn't that what Barrister Chima told her when he gave her money the other time, *take care of yourself?* She would go to the hospital and she would give them a fake name and address. She would not speak to anyone except the doctor. She counted the money Barrister Chima had given her and stuffed it into her bag.

When she walked into the hall of the hospital, the receptionist, a pinched-faced woman who threw her a suspicious look, gave her a form to fill. Her hand was steady. She wrote down the name Ijeoma Nnedi and gave an address in faraway Brigade area on the outskirts of her suburb. She did not feel nervous; her heart did not thud frantically. She bristled with such confidence that when she took a seat and waited for her turn to see a doctor, she wondered why she had bowed to fear and hadn't come earlier.

The doctor, a tall fair man in blue jeans, offered her a seat and asked what ailed her.

She stared at the cluttered desk. 'My period was supposed to be here two months ago. I want it to come out.'

For a moment she feared the doctor would fly into a rage. 'Have you told anyone this?' he asked instead. She said no.

The doctor asked if she had had unprotected sex, and how many times. She returned her gaze to his desk, and responded to each question, her mind partly leaving her body, travelling to Barrister Chima's office, to that first day she walked in and the fan whirled, scattering the papers on the desk. She should have taken that as a sign that things were going bad, that everything would float out of her control. She began to cry. The doctor watched her cry and after she was done, he asked her to lie on the table by the side of the room. She did as she was told, stared at the ceiling as the doctor felt her stomach, pinched her nipples.

When she got down from the table and returned to sit before him, he told her the cost and she handed him all the money Barrister Chima gave her. He shoved the notes into his drawer without counting, and then scribbled down an address where she must meet him by afternoon.

'We don't do that in this facility. It is illegal,' he said. 'But I want to help you. You are still young, and you just made a mistake.'

She folded the address slip into her handbag. She could finally breathe well.

The address was on Enugu Road, four streets from their home. An old woman dozed in front of a TV, her cornrows a dusty white, her neck hanging at an awkward angle. Two small girls, no older than four, chased after each other in the flat, both of them wearing plastic tiaras. They ran past Ogadinma, laughing as they made for a connecting door, and long after the doctor had appeared by the door of an adjacent room and summoned her in, she still heard them giggling.

The doctor led her to a bedroom and told her to take off her clothes. 'Lie on the bed after you are done,' he said, and then he left. The girls appeared by the door, watching her remove her underwear, both of them huddled together. They were actually twins, alike in every way. They giggled and fled just as the doctor came in with two women. She wanted to ask if the girls were his children, why they were roaming freely, peeking in to watch her undress.

She climbed on the bed and lay on her back. She drew in a breath when the doctor raised her knees and spread her legs open. She shut her eyes when he probed her with his gloved hands. Seconds slowed to forever. Cold metal slithered into her body, into her womb, churning her stomach. Sharp pain travelled down her back, singed her waist, her knees. She was trembling, sweating. Cries came to her throat. The women held her legs in place as the doctor worked metals in her body, swirling objects, and then forcing in a large syringe. Her waist was on fire, her eyes pressed with tears. The doctor and the women did not look at her face.

'She has a retroverted uterus,' he said, and the women bent over to peep. Then they carried on with their activities. If they noticed her discomfort, they did not acknowledge it, not even when the first cries slipped from her lips.

She thought of Barrister Chima, mustering all the hate she could. She thought of all the ways she could hurt him if she had the means, and then she wanted to hit herself for being so stupid.

After the doctor was done, she avoided the women's eyes as they wiped her clean, even when they slid a Comfit pad between her legs and pulled on her underwear. When she climbed out of the bed, the floor shifted under her feet, but she placed one foot after the other, out of the flat, onto the streets. There were moments when she clenched her stomach, when darkness hovered before her. At home, she climbed into bed and shut her eyes. Her waist burned, and her stomach contracted. She shivered in bed, pulled more sheets to her chest. She did not stop shivering, even by evening, when her father came home and found her in bed, sweating. She said she was menstruating, that the pain was too much. She slipped in and out of consciousness, barely remembering what she said. Her father's face swam above hers, and she was wondering why he looked so worried and devastated when her eyes drew shut.

She opened her eyes and knew she was not in her bed. This one felt hard. A fan whirled above her, the ceiling was painted white, the walls blue, and the room smelled of Izal and drugs. She sat up. Her father was standing by the door. A nurse walked into the room. Her face bore judgement. Ogadinma knew then that they had found out, that her father had found her out. She lay back in bed and shut her eyes, and wished for the floor to cave in and swallow her.

2

Her father shook her awake at past midnight, when the cries of crickets flitted in from the open window, the room illuminated by the orange flame of a smoky kerosene lantern. He sat on the chair close to her bed, his elbows resting on his knees.

'Papa,' she said, and tried to make out the look on his face, to prepare her mind for what he wanted to say. It still hurt to move, and her stomach felt as though someone had dug everything out. Still, she sat and said, 'Good morning, Papa.'

He stared at her for a long time, his face shielded by dark shadows. The last time they stayed this way was the day after the rioting boys wreaked havoc in Sabon Gari and burned down the church. He brought her home and made their meal, the first time in many years. Later that night, she had woken to find him leaning by her bedside, weeping. He didn't bother wiping the tears, or to muffle his cries. He said he had feared that something bad would happen to her. He said he had feared for her, not for his own fate. That was the first time she would see him cry. But it was a different look in his eyes this time.

'You went and got pregnant, and then killed the child. Under my roof?' He always panted whenever he was angry, but now he did not pant. He did not stutter. He waited for her to explain herself, as he always did. Heart-to-heart, he always called it. Although the night was still and cold winds sifted in from the open windows, she felt suffocated. The bed was sucking her in. The room had gotten darker. And she wondered what he would do if she told him every-thing about Barrister Chima.

She stared at her clenched hands, because she did not want to look into his eyes and see the anger and disappointment simmering on the surface, and said, 'I am sorry, Papa.'

He stared at her. For a long time, he just stared at her and she wondered what he was thinking, if perhaps he had accepted her apol-ogy and forgiven her. But then he stood and walked out of the door, his feet padding wearily down the passage. She had almost sighed in relief when his footsteps returned, heavy with purpose. The glare from the extra lantern he had brought brightened the room before he appeared at the door. He was holding a bunch of rattan canes, slim, long sticks bound together at each end with black rope. Her heart lurched painfully in her chest.

'Papa.' She stood up.

He set the canes by the door, pointed to the bed and said, 'Lie flat on the bed,' his voice barely above a whisper. 'Your aunty Okwy brought pregnancy from nowhere into my house. And you went and did the same thing? Ujo adiro gi n'anya, eh, so you have no fear in your eyes?'

She looked at the canes and searched his face as if trying to find a sign in his eyes, or the crumple of his forehead, that would tell her that this was all a mistake, that he was not about to break his promise to her years ago. 'Papa, you promised you would never flog me again,' she said, her voice choked with the beginnings of cries.

'Lie on the bed!' he shouted, his voice so loud it caused her to jump.

She climbed into bed and flattened her stomach against the soft mattress, her head turned to the side, so she could see everything he did. This was not happening, she told herself. This was all a bad dream she would soon wake up from. Outside her window, the world was so dark, so still. He grabbed a cane, a long thing that was as thick as her thumb.

'I am very sorry, Papa. I will never do it again.'

'I will give you twenty-four strokes. If you shift and I miss your buttocks, that is a minus, and I will have to start all over again.'

'Papa, *biko*. Please.'

'Where did you get that pregnancy from?'

'It was a mistake, Papa.'

He lifted his hand, the cane reaching for the ceiling, before he brought it down with so much might that it zipped through the air, before landing on her buttocks, the force lifting her skirt. She was numbed by the shock, her knees suddenly soft. And then she screamed. A hoarse cry that tore through the night, ringing throughout the compound. Neighbours jerked awake. Worried voices rose. Her father was undaunted.

'*Mechie ọnụ*, shut your mouth!'

'*Biko, biko!*'

The cane landed again with the same force, carrying the same zipping sound. Ogadinma jumped off the bed, screaming. He shoved her back on the bed, yelling threats.

Her skin broke. Cries surged up her throat. Neighbours pounded on their door, shouted from their windows, asked if he wanted to kill her.

'*Ọọ mụ mụlụ ya*, she is my child. If she dies, I will bury her body.'

She slipped into a dark place and when she opened her eyes again, he had finally stopped, and he was speaking to her.

'You will go to Lagos,' he was saying. 'I would have sent you to your grandmother in the village, but the shame you have brought will kill that woman if she learns the truth. You will go and stay with my brother Ugonna until I decide what to do with you.'

Her vision was hazy and her whole body was on fire, but she still said she was sorry for what she had done; she apologized because there was something in the way he hung his head when he walked out of the room, as if a heavy weight was pressing down on his shoulders – a sack of sadness birthed by the shame she had brought.

She stayed in bed, afraid to move her body or even raise her hands. She was still there when the sounds of night life sifted in:

the croaking toads in open drainages, the rustling of cats and rats, the flap of bats, the howls of street dogs. And then her eyes drifted shut and she fell into a dreamless sleep.

Neighbours woke her with the usual cacophony of her childhood: pots and spoons banging in out-kitchens, pestles pounding into mortars, small children bathing on the ledge in front of the compound, splashing water all over the floor. As a child, she had bathed outside too. On some days, it was Aunty Okwy who supervised her bath. Ogadinma had hated it. Aunty Okwy would sponge her until she was a frothy mass of white bubbles, before rinsing off the lather with bowls of water, and when soap burned her eyes, Aunty Okwy would smack her over the head, *kpa! kpa!*, while Ogadinma danced in pain. 'Who asked you to open your eyes, eh? Don't you have sense?' before obliging her with a soothing splash of water. Her father was careful with the sponge when he helped out, and he was easy on the soap. He would scrub her upper body, hand her the sponge and say, '*Ngwa* wash your bom-bom,' and she would sponge her buttocks and the space between her legs before he poured her bowls of water to rinse off the lather.

Now she huddled by the window, crouched on all fours because she could not sit yet; her buttocks were riddled with welts and had burned when she washed herself that morning. She wondered if Aunty Okwy had felt the same kind of pain years ago, after she got pregnant. Ogadinma still remembered that night. Aunty Okwy, thin and small and hovering by the door, her belly elevated to a strange roundness that made her look like she'd stuffed a limp ball under her dress. She had told Ogadinma's father that she didn't know the man who got her pregnant. Ogadinma remembered how her father had dragged Aunty Okwy into her room and locked the door. She remembered Aunty Okwy's shrieks, the zipping sounds of the rattan canes. After her father was done, he locked Aunty Okwy inside her room, and shipped her off to their home town the next morning. The last time she saw Aunty Okwy was in Onitsha, after her hasty wedding to an old widower.

'Are you ready?' Her father's voice broke into her thoughts.

She jerked away from the window. 'Yes, sir,' she said, and caught herself. She had never called her father 'sir'.

'Let's go,' he said, his voice oddly piercing.

She carried her bag and he followed behind her. She heard the click of the door and the turn of the key. She kept walking, never looking back or slowing her pace, and he stayed behind her too. They did not speak. The previous years, when they travelled to their village in Abagana for Christmas, they would hold hands and he would take the window seat so she could watch the trees and houses blending into each other, flitting past. Those times, she looked forward to travelling, to sitting for twelve hours on the bus with her father. But it was different this time. About the abortion and the punishment he meted out last night, he said nothing. It was as though all of that had never happened.

At the bus park, she hovered behind as he got the ticket from the counter, then they waited, neither saying anything to the other until her bus was ready to leave.

'You will stop at Jibowu,' he said. 'Don't get down at Berger or anywhere else. I have also told the driver this. Your final destination is Jibowu. Do you hear me?'

'Yes, Papa. I will get down at Jibowu.'

There was a restlessness about him. He quickly pulled her to his chest and wrapped his arms around her. She rested her head against his chest and wondered if his stomach was knotted with tension as hers was. It was the first time in their lives that she would be travelling without him by her side. He broke the hug and pulled away. 'Safe journey,' he said stiffly.

'Thank you, Papa,' she said.

In the bus, she looked out to catch a last glimpse of him. She did not see him.

The morning breeze pushed against the blinds when they arrived in Lagos. She woke to the frantic voices outside her window – wheelbarrow-pushers offering to carry luggage, the taxi drivers hounding passengers, young boys in stained clothes begging to lug bags on their heads, hawkers plastering their wares against the windows. Jibowu Park was cramped, the floor stained black as though someone had spilled a tank of grease on it. Her buttocks were satisfyingly numb, but a thousand pins of pain shot up her body when she stood up, the welts coming alive again. She got down from the bus, clutching her Ghana-Must-Go bag. Men grabbed her, boys rounded her up, all of them offering their services. Someone called out her name. She turned and saw Nnanna, Uncle Ugonna's son. She had last seen him two years ago, when they travelled to the village for Christmas, but he looked slightly different now, taller. 'Ogadinma, you are here!'

She still remembered his goofy laugh, how the dimples sank when he laughed. She hastened towards him, even though she felt a throbbing all over her body.

'Nnanna, you haven't changed one bit!' She forced brightness into her voice.

He clasped her in his arms and held her tightly against his bony frame, laughing. He smelled of Imperial Leather soap.

The hustlers, seeing this was bad market, broke away to hound another passenger. Nnanna said his father was parked across the road. He took her bag in one hand and held her with the other, and they made a dash across the busy road, narrowly missing a taxi that swerved dangerously in front of them.

Uncle Ugonna's Peugeot 505 was black and shiny. His face broke into a brilliant smile as he threw his hands open and wrapped them around her, swaying from side to side. 'Bịa Ogadinma, look how tall you have grown, like yam tendrils during the rains. *Neke, neke!*' He pulled away and tilted his neck dramatically up to look at her face. '*Ị fukwa obele nwa unyaa*, now I have to crane to look at her?' For a moment, she was staring at a happier, shorter version of her father. His face was not stretched thin with worry, and he had eyes that danced with mischief and laughter.

She grinned and did not say anything else after they got into the car. They drove into dense traffic, squeezed in between yellow buses, fought for space with taxi drivers and rode on pavements to beat hold-ups. She listened as they made small talk about the state of the roads, the corrupt government, how Nigerians were still enduring epileptic power supply. Mostly, Nnanna did the talking and Uncle Ugonna responded in the affirmative. She watched the ease with which they conversed, her chest suddenly tight. She thought of her father and their empty apartment, how the rooms would be silent now, how he would have breakfast and dinner all by himself. Would he still watch NTA News, would he still laugh when *New Masquerade* came on?

'We are entering Victoria Island,' Nnanna said later. She pulled away from the window and grinned at him. He frowned, then whispered, 'Why are you crying?'

She swiped at her face and felt wetness, then she turned away and mumbled something about being tired. But Uncle Ugonna was already looking back, his gaze darting between her and the road, a knowing look in his eyes, and for a moment she feared her father had told him everything that happened.

But Uncle Ugonna said, 'Your father misses you, too. He called ten times this morning, asking if I had already picked you up.'

'He did?'

'Yes o! He refused to let me sleep!' He laughed. Ogadinma laughed too, nervously. Nnanna rubbed her shoulder. Something lifted from her chest. Her father missed her. She wanted to believe it. She shut her eyes and tried to imagine his face, his laughter, but all she remembered was the cold look, how distant he was when they walked to the motor park. Her chest felt tight again, but she took a deep breath and tried to chase the sad thoughts away.

They reached Victoria Island. The cars here were sleeker. Glassy buildings sprang from among dull ones on dusty streets, reaching for the sky. She knew when people said that Lagos was the *New York of Nigeria*, they were speaking in the metaphorical sense because the

Lagos and New York she saw on the TV did not look alike in any way. But she pressed her face against the window and breathed the air that smelled of dust and sweat, and imagined she had flown out and was now driving down the streets of Manhattan.

They pulled up in front of an old, wide gate with a signpost that said Bar Beach Barracks. The gates were thrown open by a young boy in a stained kaftan. Nnanna gave her a mini-education on the buildings: the mammy market, the police station spilling over with black-clad officers wielding guns and batons, the apartment blocks with peeling paint and stained balconies. They drove into a quieter section of buildings with wide front yards and manicured lawns and water tanks sitting on raised metal platforms. Each apartment had an outdoor TV antenna perching on the wall. They rolled to a stop in front of a flat and Uncle Ugonna switched off the engine.

Aunty Ngozi was coming out of the building as they got down. Aunty Ngozi who often brought them *chin-chin* at Christmas. Two years had passed and she had not changed. Yellow-skinned like an overripe pawpaw, she still had light stubble under her chin. Aunty Ngozi laughed a lot, and she was laughing now as she gathered Ogadinma into her arms.

'Ah, ah, Ogadinma, is this really you?' She pressed Ogadinma to her soft bosom. She smelled of curry and Maggi. Ogadinma laughed as Aunty Ngozi swayed with her in a small dance. Her hair was gathered in a fuzzy bunch at her head, like a blob of dark cotton wool. She looked genuinely happy to see Ogadinma. What a pleasant welcome, Ogadinma thought, hugging Aunty Ngozi tighter. Relief flooded her chest for the first time since she got off the bus.

Nnanna carried her bag into the flat. Aunty Ngozi slung a hand around her waist, led her inside the house, down the passage and into a room crammed with bags. The only table in the room was cluttered with books. 'You must be tired. Make yourself at home, i nu? This is also your house. It is so good to see you again.'

'Thank you, Aunty.'

Aunty Ngozi looked around the room, picked up a lone bra from the floor, the books strewn by the side of the table. 'This is Ifeoma's room. That girl is so dirty,' she said, but her words were drenched in the warmth of a mother who had learned to dismiss her child's shortcomings.

Satisfied there was nothing else lying around on the floor, Aunty Ngozi told her to rest, that she would ask Nnanna to get some water for her to bathe.

After she left, Ogadinma looked out to find a group of teenagers in blue-and-white uniforms walking to school, their gait leisurely. It all felt surreal, her mind struggling to wrap itself around the sudden change of things. Only weeks ago, she was preparing to go to university. Now she was in Lagos, her buttocks on fire, her future as hazy as the confusion swirling in her head. Nothing made sense to her yet. She wondered what her father had told Uncle Ugonna and Aunty Ngozi about her coming, how long she would be staying here. But they hadn't shown signs that they knew what had happened with her; they carried on like she was on a vacation.

Nnanna appeared at the door later. He had changed into blue shorts and a faded white t-shirt. She could almost see the bones of his legs, the veins wiring his arms. He looked different suddenly, maybe because she was now seeing him in their house, in simple clothes. He looked painfully thin.

'Your water is ready,' he said, 'go and bathe now before the water gets cold o.' And she was pleased that he talked as if she had not just come, as if she had always visited and knew her way around the house. She smiled and thanked him.

After he retreated, she looked around the room. It wasn't much larger than her room in Kano, but it stank of dust and mould from clothes not properly dried. The reading table was stained with food and the standing mirror was chipped and caked with makeup and cream. The bed sheet smelled of unwashed skin and the pillow of sweat. Ifeoma evidently paid less attention to her room and more to her books. She had so many of them, especially novels, stacked in cartons under the bed, piled in stacks atop the wardrobe, stuffed in bags under the bed. She seemed to read everything from James Hadley Chase to Mills and Boons and Harlequins, most of them tucked away from sight.

The wardrobe was filled with bags, so Ogadinma left her bag by the foot of the bed, then stripped hastily, knotting a wrapper around her chest. When she stepped out of the room, Nnanna was carrying a tray into the parlour. He stopped and said, 'I fried some eggs for you.' She gave him a nervous grin because what she wanted to say had nothing to do with eggs or food. 'Where is the bathroom?' she asked him.

'Oh, over there.' He gestured at a brown door down the passageway as he continued into the parlour.

Inside the bathroom, she stepped into the white tub and pulled the blue bucket of water close to her legs. This place was scrubbed clean, even the spaces in between the tiles. The toilet bowl had no stains and the sink was wiped clean. Without being told, she knew Nnanna had made it so. She could almost imagine what his room must look like.

She was still sponging her body when Aunty Ngozi called out her name and said she was leaving for her shop. 'Rest well o. And don't let this boy disturb your sleep, i nu? He watches too much TV,' she said.

'Yes, Aunty. Bye-bye, Aunty!' she said, and then she wondered if the lightness in her voice was too forced.

She had just pulled on her dress when Uncle Ugonna announced that he was leaving for the office. She came out to bid him goodbye. He was dressed in full police regalia, the black outfit shiny and ironed, lacking the dusty fadedness she had seen on the police officers on the streets. He reached out to pick something from her hair. She stood still, watched every movement he made; she could not tear her eyes away from his. After he showed her the lint he had picked out, she thanked him and watched him leave. And she felt a pang. It was because of the way he carried himself like her father, his back slightly curved, his gait light and swift. Watching him from behind was like watching her father leave for work.

The flat fell silent afterwards. She sat on the bed. Had Uncle Ugonna called her father to inform him of her safe arrival? She imagined he had wanted to speak with her but ended the call because she was in the bathroom. She looked out of the window. This part of the barracks was empty, silent. The silence unnerved her. She got off the bed and went to the parlour to join her cousin.

Nnanna had arranged tins of Peak Milk, Bournvita, Ovaltine, Planta and a packet of Saint Louis Sugar on the table, and he had set out a plate of fried eggs and a loaf of bread. Her mouth watered though there was no hunger in her stomach. But she took a seat at the table and pulled the plate closer after Nnanna said, 'Your food is almost cold, Ogadinma. *Biko* sit down and eat.'

He was crouched before the large TV encased in a burnished wood shelf, picking through a bunch of video tapes stacked in a corner. 'Have you watched *Rocky II?*' he asked.

She paused and wondered what he would think if she told him that they did not own a VHS player, that she only watched American movies from the window of their rich neighbour who owned the expensive machine. 'I haven't watched it,' she said.

Nnanna smiled at her, a small, honest smile that seemed to say it did not matter if she hadn't watched any American movies at all. 'You are lucky,' he said. 'I have all the Sylvester Stallone films.' He inserted the cassette and sat back as the TV came on, flashing gritty grey like a rain of fine sand, before the pictures started rolling. 'Have you seen his other films? He is better than Chuck Norris.'

'We don't have a VHS player,' she finally said. 'But I have seen one Chuck Norris movie. I think I like him,' she said.

'But Chuck Norris is a terrible actor.' He started to laugh, and she was relieved to find that it was not a laughter that mocked her for having poor knowledge of foreign films. It was a kind, soft giggle. He turned back to the TV as Sylvester Stallone dashed across the screen, and began to talk easily about these actors, these films.

She watched from the table until she finished her breakfast. After she had cleared the table, she came to sit beside him. He continued his running commentary about the film. She listened to every word he said and followed the images on the screen. But soon, she grew tired, her thoughts often flitting to Kano, to her father and their now-empty flat, until her eyes drooped closed in sleep.

Ogadinma was watching schoolchildren trudge down the narrow street, on their way home, when Ifeoma walked into the yard. She was a slimmer version of her mother. She dragged her feet when she walked, as though sacks of garri were tied to her ankles, and when she entered the flat she called Nnanna's name in the loud, piercing voice of someone used to getting whatever she wanted, asking if he had left any food for her. Ogadinma smoothed her palms on her lap and took a deep breath to steady her nerves before Ifeoma walked in.

Ifeoma paused by the door. Her eyes clouded with a look that seemed to say Ogadinma was the last person in the world she wanted to see. 'Ogadinma, you are here,' she finally said.

'I arrived this morning,' Ogadinma said. 'How have you been?' She reached out and clasped Ifeoma in her arms, but as she made to press the girl against her chest, Ifeoma slipped from the hug just as quickly, their bodies barely touching.

'Wow, you are really here.' Ifeoma kicked off her shoes and left them in the middle of the room. She threw a quick glance around, her brows creasing in surprise. 'You rearranged everything.' It sounded like an accusation.

Ogadinma nodded and smiled. She wanted to say Ifeoma had become more beautiful, but she couldn't. They had long grown apart. As children, they spent Christmases together in their home town, shared the same bed, did chores together. Some Christmases, Aunty Ngozi bought them identical dresses and shoes. And though Ogadinma was a year older, they behaved like twins. They grew apart after Uncle Ugonna built a big house and moved out, and Ifeoma had made new friends, friends who were the children of other rich men. She talked stiffly when her family visited Ogadinma's, and did not sit with Ogadinma even when her parents urged her to. Uncle Ugonna's wealth had transformed Ifeoma into a stranger. Ogadinma mourned the girl she had once been. And now, as Ifeoma looked at her, and Ogadinma briefly wondered if Ifeoma still remembered their childhood, how close they had been; if she missed the girls they once were.

'How was school today?' she asked Ifeoma instead.

A tight smile appeared on Ifeoma's face. She had stripped to her underwear. 'Aside from the silly NYSC teacher that tried to mess with me today, it was boring.'

Ogadinma sat on the edge of the bed, leaned forward, eager to chat about Ifeoma's day. Perhaps her enthusiasm would ease the awkwardness between them. 'What did he do? I am guessing it's a he.'

Ifeoma snorted. 'He thought I was one of those small-small girls they lure into their quarters. I reported him to the principal after he tried nonsense with me.'

'Good job!'

'So how long are you going to stay here?' Ifeoma blurted out.

Ogadinma gasped because she had not expected the question. She could hear Nnanna speaking to someone outside. 'I don't even know,' she told Ifeoma.

Ifeoma seemed to consider this for a moment, then she pulled on her dress and walked out, shouting, 'I am so hungry. Is there any food in this house?' Ogadinma's face fell, but she got up and followed Ifeoma out.

'Nnanna made jollof rice,' she said.

And Ifeoma, without bothering to acknowledge Ogadinma again, headed into the kitchen. Ogadinma heard her opening pots and clanging spoons. When she stopped by the door of the kitchen, she found Ifeoma eating directly out of the pot.

A car horn honked in the distance and Ifeoma sighed and said aloud, 'Mummy and Daddy are back. I hope we are not cooking soup tonight because I don't have strength to do anything at all.' She bounded back to the room, just as Aunty Ngozi walked in lugging a nylon bag spilling with ugu leaves. 'Ogadinma, *kedụ*? I know these children did not let you rest today,' she said.

Ogadinma took the bag from Aunty Ngozi and said she rested well.

Aunty Ngozi peered into the room. 'Madam, you left your bra on the floor this morning.'

'Mummy, I forgot—' Ifeoma began.

'*Taa, kpuchie ọnụ gị*, shut your mouth! I have warned you about this over and over again, but you have refused to learn. That is how you will take this nonsense attitude to a man's house and he will break your empty head for you, since you refuse to grow yourself some sense.'

Ogadinma took the bag to the kitchen and emptied the contents, setting the items side by side on the sink – the meat tied in a black nylon bag, the mangala, okporoko, pepper, crayfish, palm oil, onion and okro. It was her first time living with her uncle's family and so she would have to behave well, she thought; she was expected to be polite. She had transferred the meat into a basin, taken a pot from one of the shelves, and was turning on the stove when Aunty Ngozi walked in, a wrapper knotted around her chest. The older woman pulled a chair close to the door and sat and talked about her day as Ogadinma worked: she did not sell a thing in her shop today and she blamed the bad market on suspicious neighbours who she believed buried ogwu in front of her shop to drive away her customers.

'God will shame all of them,' she said. 'God will expose all of them and destroy their evil charms.'

Ogadinma did not say anything as Aunty Ngozi talked, but she gave perfunctory smiles and nodded when she felt it was necessary. She sensed her contribution was not needed in the monologue, that Aunty Ngozi just wanted her to listen to her chatter about her tedious day. So, Ogadinma sliced onions into the pot, wiped onion tears, added Maggi cubes and salt. Then she washed the okro, dicing each into thin slices. She pounded the crayfish and peppers and sliced the ugu. She cooked the soup, nodded or smiled, and all the while Aunty Ngozi talked.

Uncle Ugonna peeped in later, after the soup was simmering and Ogadinma was stirring garri in a large bowl. '*Daalụ kwa nụ o.* This soup smells good,' he said. 'Did Ogadinma cook it?'

'She did o! See how neat the kitchen is! She has even washed all the utensils she used. But that girl Ifeoma, who has refused to come here and learn how things are done, will leave them lying around until you buy her drinks, kneel and beg her to wash them.'

Uncle Ugonna smiled and left, and Aunty Ngozi followed. Ifeoma snuck into the kitchen later. 'Mummy has finally carried her *wahala* and go,' Ifeoma said. She opened the pot and sniffed the steam. 'Can I take mine now? Because if Uncle Tobe comes now, this soup will be finished this night.'

'Who is Uncle Tobe?'

'Mummy's younger brother. He is a contractor. He comes here every evening to eat.'

Ifeoma took some soup, scooped some garri and fled into her room before her mother returned. Ogadinma returned to the room too, to wait for Aunty Ngozi's next command.

'The soup is very sweet,' Ifeoma said after she had finished eating. 'You cook so well.'

Ogadinma was too unnerved by the sudden warmth to smile, and instead asked Ifeoma if she wanted more soup. Aunty Ngozi's voice floated into the flat later, unusually loud. She was speaking with a man whose voice had laughter clinging to the end of each word. Though Ogadinma could not hear what they said, she knew they were speaking about her because shortly afterwards, Aunty Ngozi peeped into the room and told her to come and meet Tobe.

'You can change your dress,' Aunty Ngozi said and left.

Ogadinma rubbed one sweaty palm on her dress, her stomach suddenly queasy. Why did she need to dress up for Aunty Ngozi's brother? And why did Aunty Ngozi say this so casually, as if it was totally normal for a girl to dress up for a man she had never met? She stood up and went over to her bag, and began to search for what to wear. She did not know the appropriate thing one should wear on such an occasion. After rummaging through her clothes, she settled for a pink dress, a gift from her father last Christmas.

Ifeoma lifted her face from her book and watched as Ogadinma gathered her braids into a bun. 'This one, you are dressed like you are going out this night,' she said. She was looking at Ogadinma, but her gaze was softer than earlier.

Ogadinma was suddenly unsure of her choice of clothing, and she thought of changing into something simpler. But Ifeoma said, 'The dress is very pretty. It hugs your body well.'

Ogadinma's palms became clammy again. As she came out of the room, Aunty Ngozi and Tobe's voices floated in from the open door of the parlour. They were talking about the executions being shown on the TV.

'I will never understand why they televise these things,' Aunty Ngozi was saying. 'Yes, you have condemned these people to death, but why must you televise their execution, eh? Just *negodinu*, see how they strung them up like chickens and riddled their bodies with bullets. These are people's children *bikonu!*'

'What do you expect?' Tobe said. 'These soldiers do not think like civilians.'

Ogadinma waited for a moment by the door because she did not want to see executions. She had read about the men when they were condemned to death by the military tribunal for smuggling drugs. She still remembered them, the small-boned men who looked like university undergraduates, their pictures splashed on the covers of newspapers. Her father had raged when the men were condemned, and she remembered him staring at their faces on the cover of *Daily News*, muttering, 'So, they are going to be shot because of low-level drug offences?'

After Aunty Ngozi and Tobe had resumed making small talk, she walked into the parlour, feeling a sudden headache. What should she do? Aunty Ngozi and Tobe had their backs to her, so she wondered for a moment if she should stand behind and greet them, or walk over and stand in front of them. She was still contemplating what to do when Aunty Ngozi sensed her presence, turned and saw her and leapt from her seat.

'*Ezigbo nwa*, good girl!' Aunty Ngozi sang, her laughter layered with extra notes. 'Tobe, meet my niece, Ogadinma. She has home training and she is a great cook.'

Ogadinma muttered greetings and kept her eyes on her hands. Her fingernails were still tinted a deep green, the same colour as the ugu leaves she had cut earlier. She was not sure why Aunty Ngozi spoke about her cooking.

Tobe sat forward in his seat and said, 'I can't wait to eat your delicious food.'

She nodded, settling her eyes on a spot on his chest, so she wouldn't be flustered by his direct gaze. She wished they would both stop looking at her in such a brash way. She was not used to this kind of scrutiny. This had never happened to her before.

'You are welcome to Lagos, *nne*,' Tobe said softly. That soft voice prompted her to finally look up and meet his eyes.

Tobe was built like his sister but slimmer, taller. He was handsome in a soft, relaxed way and had the kind of perfectly symmetrical body that seemed suited only for royal regalia. Perhaps it was the way he carried his upper body, as though his shirt was fortified with shoulder pads. There was something about him that eased the tension simmering in her body. It was the way he smiled at her, how he arched his neck when he spoke. She exhaled. 'Thank you,' she said.

This seemed to please Aunty Ngozi because she brimmed with the satisfaction of one who has done a good job. Ogadinma stood before them as Aunty Ngozi resumed telling him stories about her upbringing, as though she was no longer in the room. '*I makwa na* this girl *na-eje sọ ozi*, she does everything in her father's house, from cooking to washing. Everything.'

'Looking at her, you already know she was raised well,' Tobe said, and turning to her, he asked, 'How was your trip, *nne*?'

'It was fine.' Ogadinma tried to smile, though in fact she was becoming unnerved by how steadily he looked her in the eyes.

Then Uncle Ugonna entered the parlour, a wrapper wound round his waist. The tufts of hair on his chest were coiled and sparse and dusted with grey. 'Ha! My in-law, you are here already,' he said, and Tobe stood to greet him.

Ogadinma took the cue and made for the exit. Aunty Ngozi followed closely behind her. 'We are coming o,' she told the men. As they left the parlour, she took Ogadinma's hand in hers. It was callused and warm, like the hand of someone who farmed the land every day. Aunty Ngozi did not speak until they reached the passageway, then she turned around and her face broke into a smile. '*Akwa gị nke a amaka!* Such a beautiful dress. You chose the perfect outfit,' she said. '*Ngwa*, come, let us serve them food.'

Ogadinma felt a rush of relief that made her dizzy. It had been a long time since she felt companionship with an older woman. She did not understand why she needed to play dress up, but she was glad that she had pleased Aunty Ngozi. And when they went into the kitchen, she liked the comfortable silence they shared as they got the food ready. Aunty Ngozi brought out the prettiest plates from a shelf, ceramic bowls and dishes that looked as though they had never been used. She passed them to Ogadinma, who rinsed each one and handed them over for her to dish out soup and garri, before setting them on a brand-new tray. Aunty Ngozi flicked her thumb at the edges of the bowls to wipe off soup stains, then stood back to examine her handiwork.

'*Ehen*, you can carry them to the dining room,' she said.

Tobe was sitting cross-legged, talking with Uncle Ugonna, when Ogadinma returned. He was watching her, and she knew that he was doing that to get her attention, perhaps for them to lock eyes. After she kept the tray and returned with a bowl of water for hand-washing, she cast a quick glance in his direction and found his waiting smile. She looked away quickly, her face suddenly hot with embarrassment. She had never felt that way before with any man, not even with Emeka, her secondary school classmate. Later, she would ponder over and over about that look and how it made her feel. But for now, she went into the bathroom, stood before the mirror and pulled up her dress. She stared at the purpling bruises, like overripe avocado, streaking her lower back and her buttocks, and wondered how long before her body fully healed, before her stomach stopped quivering like everything inside it had been dug out.

Aunty Ngozi came to take a last look at the table. She moved a plate to one side, set down the cup of toothpicks and a packet of serviettes, before turning to the men. 'Food is ready, come and eat.'

Ogadinma returned to the kitchen to get her food. Back in the room, she picked at the meal. The soup tasted like paper because she felt so many things swirling inside her, emotions that made her face hot and caused her stomach to jump every time she heard a shuffle of feet. Later, a knock came at the door. When she got it, she found Tobe in front of her.

'Nne, do you want to step outside for some fresh air?' he asked, and quickly added, 'I already asked my sister and she is fine with it.'

She stared at him. She did want to step outside with him, to listen to his gentle voice and enjoy his warm smile and listen to him talk about important things. Yet, she did not want to be left alone with him. She should not mingle with any man that was not family, not after what happened the last time. But he was looking at her with an open, honest look. He would not harm her in her uncle's home.

'Yes. I want some fresh air,' she finally said.

Outside, the porch light flooded into the front yard where some-one had set a short bench. Winged insects butted their heads against the fluorescent lamp. Tobe sat on the bench and patted the space beside him. She went and sat. The bench was so short their shoulders touched.

'How was your trip?' he asked. 'I know it must have been very tedious.'

She tried to remember if it was tedious, but the back of his hand kept grazing hers. It was too disturbing, how their bodies touched. Her mouth had gone dry again and she licked her lips and sat forward, so that they would no longer touch, so the cobwebs in her head would clear and she'd be able to give an intelligent answer to his question. 'It took twelve hours to get here,' she finally said.

'I went to Kano once, in 1981. For a friend's wedding. After that trip, I swore I would never ever set foot in Kano again.'

'Something bad happened?'

'No, just the sun and heat and the smell in crowded taxis. I almost passed out many times.' He laughed. 'When I got back to Lagos, I could not recognize myself in the mirror. I was roasted black like a Christmas goat.'

'We are used to the extreme weather,' she said, and then wished she had said something smarter.

'What does your father do in Kano?'

'He sells building materials.'

'Oh, he must be a big man.'

She should tell him that her father was not a rich man, that he sold only nails and bolts and keys and aluminium roofing washers, but she said again, 'He sells building materials.'

Tobe talked more about his experience of Kano, how he had been put off by the sea of flies that hopped on everything, the mosquitoes he endured in dank hotels on Abeokuta Road. But when she told him that they lived on New Road, three streets from Abeokuta Road, he sighed, almost in relief, and said New Road was the only nice place he remembered. He talked long into the night. And he had moved closer, their arms pressed tightly, their faces inches apart. It seemed too intimate, to have him this close to her. The last time she sat this close to a man, something bad happened and caused her father to punish her. Tension fell from the sky and stifled her. Where was her uncle? Would he be disappointed if he found her talking with a man she had only met that evening?

She sat up. 'I think Aunty Ngozi will be looking for me now.'

He touched her shoulder and squeezed. 'I will see you tomorrow,' he said.

She nodded and hastened inside. What had he meant by 'I will see you tomorrow'?

He strode into the flat, talked in low tones with Aunty Ngozi. After he left, Aunty Ngozi's voice floated through the flat, drunk and happy. She sang an Igbo song of praise, '*I meela, i meela. I meela Okaka*,' her voice squeaky.

Ogadinma stretched out on the bed beside Ifeoma, who had long since fallen asleep. She stared at the door which stood partly ajar, wondering what her father was doing at that time, if he was still awake. She wished she could get up and ask Uncle Ugonna to call her father, so she could tell him about Tobe and everything that was happening to her, and yet she didn't want to speak with him because she feared he would disapprove of how she had conducted herself, that he would consider her a disappointment for the second time.

That night, she dreamed she was running and crying and her father was chasing her with a rattan cane. Her cries were loud and hoarse. She had never heard anyone cry so loud.

3

She woke to the morning call to prayer from a nearby mosque. The voice, amplified on a loudspeaker, cracked as though it hung from the window of their room. She didn't have problems with the noise levels of mosques. Her street in Kano had three of them close to their home. The calls were always distant, and over time became the neighbourhood's alarm clock, because it was when Mama Nkechi, their neighbour, began preparations for the food she sold at the kiosk opposite their gate; when small children washed the plates and pots used the night before, and older children swept the rooms and rinsed the mats they slept on; when they all hurried with their tasks, in time for school at the break of dawn. But the call was louder this time, screeching and stretched out, without ceasing.

'The noise from the mosque is so loud,' she said to Ifeoma, who was at her reading table, notebooks splayed out before her.

'We are used to it. Don't worry, in one week, you won't even think about it.' Ifeoma did not lift her head from her books, but her voice was no longer brittle with the irritation of the day before, the one which showed how upset she was about Ogadinma's arrival.

Ogadinma returned to bed and pulled the sheet over her body. But she woke again when Aunty Ngozi's angry voice pierced the air. She was scolding Nnanna, who had stayed up all night to watch TV.

Ifeoma hissed and said, 'She is awake and we will not hear word.' Ogadinma was startled by her tone, how anyone could speak of their parents that way. She thought to berate Ifeoma, but she feared that would tear down their silent truce.

Aunty Ngozi entered their room. Ifeoma mumbled, 'Good morning, Mummy.'

'*Ehen*, morning,' Aunty Ifeoma said. 'Are you not late for school already, *ka ọ bụ na* school *agụrọ gị agụụ taa?*'

'Mummy, I am going to take my bath now,' Ifeoma said. She packed up her books and left, her face scrunched up in irritation, her feet shuffling angrily down the passage.

Aunty Ngozi came and sat on the bed and Ogadinma blinked to make sure she was not dreaming. Why was Aunty Ngozi ignoring Ifeoma's rudeness? Why did she always allow Ifeoma to talk to her elders in such a manner? The women in their compound in Kano would smack the snot off their daughters' noses if the girls dared to talk back at them that way. Ogadinma quietly pulled the sheets off her body, smiled and asked Aunty Ngozi if she slept well.

'*Nne*, I didn't. This back is beginning to give me problems. My doctor has recommended an orthopaedic mattress. I think I should check that out today.' Aunty Ngozi sighed. 'You know what? Tobe will soon be here to pick up Ifeoma. Do you mind joining them? He will drop Ifeoma off at school and then go shopping for the things he needs in his new house. I will tell him to also check out an orthopaedic mattress for me.'

Ogadinma said, 'Okay, Aunty. I will join them,' but her heart had begun to thud frantically. She got off the bed, feeling a sudden weakness in her knees. What was she expected to do, since Tobe was the one doing the shopping? The memories of the night before played across her mind. Tobe smiling, looking her straight in the eyes. Their bodies touching. She had felt light in the head when they sat together, and long after he left, the back of her arm still tingled from the touch. Now, she was going to shop with him. She felt a mix of emotions, worry and excitement swirling inside of her until her stomach gurgled.

Sponging her body in the bathroom, she wondered what she was going to wear. She liked to coordinate her outfit before an event – the right shoes or sandals, how best to wear her hair. But this outing was not planned. Back in the room, she changed and discarded dresses, and her clothes lay in a pile at her feet when Ifeoma peeped in moments later. She quickly snatched up a wrapper and threw it over her body, to hide her welts.

'We have to leave quickly or we will get stuck in traffic and I will be punished if I get to school late,' Ifeoma said, and left.

Ogadinma settled for the dress from the night before, applied deodorant generously under her arms and bunched her braids in a bun on top of her head. She pulled open her makeup bag, picked up a lipstick, but dropped it when footsteps approached. She grabbed her sandals and hurried out of the room.

Tobe was in his car, a black Peugeot 504 that sat glinting in the morning sun as if it had been wiped down with groundnut oil. Ifeoma was seated in front and reached over to open the back door.

Ogadinma got inside and greeted Tobe.

'Nne, kedụ? I hope you slept well,' he said, staring at her from the rear-view mirror. She muttered in the affirmative and looked away. Locking eyes with him made her feel heady, caused her hands to shake and her mouth to go dry. She stared at her hands, and she was grateful when he started a long talk about his night: he did not sleep well because he sweated all through the night. NEPA had yet to restore power. Nigeria was hellfire. No Nigerian should go to hell after death because that would be unfair.

Ifeoma laughed all through the talk and sometimes chided him. Ogadinma fixed her eyes on the bird shit smearing his windscreen, and wanted to tell him that complaining about power outages was a waste of time because it was the way things were. To have electricity for a few hours was a luxury everyone looked forward to. Everyone knew this, the workers at the power company knew this, even babies knew this. It was why everyone chanted 'Up NEPA!' in gratitude to the power company, when they restored power. But she didn't tell him, though; her mouth could not form the words.

They rolled to a stop in front of Ifeoma's school in Yaba, where cars disgorged girls at the gate, causing a bottleneck. Tobe complained about the drivers who parked their cars in a haphazard manner. He called them 'bush men' and stuck his head out of the window to shout when the traffic wouldn't give.

'That is the problem in this country, everyone is acting like an animal! Simply queue up in a straight line, this they cannot learn. They are always rushing and rushing and doing nothing but being an absolute nuisance everywhere.' He pounded his horn, stuck his head out of the window again to cuss the driver in front. 'Bịa this idiot, if you scratch my car with this gwụla gwụla, I will wipe the floor with your butt!' He turned back to her, sweating, mopping his brow. 'That is the problem. Simple orderliness, they do not know. When you get on a plane filled with Nigerians, you will hate your life. This same thing they do here, is how they rush inside planes like bush people from the village.' He stuck his head out of the window again, shouted, fought for space. There was a sweat patch under his arm, the light fabric tinged a wet brown. His theatricals were excessive and exhausting, even unsettling. She wished he would stop shouting; he was clean-cut, with his obvious grooming, and so should not lower himself to the level of street touts. She held his gaze and smiled nervously. But he did not smile back. She turned away and looked out of the window.

Every driver was doing the same as him, struggling and cussing. Just then, an army van pulled up in front of the school and soldiers clutching long guns and horsewhips jumped off from the back of the vehicle, their booted feet landing with thuds on the ground. Passers-by scuttled for safety. The soldiers went after the reckless drivers with their horsewhips. Zipping sounds slashed through the air as the whips landed on bodies. The men thrashed out. The women held tightly to the ends of their wrappers. Passers-by hung at the edge of the road to watch the spectacle. Ogadinma saw a soldier butting the head of his gun against the cars' headlamps, smashing them to pieces, before ordering the owners to move their vehicles.

In minutes, Tobe drove out seamlessly.

'You know, if there were a warden at that junction, there wouldn't have been a jam and people wouldn't need to break the law,' Ogadinma said.

Tobe looked at her. Something softened in his eyes. He was no longer sweating. 'Well, that's true,' he said. 'And it's good to hear you speak. You are always quiet, always watching. It's good to hear you speak.'

She looked at him and a smile began to stretch her cheeks, her lips. He was smiling too. For a moment, she remembered riding in Barrister Chima's car a long time ago, how uncomfortable it had been. This one felt different. He did not barrage her with unnerving questions, did not make her feel like she was so insignificant, so tiny, something to be used and discarded.

They rode in silence past traffic jams, past cars stuck in potholes, past small children hawking oranges and mangoes, past mothers setting up vegetable and fish stalls at the edge of the road, past girls lugging gallons of water with their babies strapped to their backs. And when they joined the expressway, Tobe turned to her, as though only just then realizing that she had been sitting behind him: 'You should be sitting in the front with me. I am not your driver.' He laughed and rolled the car to a stop at the side of the road. 'Come to the front.'

She joined him in the front.

'We are close to Alaba Market. I will have to look for a good place to park my car,' he said as he worked the stereo blindly, fumbling with the knobs. All the channels were broadcasting news items. He brought out a pack of cassettes from the pigeonhole and dumped them on her lap. 'Check for Osadebe,' he said, half-watching as she inspected the writing on the cassettes. 'I am moving to my new house. The only items of furniture I have there are my bed and a stove. You are going to help me select what to put in that empty house, i nugo?'

'Okay.' She was not frightened to be alone with him, not in the least. Aunty Ngozi had planned for them to spend the day together. She did not know their intent, and now did not care to know. For a long time, her mind had been knotted by worry, so it felt good to sweep her mind clean and chase all anxious thoughts away.

The traffic on the expressway was impenetrable. She looked at him. He no longer seemed upset. Perhaps it was because he sang along as Osadebe crooned from the radio. Perhaps, too, it was because of how closely they sat. Outside her window, hawkers, mostly older boys in stained clothes. Some tapped the glass, pointing out their wares in case she missed them.

'You know you can sit in a Lagos hold-up and cook a pot of soup?' she said. 'Everything you need is sold here, from a cooking stove to pots and even the ingredients for soup.'

He began to laugh, a rumbling sound that made his stomach quiver. He touched her shoulder, his hand resting softly on her body.

'I agree with you,' he said. 'The only thing missing in a Lagos traffic jam are the mobile bathroom hawkers offering you space to take your bath.'

He laughed again. She chuckled too. Then she leaned back in her seat, her gaze on the window, and as they drove to Alaba Market she listened to the melancholic voice of Osadebe. She liked that she made him laugh.

The hustlers outside the Alaba Market rushed forward when they saw Ogadinma and Tobe approach. They clustered around, all of them speaking at the same time, pulling Tobe and Ogadinma towards their shops.

'We have original Austrian and Italian laces. I go sell am for cheap price!'

'We have London baby clothes, original ones. We just import am!'

'Come, na me you dey look for. We have Italian shoes. For husband and wife!'

Tobe held her hand, shoved past the hustlers who trailed behind them, pleading and plodding along before giving up the chase when Tobe wouldn't budge. They walked into the first shop, a cramped small room with electronics stacked from floor to ceiling. The space left inside was so narrow Tobe would have to walk sideways if he were to go inside. A fair woman who was so tall she stood hunched at the shoulders offered them seats by the door and bottles of Maltina. She didn't have the brand of Thermocool refrigerator Tobe asked for but sent one of her boys to get it from her second shop down the road. When she went inside to get the other items Tobe requested, Ogadinma took a sip of her Maltina, but choked on the drink; Tobe was watching her keenly, his gaze following the lift of the bottle, how the drink poured into her mouth. She coughed, her face suddenly warm with embarrassment. 'It is very cold,' she said.

Tobe moved his seat closer. 'Shagari's government was kind to us,' he said. 'My company did so many jobs for the government. *I makwa*, some of the roads in Lagos were not motorable and residents had to park their cars on the outer streets because the potholes were large enough to sink a vehicle. But we repaired them. Now the military is back again. I hope they will treat us better than they did the last time they were here.'

Ogadinma nodded with some enthusiasm, even though all she remembered of Shagari's regime was how expensive foodstuffs became, and how she and her father hid in his shop as Hausa Muslim boys wreaked havoc on properties belonging to the Christians in Sabon Gari.

Two small boys lugged the refrigerator on a long wheelbarrow. They kept it by the door, kicked off their slippers and wiped their feet on the doormat before going inside to get the woman. She emerged, smiling. 'You can see it is the original Thermocool,' she told Tobe, then glanced at Ogadinma. 'I am sure madam will like this colour. It is pure white.'

Ogadinma looked at Tobe and then at the woman. Tobe was grinning. He should not, because she was not his madam. The very word unsettled her, made her tongue thick and speech difficult. Tobe was nodding and saying, 'Yes, madam really likes it,' and looking at her, and she was unsure of how to react. It was a joke, she thought, because his eyes seemed to twinkle with mischief. But when the woman brought out other kitchen appliances and held them out for her approval, she looked at Tobe and saw that he was watching her, that he was serious about playing this strange game. She said 'okay' to the woman or 'this is fine', before he agreed to take things she brought.

After what happened with Barrister Chima, she should be wary of men. But it was hard to feel that way now, with him looking her in the eyes. She felt calm instead and it pleased her that she made him happy.

After they had gotten everything he wanted, they went to other shops to buy Aunty Ngozi's mattress and a new transistor radio for Uncle Ugonna. The shop owners all addressed her as 'madam', and as before, Tobe did not object or correct them, but leaned back and waited until she had declared she liked an item before he accepted them.

But a thought soon crept up her mind that this bonding with Tobe, which she had no name for, was moving too fast. At the last shop, where they bought kitchen utensils, she drank slowly from her glass of water and stood behind Tobe so that she would not have to speak, so that Tobe would not have to rely on her to make his choice, and the sellers would not call her 'madam' and ask for her opinion. Tobe hired a truck and the men loaded the items onto it. Ogadinma went to his car and leaned on it. Alaba Market reminded her of the Sabon Gari Market in Kano – the rowdiness, the hustlers and the barrow-pushers lugging goods for visitors, the roadside sellers who stacked their goods by the edge of the road and constantly moved their tables and kiosks so that goods-laden vehicles could go in or out. She missed Kano, the comforting silence of their yard when all the children had gone to school, and the chaos in the afternoon when they came back, the evenings she spent watching soaps with her father and the meals they shared. She was still leaning on the car, looking around at nothing, when Tobe returned.

His white shirt was now creased at the hem and stained with splotches of brown. He hugged her briefly. Surprised by the sudden embrace, she looked down at her feet, which were now covered with a film of dust.

'The men are taking the things to my house. We have to follow behind in case the soldiers ask them for the receipts.'

They got in the car and he looked at her for a moment before turning the key in the engine. 'After we get these things home, we are going somewhere nice to eat. I am so hungry. *Ọ kwa agụụ na-agụ gị*, you are hungry too?' he asked, before he revved the engine and wound down the windows to let out the heat that had accumulated.

'Yes, yes,' she said. She stared at the bird shit still staining one side of the windscreen. She did not want to go to his house because she feared what would happen when they got there, when they were alone with no one to watch them. And yet, she wanted to go with him, to spend all evening listening to his gentle voice, or to drive around town, just the two of them and the small space between them. She wondered what he would think if she moved her hand closer so that their hands would touch each time he changed the gears. Alarmed by her wild thoughts, she clasped her hands and left them on her lap.

The woman from the first shop came to Ogadinma's side of the window to bid them bye. '*Daalụ nụ o*, thank you o! You have done well, madam.'

The woman's face had reddened and was beaded with sweat, and her makeup had melted and dripped down the sides of her face, staining the collar of her blouse a dirty brown. Ogadinma waved, and then wondered if this was how the woman hustled every day, lugging large electronics; her blouse was soaked with sweat, so much so that her bra was visible under the now-transparent fabric.

'She works very hard,' Ogadinma said. 'She needs to install an air-conditioner in her shop.'

'That is true, but what electricity will she use to power it? I hear they have not had electricity in this market in four months.' He eased the car onto the road. Ogadinma looked at the side mirror and saw that the woman was still waving at her, a fat smile stretching her lips from cheek to cheek. She waved back.

'I am so hungry,' Tobe said. 'I could finish a pot of food right now.'

But Ogadinma was not hungry, not even after the long trip to his home in Falomo, where hired hands moved the items into the large compound. She was so dizzy with nervousness that she could hardly pay attention as he gave her a small tour. He showed her the parlour that was twice the size of Uncle Ugonna's, the marbled floors of the rooms that gleamed like mirrors, the beds that stretched from wall to wall, the kitchen with generous white and matching grey shelves; it was the biggest house she had ever seen. They went to the outer balcony, a space that could easily fit two cars.

'I will put some chairs and a table here, so that when it gets too hot, we can sit out here and enjoy the fresh breeze,' he said.

She was dazed by the pronoun 'we'. She thought about it when they trekked to the restaurant very close to his home for a late lunch, and even when he placed the order for their food and drinks. She should ask why he was talking about them as though they were a couple, but her mouth could not form the words. When their food arrived, she picked at it, moulded her fufu into small balls and dipped it into her soup. She kept her eye on her plate, and when he reached over to wipe soup from the side of her mouth, the ball of fufu surged down her throat. She grabbed a glass of water, drank it in one gulp, and began to cough. Tobe held her hand and said, '*Ndụ gi, ndụ gi.*' He held her hand until she stopped coughing. Then he brought out his handkerchief and wiped the tears that had leaked out of her eyes. She had never felt this nervous around a man before. And this was not the discomfort she experienced with Barrister Chima. This one flooded her with warmth that encircled her stomach before travelling down the bridge of her legs, staining her underwear with an embarrassing wetness.

They returned to Uncle Ugonna's home at past six in the evening, when the tangerine sun had grown weary and darkness crept over the sky. Aunty Ngozi emerged from the door, a wrapper knotted around her chest. She hugged Ogadinma and then she hugged Tobe.

'You must both be tired. Come inside, I cooked jollof rice and fish.'

He joined Aunty Ngozi in the parlour and Ogadinma fled into the room to stretch out beside Ifeoma who was fast asleep. She tried to remember how the day had gone, what she had said and how Tobe had felt about it, but she could not remember it all.

Tobe knocked on the door later, looked in and said she should escort him to his car. Outside, they lounged by the door. He asked if she would like to join him the following day for another round of shopping.

'It will keep you busy, you know. Rather than sit at home when no one is around.'

Nnanna was always around, she began to say, and there were also the stacks of books in Ifeoma's room which should keep her busy, but he was looking her in the eyes and she knew that she could not refuse his request. She did not want to refuse his request.

'Yes, I would like to join you.'

He enfolded her for a brief hug and she did not melt against him or rest her head against his shoulder, because she was afraid she would wrap her arms around his waist and refuse to let go. After he broke the hug and got in his car, she stood outside, in the dimly lit night, long after his car had turned at a corner.

It became a routine. Tobe would come every morning and take her with him to the market, or they drove around town and he showed her landmarks and his old neighbourhood in Yaba. One evening, after he dropped her off and she walked into the room, she found Ifeoma reading in bed.

'Ifeoma, kedụ?' she said casually, kicking off her shoes.

Ifeoma looked up from the book. 'Hmm,' she said. 'So are you two going out together?'

Ogadinma did not respond immediately. Tobe had not formally asked to date her, had yet to define their relationship. Once, she had a feeling that he was only being kind to her because Aunty Ngozi wanted him to do so. Aunty Ngozi was not the conventional kind of mother, the type who punished their daughters for talking to boys; she even ignored it when Ifeoma talked down to her, something many mothers would never tolerate. She stared at the wall and tried to remember how Tobe always looked into her eyes, the way his arms encircled her in brief hugs at the end of each evening. She searched her memories for signs that Tobe really liked her, but that could not clear the confusion clouding her mind.

'I don't know what we are doing,' she said.

'You don't know!' Ifeoma shrieked and began to laugh. Ogadinma was stunned by the laughter, because it sounded genuine. 'You should see the girls killing themselves to be Uncle Tobe's girlfriends. Big Lagos girls who are ready to use juju on any rich man they set their eyes on.'

Ogadinma laughed nervously. 'I haven't seen any girl around him.'

'That's because he chased them away! Mum doesn't like those girls. She thinks they are too wild. Uncle Tobe likes you very much.'

Ogadinma felt a new, numbing rush of hope. 'I think your mum just wants him to keep me from getting bored,' she said, though in her heart, she wanted what Ifeoma said to be true.

And Ifeoma knew this too, because she yelled, 'Story for the gods! He likes you jor.'

Tobe turned on the radio and Osadebe's soothing voice filled the car. She knew the song, it was her father's favourite. A memory of her father ironing and singing came back to her. She had yet to speak with her father since she came to Lagos. Whenever he called, which was rarely, it was to relay a message through Uncle Ugonna. He was still angry with her. Sometimes she longed to speak with him, to cry and beg for his forgiveness, so that they could return to being as they used to be. But Tobe had since swept up her attention, and now she realized she no longer felt that intense pang.

Tobe's quavering voice broke into her thoughts, so she lifted her voice, singing along, until their voices melded as one.

They rolled to a stop in front of a faded office complex in Ilupeju. 'My father used to work here,' he said. The guards sitting by the gate looked tired. They did not approach Tobe even though his car was parked right in front of the entrance.

'The week after my father was promoted to the post of regional director, he fell ill with a strange disease that made his tongue fall to his chest and his legs swell to the size of three yam tubers. I think they used ogwu to kill him. They couldn't stand having an Igbo man as their boss. My father died two weeks later – his ailment had no cure. He worsened when he was given Western medication,' Tobe said.

Did he really believe in ogwu? She remembered how her father tipped his head back and laughed when her grandmother dug up a rusty padlock on their farmland. Her grandmother had said that enemies were after their lives, that they used the ogwu to jinx her father's destiny. But her father never believed in that, just as he never believed in preachers. She doubted if her father believed in anything, because he went to church perfunctorily, showing up only when neighbours invited him for special services like child dedications, weddings and harvests. The only time he took her to church was on Christmas and New Year eves, when he brought her firecrackers. After the services, he would sit outside with the neighbours, and watch the children light the cigarette-shaped crackers and toss them in the distance. She knew her father would have scoffed at Tobe's story.

They returned to the car and drove for a long time; his brow was creased in worry. 'I hear they no longer pay staff salaries. The place has been run down by tribalistic cowards who wanted to keep the job for their people. That's what kills this country: tribalism. You should have seen this place when it was working. It was one of the best beverage companies in the whole of Nigeria, but tribalism killed it.'

Ogadinma agreed with him; she had seen first-hand how tribalism and religion could turn bloody, but she did not tell him her story. She did not want her gory memories to ruin their day.

He changed stations and King Sunny Ade's sonorous voice swam into the car. Sometimes, they rode in silence, watching people. Other times, they stood in front of old buildings and he shared the stories behind them, how he had played at the field with his mates and rushed home to bury his nose in his books before his father came home. How they trekked to school and saved their transport fare, only to use the money later to hire bicycles for a ride around their neighbourhood.

'What of your mother?' she asked.

'She was a housewife,' he said.

'She didn't run a business?'

'Why should she? Is it not the job of a woman to care for the family and for the man to provide? Is that not why we call our women "*Oriakụ*", the ones who enjoy the wealth? Am I mistaken?'

A drop of rain plopped on her arm, and then her face. A light drizzle started. She believed that a woman should run a business and earn her own money. But Tobe believed otherwise and she did not want to worry so much about this, because she did not want him to appear smudged before her eyes. And also, thinking about his ideals would mean she was imagining herself in his life and how those ideals would affect her. And she was not sure she wanted to think about that.

In the car, he left his hand lazily on her shoulder and steered the wheel with the other. Then the rains came, heavy and urgent. The windscreen misted over, and he turned on the air-conditioner. 'Tell me about yourself,' he said. 'You haven't really said anything about yourself.'

Cool air gushed out of the vents. There was a slight dusty smell before the air began to chill.

'There isn't really anything to say,' she said.

'Then say anything. I am tired of talking.'

Outside their window, a man got out of his car, stomped over to the car in front of him and pounded on the window, his hands drawn into fists. He made to pound the car again, but the driver rushed out and lunged at him. They wrestled. Cars honked, warning signs to the fighters who stumbled and tussled, falling against sitting cars. The traffic gave way at that moment. Tobe slammed on the accelerator and raced to escape. Other drivers curved past the wrestling men who were still swinging and sizing each other up.

'I don't swim,' she finally said.

He looked at her. 'Why?'

'Each time I stand by a pool, I get this feeling of falling. I fear I will drown if I ever go into a pool.'

He laughed. 'So, you drowned in a previous life?'

'My friend Ifedi drowned in a well when I was twelve. Since then, I never go close to wells or pools.'

'Then it is my job to cure you of that fear. We will go swimming tomorrow.'

'No!'

'I'll bring you a suit on my way tomorrow.'

'No, I will not go with you.' She had spoken so loudly, her words came out as a yell. She clamped a palm over her mouth, but he only looked amused.

'You are such a child. How old are you?'

'Seventeen.'

'Seventeen! You are a small *pikin o. Nekwa*, you are so young.' He looked at her curiously, as though seeing her with new eyes. 'Guess how old I am.'

A pause. 'Thirty.'

He threw his head back and laughed. A car honked from behind and he gripped the steering wheel tighter. 'That is the nicest compliment anyone has ever given me. I am not thirty, *nne*. I just turned thirty-five.'

Aunty Ngozi was at home when they returned. 'Your father called an hour ago,' she said.

Ogadinma's knees buckled. She had been in Lagos for a month, but it felt like a year had passed. 'Did he ask to speak with me?'

'Yes, and I told him that you are doing fine.'

'Can I speak with him?'

The telephone on the bedside table was covered with a light film of dust and handprints. Aunty Ngozi sat at the edge of the bed and began to dial the number. Ogadinma felt nauseous, with an urge to run out and lock herself up inside Ifeoma's room, and when Aunty Ngozi began to speak into the phone, her voice awkwardly high, Ogadinma felt a need to pee. She held the phone against her ear after Aunty Ngozi handed it to her, and she could not hear a thing from the other end for many seconds.

'Papa,' she said into the phone. 'Papa, good evening, sir.'

Her father drew a tense breath. '*Kedụ*? How are you?'

'I am doing fine, Papa. How are you too?' she asked. Outside, Aunty Ngozi was speaking with Tobe, both of them standing closely, their faces set with tense lines. 'I am fine, Papa,' Ogadinma said into the phone again.

The conversation was short. Her heart pounded furiously, and there was a whirling sound in her ears. Everything was floating away into a wave that howled and howled. She sat forward on the bed so that her elbows rested on her knees, because she feared that if she didn't, her knees would give way under her and she would slide to the floor and the line would cut and she wouldn't be able to reach her father again. Her hands shook. She should tell him about Tobe, about Aunty Ngozi's matchmaking, how Uncle Ugonna seemed to have approved of it. She should ask if he knew about it, if that was why he sent her to Lagos. But so much had changed between them. Now he talked in a clipped voice, his words punctuated with long, impenetrable silences. She had never heard him speak like this before, no longer knew how to talk to him, and could barely hear herself above the din in her ears and the heavy pounding in her temples. The call ended. After she put down the phone, she stood up, wishing she had said more and had asked what he ate, if he cooked his own meals. Her throat choked up and her eyes burned with tears.

She returned to her room and sat on the bed, staring into nothing. Aunty Ngozi walked in later.

'How is he?' Aunty Ngozi asked.

'He is doing fine.' She tried to smile.

'*Nne.*' Aunty Ngozi came to sit beside her. 'Tobe was invited to a wedding and he wants you to go with him.' She draped her hands over Ogadinma's shoulder. 'He has promised to buy you a dress and all the things you need for the occasion. Will you go with him?'

She stared at Aunty Ngozi. Something warm began to bubble in her chest, gradually chasing the previous sad feeling away. She did not ask why Tobe would want her to go with him to a wedding because she already knew why. And she wanted to tell Aunty Ngozi that there was no need to beg or cajole her into going with him because she wanted to. With Tobe, she was always happy, and she felt she was where she was meant to be. But she simply said, 'Yes, Aunty. I will go with him.'

The wedding party was rowdy. The hall, a makeshift tarpaulin dome set in the middle of a large field, was decorated with a sea of plastic red and white roses. The chairs were clothed in creamy satin and red bows, the tables packed with drinks and plates of small chops. It was a big-man wedding.

Tobe knew almost everyone. He swarmed from table to table, shaking hands, hugging friends, patting shoulders. He introduced Ogadinma as 'Nkem', 'his own', and his friends hailed him as one would a hunter who brought home the best bush meat. 'Tobe, my man! You picked the ripest udala. You have good eyes,' the men said. The women, dressed in overly embroidered stiff brocades and dresses, passed cursory stares at her dress, a silky red thing that flowed all the way to the floor, dragging extra length as a train, with a cut-out that left her back exposed all the way to her waist. One of them – the one wearing rows of jewellery that lay thick on her fat, sweaty neck – pursed her lips and said, '*Nne*, your gown is so fine! Is it London or Turkey?'

'It is London,' Ogadinma said.

Tobe held her hand and did not let go. He led her to their table, where two other couples sat, and he pulled her chair close, keeping his hand slung permanently over her shoulder. He smiled at her and whispered something. She did not hear him above the cacophony around them, but she thought about the workings of his mouth, how his eyes brightened and his lips peeled back when he smiled at her.

The women talked about their trips to America and London and how they would be travelling abroad to have their next children. Tobe talked with the men, and he turned often to ask if she was having fun.

They did not waste time at the wedding. When it was time for the money-spraying dance, he spoke in an exaggerated voice, carrying his shoulders higher as he walked, a big-man swagger in his gait. 'Let's go and spray them with some money and leave this place,' he said.

At the stage where the new couple danced, Tobe tore the wrappers off stacks of naira notes and flung them high above the couple. Money rained on the dancing floor. The crowd cheered. Some guests stood to watch the spectacle. Ogadinma was giddy as she sprayed the couple from the stack Tobe gave her. The couple, unashamedly ecstatic, hugged them and, though she did not know who they were, she told them, 'Congratulations.'

As they left the hall, the women watched them, their gazes flickering from her head to the train of her dress. She had never been to such a lavish ceremony, never walked beside a man like Tobe, never had other women look at her with so much envy in their eyes. She clung tighter to Tobe's arm as they left the hall, and for a moment, she wished he would slow his footsteps so they would take longer to make this grand exit. She had never felt this lucky in her entire life.

Back in the car, Tobe's eyes shone. 'I am so happy you came with me. You saw how everyone was looking at me as if I had brought Princess Diana with me? I am so happy.'

He sang to Osadebe and when Onyeka Onwenu came on the radio, Ogadinma sang at the top of her voice. They drove, singing to song after song.

The track was cut off abruptly and the news came on. Tobe turned up the volume of the radio. The newscaster, a woman with a thick Hausa accent, said that the federal government had launched a campaign called *War Against Indiscipline* to crack down on corruption, and would begin to arrest people who diverted public money during the previous government.

Tobe clucked his tongue and shook his head. 'Chief Adebiyi will not escape this. You remember him? He is the fat man at the wedding that was groping your hand when I introduced you.'

Ogadinma did not remember the man, or that anyone groped her. She was fleetingly disconcerted by the idea of Tobe watching every move she made, who she talked to.

'He was awarded the contract to repair the roads in Badagry but he totally diverted the money, filled up the potholes with red mud and plastered it with a film of tar,' Tobe continued. 'He must be pissing his pants now.'

Ogadinma stared ahead. She became aware of how close they had grown as the weeks passed, how he shared details about his life with her, and this excited and confused her.

'You are not here with me,' Tobe said, breaking into her thoughts. 'You are tired?'

'No, no. I just remembered how the women looked at my dress.'

He laughed. 'When I said you looked like Princess Diana, you thought I was joking? Let's go to the beach.'

It was early evening and the beach was still packed. He kicked off his shoes and she did the same and bunched the hem of her dress in her hands. The waves swept past the bank piled with sandbags and licked at the edges of the wooden stalls several feet away, then dragged dirt into the sea. Young boys on horseback rode past. Little children dashed to the mouth of the water, scooped wet sand before the waves returned.

'Before I left Nigeria, this water you see here swelled and swallowed all of this space, flooded the expressway and swept into houses on the other side. It even entered the Police Barracks,' Tobe said.

'Up to where Uncle Ugonna and Aunty Ngozi live?'

'Not up to their front door. But it flooded the front of the barracks. The government of that time dredged up sand from the sea and sent the water back. They filled these bags you are looking at, to keep the water away. But that's not enough. This place will be flooded once the rains fully return.'

He looked back; they had come quite a distance, away from the beach noise. 'I have always said to myself, whenever I am ready to marry, I would bring my woman here and ask her to marry me,' he said. 'I want to marry you. What do you think?'

The waves swept water around her feet, washing off the sand that clung to her toes. Something began to bubble inside of her, rising and swirling, filling her mouth with a sweet taste. She wanted to jump up and down and chant 'Yes! Yes!' But she feared that a wanton display of joy would come out as undignified, very unlike Princess Diana. So, she blinked and tried to pace her breathing, and when she spoke, her words came out as a near whisper. 'Yes,' she said. 'Yes,' she said again, unsure he heard her the first time.

He wrapped his arms around her, swayed. 'We will tell your uncle and my sister once we get back,' he said. When he began to break the hug, she held him. For a long time, she held him. She had no name for it, this feeling that made her want to slide into his body and become one with him. She pressed her lips against his neck. Then he pressed his lips against hers.

It was only after he had dropped her off and left and she was sitting between Uncle Ugonna and Aunty Ngozi that she realized the seriousness of all that was happening. Uncle Ugonna was staring at her, his eyes clouded with worry.

'Did it come from your heart?' he asked. 'No one should force you into doing what you don't want. So, I ask again: did it come from your heart?'

Aunty Ngozi held her hand, rubbed it, smiled.

'Yes, Uncle. It came from my heart,' she said.

She sat, slouched. How would her father feel about this?

'Go and rest. Sleep on it,' Uncle Ugonna said. 'We will talk again by morning.'

But she did not sleep well that night. She gazed at the ceiling until morning came; she was too giddy, too wired to close her eyes. And when Uncle Ugonna called her into the parlour again and asked if she willingly accepted to be Tobe's wife, she still didn't feel any different, and so she nodded.

'Yes, Uncle,' she said. 'It came from my heart.'

'Then I will send a message to your father to inform him. Tobe will go with you to Kano to meet your father.'

4

Ogadinma looked out of the window as they drove in the slow traffic. A man was rolling in the dirt, thrashing and kicking out as a snarling soldier flogged him, the horsewhip curling in the air before landing on the man's body. The windows of their car were up, otherwise Ogadinma would have heard his shrieks. On the other side of the road, another man was hunched over on his knees, frog-jumping at the command of a soldier who followed menacingly behind, caressing his gun.

Tobe rubbed her shoulder. 'You are not here with me. What are you thinking?'

She looked at him and smiled. Things felt different this time, maybe because the condition of their relationship was now clearly defined. Or maybe because her status as a wife-to-be meant she was supposed to behave in a certain way, even though she didn't know exactly how a wife-to-be was supposed to behave. Perhaps it simply meant obeying Tobe. Still, she felt the weight of expectation pressing down on her shoulders. And it started when he began to take her home to cook his meals. Once, his friends dropped by and Tobe introduced her as 'the girl I am going to marry'. The men praised him for 'having a good eye' and thumped his back. 'Tobe, she is easily the most beautiful woman out there,' said Segun, who spoke in a voice that rumbled. There was also Femi who fondled his goatee when he spoke. There were others, too, who dropped by at different times. She would sit in the kitchen and nibble on a piece of fried meat or

fish because she sensed the men needed the privacy to discuss important things, and also because Tobe never invited her to join in their
discussions. After they had eaten and left, Tobe would kiss or hold
her firmly against his chest. But he never peeled off her clothes, was
not in a hurry to know her body.

He parked the car in front of a row of stores and they entered
the one lit with neon fluorescent lamps. The shop owner, a thickly
built man with a stubby beard, offered them seats and mineral water.
Tobe asked to see some of the dresses and the man brought them in
piles, holding out each one before Tobe, turning it this way and that.

Ogadinma touched a red structured dress. 'I like this one. I think
it is the prettiest.'

The seller agreed and thrust the dress into her hands.

Tobe snorted. 'What do you even know about fashion?' Then he
laughed in the way that said he was making a joke, but he shoved
the red dress back into the hands of the seller and reached for a
green one instead.

Ogadinma sank in her seat, suddenly wishing she had not spoken.
And when Tobe asked her to try on the dress, she did not object. In
the narrow changing room, the lights were too bright, and she thought
she looked gorgeous in the dress. She was worrying too much, and
so her mind had become a haven for foolish thoughts. She should
chase them away, set herself free. She turned at an angle, and then
hurried out to show him the dress.

The following day, a Sunday, Ifeoma shook her awake and pointed
at the bloodstain on the bed. She had overslept. There was a pulsing
ache in her lower abdomen. She clutched her stomach as she got off
the bed. Ifeoma removed the sheet and rolled it in a bunch.

'You have cramps,' Ifeoma said.

'The first day is always hell for me.'

'Ndo. Go and take your bath. I will get you paracetamol.'

In the bathroom, she sponged and massaged her stomach with
warm water until she was numb. When she returned to the room,

she found the cup of water and the packet of paracetamol sitting on the table.

She had just swallowed two tablets when Tobe drove in. He wore a blue kaftan that was starched and ironed into crisp lines, black embroidery threading the neckline and the cuffs. Even in the simple outfit every man in Lagos owned, he looked kingly and flamboyant. Perhaps it was because of the way he carried himself, his hands slightly stretched out, as though he had tennis balls glued to his armpits. Ogadinma watched him through the window as he approached the entrance, her face so close that she could smell the layer of dust coating the criss-cross netting which would give off the smell of fresh earth and rust when it rained.

Aunty Ngozi came out to meet him. They talked in low voices. She should go and greet him, but she stayed in bed. She could not believe she would be marrying this man. She could not believe how quickly everything had changed. When she told her father about Tobe's proposal, she could not tell if he was happy or disappointed and this had left her feeling uncertain, nervous, a dampening feeling that continued to trail her to this day.

She was still lying in bed, pretending to be asleep, when Tobe looked in. 'Ogadinma.'

She opened her eyes and sat up. 'Good morning.'

He came and sat beside her. The collar of his kaftan was buttoned too tight, so tight that his neck bulged. 'I want to take you to meet my good friend who is visiting from the east,' he said. 'I have told him about you and he is eager to meet you.'

'I can't go out today *biko*,' she began. 'My period has started and I am bleeding heavily.'

His brows crumpled, his face folding in. 'Since when did menstruation stop people from going out? Or are you now the first woman to see her period?'

She opened and closed her mouth. Tobe was looking at her, his gaze so blank, so vacant. Ifeoma's laughter carried down the passage, piercing the tensed air. Ifeoma didn't have to seek anyone's permission before she laughed, before she did anything at all. Ogadinma wished she could be a little strong-willed like Ifeoma so that Tobe would understand when she didn't want something, when she must be by herself. But she pushed herself off the bed and said, 'I will get dressed now.'

After he left, she took her time putting on the green dress. Now it looked dull, and the fabric was too heavy. Tobe was speaking with Aunty Ngozi. She put on her shoes, and then stood in front of the mirror, turning from side to side, searching for her best angle, an angle that would make the outfit look more appealing. She did not find it.

When she came outside, Tobe was still speaking with Aunty Ngozi. He looked grave. And Aunty Ngozi was holding his hand, speaking in low, calming tones. Ogadinma ducked back into the house, her palms suddenly clammy. She knew Tobe was complaining about what just happened because when Aunty Ngozi returned, she did not say that her dress was fine or her shoes were pretty as she always said of the things Tobe gave her; she did not look at Ogadinma at all. '*Jee nụ nke ọma*,' she simply said. 'Go well.' And she entered the flat, her slippers making angry *slap-slap-slap* sounds under her feet.

For a long time as they drove out of the estate, Tobe did not speak, did not look in her direction. His jaw was grinding, his back was straight like cardboard. She should be angry with him for being so insensitive and callous, but being as naïve as she was, she cared more about his feelings. She wondered why something as simple as her menstrual cramps would make him mad.

They were nearing Ikeja when he pulled the car over at the side of the road and turned sharply to her. 'Why did you have to disrespect me like that?' he asked, but before she could speak, he was wagging a finger, saying, '*Nekwa anya*, I don't want it to look like I am forcing you to do things you don't want to. So, if you feel this thing we are doing is not from your heart, you better speak up now. Do you understand me?'

She was too stunned to speak, so she simply nodded and faced forward, blinking rapidly to chase away the urge to cry. Tobe drove off again. An uncomfortable silence wedged itself between them. He turned on the stereo but did not sing along as Onyeka Onwenu's melodious voice sifted from the speaker. He did not look in her direction again until he pulled up in front of a hotel, then he killed the engine and sat staring out of the windscreen, still gripping the wheel. Ogadinma held her breath, afraid to look at him again or even move, so he would not explode in more rage. It seemed a long moment passed before he turned and wrapped his arms around her.

'I don't want to shout at you again, i nu?'

She sighed, dizzy with relief.

He broke the hug, held her face in his hands. 'Are you okay now?'

Her eyes stung with unshed tears, but she said yes, that she was fine. It was because of the way he looked at her, his eyes mellowed with remorse, his lips thinned out in sad lines.

The bar was dim and the air was thick with smoke and music and voices. His friends were seated at the table at the far end of the room, talking over bottles of beer and plates of barbecued catfish.

'Here comes the finest couple in town,' said Femi. His words were slurred.

Segun shook her hand. The third man, Kelechi, was striking in a way that was disconcerting: warm eyes hidden behind bold-framed glasses, muscles rippling underneath his white kaftan, stretching from shoulder to shoulder. He was a head taller than Ogadinma, who was taller than Tobe and his other friends. Her first reaction when Kelechi reached out to give her a hug was to melt against him. And this startled and embarrassed her. She stood stiffly when he enfolded her in a perfunctory hug and broke away quickly after a brief touch of their bodies. She had never seen a man so beautiful.

'I can see the Lagos sun has yet to give you a proper welcome,' Tobe said, hugging Kelechi, his voice drowsy with affection and joy. 'It is so good to see you again, my brother.'

'It is so good to see you too,' Kelechi said. 'Your fiancée is very beautiful. You have picked the ripest fruit, my brother.'

Ogadinma could tell it was pride that crinkled Tobe's eyes at the corners. She was usually amused when people talked about her beauty, but when Tobe said, 'Oh, please don't praise her too much before it enters her head. You know these women, they begin to feel too big when you overpraise their beauty,' laughing in that way that said it was a joke, she flinched, and sat down.

'When are you guys getting married?' Kelechi asked.

'Probably next month. I have to travel to Kano to see her father. I look forward to meeting him, but I dread that visit. I hate Kano with a passion.'

'Come on, man! That was my city,' Kelechi said, and before Tobe could reply, he turned to Ogadinma: 'I guess you live in Sabon Gari.'

'Her father lives in New Road. That's the only nice place in that city,' Tobe said.

Femi laughed. 'Sabon Gari is very cosmopolitan now.'

'I visited in '81,' Tobe said.

'Sabon Gari is very cosmopolitan now,' Femi insisted.

'Since when, after all the riots and mindless killings?'

'You really hate the place, don't you?' Segun said.

'I think you would too, if you had lost a relative in one of their religious riots.' Everyone looked at him. He pulled a plate of fish closer and dug in. 'This fish is not going to eat itself,' he said.

But his attempt at humour fell flat because everyone was watching him. Ogadinma touched his arm. She wanted to ask which of his relatives he lost in the Kano riot, but this was not the place and time for that question, so she held his hand and squeezed, willing him to feel how sorry she was. He looked at her, patted her arm and told her to eat the fish. She began to eat.

'These new guys are already flexing their muscles, threatening everyone,' Kelechi said. 'Did you hear the announcement about prosecuting civilians and censoring the press? I don't think that Head of State has his head screwed on right.'

Tobe thought it wasn't a bad idea for the military to go after corrupt civilians, but Kelechi said the plan would backfire.

As they talked, Ogadinma's gaze kept drifting to the bulging vein in Kelechi's left temple. Her worst memories of the military rule were when a group of soldiers punished her father for overtaking them at a junction. They had kicked him around, his long spindly legs rolling in the roadside dirt, his body caked with dust. After they left, he brushed his clothes, patted his hair, and told her to wipe her tears. Then he said that nothing good came out of a military regime, that soldiers were all thugs.

The bar had become crowded. The fan above them whirred noisily and so did the standing fan at a distance from their table. Back in Kano, only girls who wore tight jeans and red lipstick and hoop earrings walked into bars, the type of girls many parents warned their daughters to stay away from. Now Ogadinma was sitting in a bar, and in the company of men. There was nothing fun about this place, not the smell, not the noisy Highlife music nor the overpowering heat, and definitely not the men, who had begun to argue about politics again. She ate her fish and drank her malt, half-listening to them, wondering if her pad had soaked too much.

'Your fiancée is so quiet,' Kelechi said later. 'She just sits and watches.'

'She is not like those women who put their mouths into conversations that aren't their business and nag like market women,' Tobe said. 'She has home training.'

Ogadinma smiled; it was the only thing she could do. She glanced at Tobe and then to Kelechi, who was watching her steadily, curiosity wrinkling his brow. 'I used to live with an uncle in Yankaba. Have you ever been to Yankaba?'

'It is not so far from Sabon Gari,' she said.

'Did this big-head ever tell you how we met after the war?' He gestured at Tobe. 'He was so thin and rough, his skin diseased from eating rodents and lizards in Biafra. We were friends in primary school.'

Tobe laughed. Ogadinma looked at him. She had no memories of the war, and her father never spoke about it. She tried to imagine

Tobe as a young boy with diseased skin, climbing trees and combing bushes, hunting rodents and reptiles, but she could not.

'His family hid in Lagos throughout the war,' Tobe said.

'He was playing football with us,' Segun chirped.

'That's when we weren't dodging the Nigerian soldiers on the streets of Lagos,' Kelechi said.

'And you and your siblings stopped speaking Igbo, so no one would identify you,' Tobe said.

Kelechi grinned and said, 'My little brothers don't speak Igbo any more. They understand the language but don't speak it because my parents discouraged it during the war. They did that so we could survive.'

'Well, you didn't turn out bad.'

'You are going to marry the most beautiful woman in the world and I have yet to make meaning out of my life,' Kelechi said.

It was a genuine comment. Kelechi was smiling. Femi and Segun too. But Tobe did not smile. 'You make it sound like I am doing what nobody has ever done,' he said. Bruised, Ogadinma bent over her plate and continued to eat her fish.

'Well, it means you are at least getting one thing right. Plus, you did make a killing from the Shagari government,' Kelechi insisted.

Tobe hissed. 'And didn't you win the contract to build the Anambra State Broadcasting Service and Television Studio? Come on, Kelechi! We all made money from the former government. Legitimate money.'

They laughed.

'I think this *War Against Indiscipline* campaign will end up being a tool for witch-hunting,' Kelechi said. 'The Deputy Head of State is the one I am worried about. He is a show-off, a dangerous show-off. He just sent my friend to prison. You remember him? The former Anambra Governor who gave me the radio contract.'

Tobe sighed. 'I read about that.'

'Hopefully they will not get power-drunk,' Segun said.

'I think they are already drunk.'

The topic clearly disturbed Tobe, and Ogadinma wondered, briefly, if he worried that he would be affected by the campaign. She slung a hand around his waist, nervously tightening her arms around him. He was so surprised that, for a moment, he did not hug her back. She had never initiated an embrace before, and now she had shocked herself. But then he encircled her with both arms, pressed her head against the soft of his chest. When he spoke again, his voice lifted, his eyes bright with laughter.

That night, after he dropped her off, Aunty Ngozi came into the bedroom. 'My brother is spoiling you silly,' she said. 'He has a good heart, but he has only one problem: he has a temper. Be a virtuous wife, and you will enjoy him well-well.'

'Thank you, Aunty.'

Later, when she stretched out beside Ifeoma's sleeping form, she thought of that hug at the bar, how Tobe had leaned against her, how his tensed breathing had calmed. And the beginnings of a smile curled her lips.

5

They arrived in Kano on a hot morning, when a light breeze swept up dust in spirals and the open gutters at the park smelled like they had not been cleaned out in years.

The walking distance to her home was seven minutes but Tobe flagged down a taxi, a green-and-yellow wagon that shivered, its loose bolts jangling as it ferried them to her compound, the two-storey building whose paint had faded so badly it was difficult to tell the original colour.

Her father was standing by the gate when they arrived. He shook Tobe's hand and hugged her. When he pulled away, his eyes were wet with delight. And she sighed. He was pleased by the news of the proposal.

She walked inside their apartment and, for a moment, was jarred by the state of their parlour. The ceiling was stained with puddles of water from the bathroom of the flat above theirs, the only two sofas in the room were splitting at the seams. The curtains were old, and the carpet had cracked in places. She had lived there all her life and for the first time she saw how they lived. She flinched when Tobe sat stiffly, his legs pressed together, his hands on his lap, as though he was avoiding further contact with the old sofa.

'I have never seen my daughter like this,' her father was telling Tobe, his voice wistful. 'I have never seen my daughter this happy.' He was smiling too much. And Ogadinma did not know how to feel about this. They had parted on sad terms, and he had refused to speak to her over the phone until one month passed. When she told him about Tobe's proposal, he had responded in a clipped voice. Now he was smiling, his eyes twinkling, the dimples in his cheeks deepening. And she did not know how to feel about this sudden change.

She muttered excuses and silently walked to her room. The cement floor was rough. She remembered how smooth the tiled floor of Uncle Ugonna's house felt under her feet. She reached under her bed for her copy of Flora Nwapa's book, *Efuru*, and tried to read. But her father's and Tobe's voices floated in, interrupting her concentration. Sometimes, they shared laughter, but Tobe's laughter was subdued; it was not the loud, free celebration she had come to know. This one was tamed, as though he only laughed because it would be awkward if he didn't.

'He is a good man,' her father said later, when he came into the room and found her staring out of the window.

'Yes, Papa. He is a good man.'

They stared at each other, saying nothing. She searched his face for evidence that their relationship had returned to how it used to be. But she could not tell, from the way he smiled, if he was happy because he missed her or because she brought a suitor home.

'He is taking his shower now,' he said. 'He tells me he will be taking the night bus to Lagos.'

'I guess he has important things to do in Lagos tomorrow,' she said.

They looked at each other for a while, before he stood. She watched him walk out of her room, how his back seemed straighter. His shoulders no longer seemed crushed in, and his gait was swift and sure. He looked energetic.

Later, after Tobe and her father had talked for a long time, he called out her name. She went to the parlour. Tobe was finally slouched on the sofa. There were dark circles under his eyes; he had barely slept during the long trip here.

'*Ada m*, come and sit.' Her father patted a space on the sofa and she went and sat. He said Tobe had told him of his intention, he said Tobe wanted their wedding done in two weeks.

'What do you think?' her father asked her.

It was so sudden, she thought, but her father's eyes shone when he spoke, the brightest she had seen him since she came home from the hospital. She looked at Tobe and felt, for the first time, that he was the one who had come to repair the dent she had made on her father's name, the reason her father was finally smiling with her. This filled her with a mix of feelings: she was glad that her relationship with her father had been repaired, yet she was sad that they needed Tobe to mend their relationship. She knew then that his appearance in their life meant she would no longer go to university. And she blamed herself for how everything had turned out.

'I love him, Papa,' she said, looking at Tobe, her eyes filled with gratitude. 'I am okay with the plans.'

She walked Tobe to the park that afternoon, when the sun had come out, angry and blazing. Even the soles of her slippers burned from walking the short distance to the park. Tobe bought a ticket and they stood under a tree, talking, until it was time for his bus to leave.

'Keep well,' he said, hugging her. 'I will see you soon.'

He got into the bus and her chest felt tight. She wanted to run after him, to tell him to take her back to Lagos, but she didn't. They would be married in two weeks in her home town, but for now, she was expected to stay at her father's house until Tobe had paid her bride price and concluded all the marriage rites.

'See you soon,' she whispered. But he had already got onto the bus. And so, she stood there, waving and waving, as the bus pulled out of the park. She was still waving when the bus joined the main road and turned at a corner.

The rains came that March, heavy and fervent, flooding everywhere, until everyone waded through the streets knee-deep in muddy water. No one fetched water during the first two days because it was when the rains washed the corrugated roofing sheet, cleansing them of the thick layer of harmattan dust, until clear, drinkable water rushed down the gutters. Ogadinma had always liked this season. As a child, she and other children danced naked under the rain. It was when they filled their tanks and basins and gallons, when they didn't need to fetch salty water from the well down the street. This time, smaller children enjoyed her childhood pastime. Her mind was preoccupied with her upcoming wedding.

Tobe called every day to talk about their preparations, how she was, the plans he had made. He also told her about the tension at his office, that soldiers often stopped by to check his books. He didn't sound worried, though; he had executed every government project and had not diverted a kobo. If anything, it was the past government that still owed him some money. He didn't seem worried, and she was relieved that he wasn't. The week before they travelled to their home town, he sent her a bag of clothes, laces and Ankara fabrics that had been sewn into ogodo and blouses with puffy sleeves, and ichafu that she would need to tie in pleats and layers until it sat on her head like a pineapple, like the women at the church.

It rained in sheets on the day they left, the winds howling, slapping against the window shutters, banging doors, causing electric wires to slap together. Their front yard had flooded, and they had to remove their shoes before wading into the pool. Her father had told her to check the rooms to make sure she had not forgotten anything important. She walked from room to room, but she did not spend too much time in her own because she feared she would crumple on her bed, hold her pillow tight against her chest and refuse to travel again. So she carried her bag and hurried out of the flat.

They arrived at Abagana after seven the following morning, when small children in dust-coloured uniforms were marching to school. Her family's home, a brown-painted bungalow, was at the end of a bumpy dirt track some ten electric poles from the main road, with two coconut trees flanking the entrance of the gateless compound. The house was bordered by a fence of short ogirisi trees strung together with omu stalks, the fence so short she could see into the yards of the neighbours on either side. Older men and women were sitting in front of their thatched huts, cleaning their teeth with chewing sticks and spitting out in their front yards. They rose and greeted. 'Ụnụ anatago? I hope you journeyed well? Welcome!'

Ogadinma muttered greetings. Her father went to shake hands with the men. Her grandmother limped into the sunlight, squinting. For a moment, Ogadinma did not recognize her. Two years had passed, and her grandmother had grown gaunt, her cheeks sunken, as though she sucked them in, making the angles of her eyes stand out eerily.

'Mama,' her father cried, hurrying to her.

And her grandmother began to shout.

'My son! Have you come back?' Barefoot, she limped towards them, her hands stretched wide as she embraced her father first, turning him around and around and singing hearty songs, before crushing Ogadinma against her long breasts. She smelled of snuff and pomade.

'Ogadinma, neke! You have grown so tall,' she said. The whites of her eyes had browned, and were streaked with red veins, and she blinked too often, touching Ogadinma's face with a quivering hand, as though struggling to make out her features.

Ogadinma carried their bags into her father's room, smaller than her own in Kano, the ceiling so low she could touch it if she stood on tiptoes. She threw open the windows. The mosquito netting was caked with red dust, and so were the curtains and the windowsill. She made a note to clean the entire room and wash the curtains later. For now, she stood by the window, looking into the yard. Their village looked different this time, dull and dusty, and emptied of people, as if everyone had packed their things and left, leaving behind only the old, tired folks and their children. But then, she only came home with her father during Christmas, when people living in the cities travelled down to their villages to celebrate the holidays with their old parents. During Christmas, she had too many places to go, too many people to visit with her father, too many carnivals and festivals to attend. But now, everywhere looked dry and empty, and the layer of red dust coating everything was hard to ignore.

Her grandmother and her father were sitting on the bench by the veranda, talking. Her grandmother's health was worsening; she had woken with pains all over her body, and this had been going on for over a month.

Her father was upset. 'But, Mama, I have told you to always telephone me from Nwude's house if there is any emergency, so why didn't you mention this when we spoke last week? And where is that girl staying with you, Chinelo? Why didn't she call me? Has she run away again? I haven't seen her this morning, where is she?'

Her grandmother flicked away an insect that was crawling up her leg. Her cornrows were fuzzy and loosening at the ends, her hair an uneven mix of black and white, like someone had poured a can of powder on her head. 'N'eziokwu, I should have called you, but I didn't. You have spent too much money caring for me. Nee anya, I am an old woman. I will soon go to sleep and join my mothers.'

'Mama, stop talking like that. Stop talking nonsense. You still have many years to spend with us. Stop talking like this, biko.'

She squeezed his hand. 'Look how well you have done for yourself and your daughter, at this time girls are spoiling like old beans and disgracing their families, see how well you have raised that girl.' She rubbed his shoulder with unsteady hands. 'If only you will let me find you another wife who will give you a son. Ugonna, he has a son. His name will not die off when he joins his fathers.'

'Mama, stop all this talk, it is not the reason we came home.'

She sighed. 'You speak like your father. He did not listen to his stupid brothers when they tried to get him to marry a second wife. You know it took years before you and your siblings came, and during that waiting period, your father did not care at all that there was no cry of a baby in his house. In fact, he chased his brothers away when they tried to come between us. You are your father's son.'

All the wistful talk reminded Ogadinma of her mother. It had been a long time since Ogadinma had thought of her. She brought out her parents' framed wedding photo from the bedside chest, wiped the dust coating the glass covering, ran a finger over the unsmiling face of the woman who looked not much older than Ogadinma herself. Every time Ogadinma stared at this photograph, her heart skipped and her mood dampened. It was the way her mother stood rigidly beside her father as if she wanted some distance; she did not seem to want anything to do with him. Sometimes, Ogadinma wished she could run a finger over her mother's face and transform the sad mien into a happy expression.

She still thought of her mother when she showered in the narrow bathroom, when she prepared meals in the afternoon with Chinelo, the small, soft-spoken girl who had lived with her grandmother since forever.

The thoughts of her mother haunted her in the following days, even on the morning of her wedding day, when Tobe and the men of his umunna came to pay her bride price. The ceremony was performed in their parlour, away from the curious eyes of women and girls, by the men of both families because only the men decided the price of a bride.

Aunty Ngozi came that morning with the pickup van full of food-stuffs for the wedding party. She ran a hand over Ogadinma's newly braided hair, nodding and making approving sounds.

'The hairstyle suits your face, but I would have preferred a wig. There is this reigning style young girls are making in Lagos. It sweeps over the forehead like this.' She demonstrated. 'Ọ maka. The style is called Diana Ross. But this one is also okay. It suits you well.'

The wives of the umunna, seven women who were dressed in faded wrappers knotted over old blouses and scarves tied lazily over their heads, came to help with the cooking, as custom demanded. The women all looked alike, these women with sun-baked skin and wiry hands that had callused from tilling the land and planting crops. Did her mother go on such customary duties dressed like them, when she was still here? She wondered if the women still remembered what her mother looked like. Then she wished her mother was here, cooking with them.

The women brought out the metal tripods and firewood and huge ite ọna pots from the kitchen and set them in the open. They mixed palm oil and detergent and slicked the paste on the bodies of the pots, so that they would be able easily to wash off charcoal stains after they had finished cooking.

Her grandmother sat on a low stool, telling the women what to do, her lips set in serious lines as she pointed from basin to kitchen. 'We will make onugbu soup first, and then the moin-moin and ukwa and pepper soup, and then cook the jollof rice last. Mama Nkechi, please bring out the basins of meat. *Nwunye nwa m* said they brought five basins. Bring them out, let's cut them into pieces.'

Her grandmother entered the room later carrying a bucketful of fried goat meat. 'This one you are sitting and staring like this, is everything all right? Your face is not bright, what is wrong?'

'I have been thinking of my mother,' Ogadinma said.

She put the bucket down and limped towards the bed and sat beside Ogadinma. She touched Ogadinma's face, ran a trembling finger along the ridge of her nose. When she spoke, her voice was weighed down with old pain. 'You know what your mother's problem was? She was too ambitious. She wanted to do everything in the world as though she was a man, reducing my son to the wife, and it did not work.'

Ogadinma swiped at her tears.

'*Nee anya*, you are getting married to a good man. A woman cannot sit on top of the man. It does not work like that – do you understand what I am saying?'

'Yes, Mama Nnukwu,' she said.

'Now, wipe your face. It is your wedding day.' She pulled Ogadinma to her chest. 'Take some goat meat. I will bring you some moin-moin to eat.'

Pestles pounded into mortars, the women sang as they cooked, and the men worked on putting up a makeshift venue. Loudspeakers crackled, a voice kept speaking into the microphone, saying, 'Testing the microphone, 1, 2, 3!' over and over again, as though he could not hear his voice echoing around the whole neighbourhood, as though he could not hear excited children from the nearby compounds running around and laughing and laughing, all of them chanting, 'Testing the microphone 1, 2, 3!'

Ogadinma was not hungry. She shut her eyes and tried to sleep but when sleep eventually came, hands shook her awake. Faces hovered above her: excited faces, moving mouths. It took her moments to make out the faces – Ifeoma and Nnanna and four other girls. Ogadinma recognized the girls, their familiar noses, the long jaws, the thick eyebrows. Nkechi, Adaobi, Nkoli and Nnenne. They were the daughters of one of the wives of the umunna.

'*Nekwa*, it is past twelve and you are still sleeping!'

'Have you even taken your bath?'

'She has not even done anything!'

'Don't you know that people have started to arrive?'

'*Kunie*, Ogadinma! Sit up. Why are you staring at us like that?'

They were all speaking at the same time. She hugged each of them. Everything was moving so quickly. When she broke the hug, Ifeoma asked if she was crying and Nnanna said he would go and sit with the men. Nkechi told her to go and take a shower. Nnenne asked where she kept her dress. Ifeoma was already pulling open the bag, getting out the dresses, the pale blue lace buba, the red ichafu and matching red shoes and handbag.

'*Nne*, go and take your bath. Your in-laws will be here soon,' Nkoli said.

Ogadinma hastened out of the room, dizzy. The wedding was really happening. She really was about to become Tobe's wife.

In the bathroom, she barely let the water run over her body, barely scoured her body with the sponge and soap, before rinsing off and hurrying back into the room.

Ifeoma had laid out the ogodo and blouse and the ichafu on the bed.

'You chose the best colour,' Nkoli said, her voice wistful, as she ran a finger over the heavy material.

Ogadinma began to say she hadn't chosen the colour, that she hadn't chosen anything at all, but Nkoli had already turned her attention to Ifeoma.

'You are going to be beautiful in them,' Nkoli said, stroking the dress longingly. '*Ngwa*, come. Let's get you ready.' She removed Ogadinma's towel with one tug, causing her to hurriedly cup her breasts and crotch, and the girls began to laugh.

'What are you hiding that we don't have?' Nkechi said.

Ogadinma gave them a nervous grin and reached for her underwear. She had never played that way with any other girl, not even with Ifeoma, who sat with the girls, laughing.

Ifeoma helped wrap the ogodo around her waist and knot it at one end, and then pulled on her blouse. Nkechi held up the mirror, Nkoli wrapped her head with the ichafu and Ifeoma applied her makeup. She lined Ogadinma's brows with pencil, dabbed her cheeks with loose powder and smeared her lips with a nude peach lipstick because Nkoli said red would be too '*shouty*'.

After Ifeoma was done, she stood back, then dabbed at the smudged lipstick. '*Ehen*! Now you look like somebody's wife.' She straightened the ichafu and the ogodo.

'I think they are going to play Osadebe's "Ọsọndị Owendị" when it is time for you and your husband to dance,' Adaobi said.

'Make sure you dance well-well. Bend down and shake your waist well-well, *inu*?' Nnenne said.

Ogadinma gazed at her reflection in the mirror. Her eyes no longer looked swollen; Ifeoma's eyeliner had worked magic. She laughed and forced brightness into her eyes.

'Another important thing: once you get back to Lagos with him, just make sure you get pregnant before next Christmas, or people will say you went to his house to watch TV,' Nnenne said.

'Yes o,' Nkechi said. 'Do not let your husband rest once you go to Lagos, because when nine months has passed and you are not breastfeeding your baby, or at least sporting a huge stomach, people will begin to say something is wrong with you. You don't want that.'

Ogadinma felt a gnawing in her stomach, but she nodded and said okay, that she would do as they said. Her grandmother walked in and the girls swarmed to her, to help her get dressed up. Ogadinma watched them flatter her grandmother but she hardly heard what they said, why they speckled their words with laughter, because the memory of her abortion and the complication played across her mind. And for the first time, she feared that something bad had happened to her body.

The wedding party soon started. 'Nke Onye Dili Ya' boomed from the speakers. Tobe and his people had arrived. Tobe, in his short-sleeved isiagu and red cap, danced to where her father and his brothers sat. He waved a glazed elephant tusk, cheered at the beaming crowd. He danced like he was royalty. Her father and Uncle Ugonna and the men of her umunna stood to welcome them. They shook hands. They hugged. Ogadinma sat back on the bed, relieved.

Ifeoma returned. She pinched Ogadinma's cheeks. 'Come, it's time to take the wine to him.'

Her knees became weak. Outside, Ifeoma and the sisters, and some other girls, whose names she could not remember, all dressed in elaborate ogodo and blouse and ichafu, had lined up, singing the Igbo wedding song. 'Ọ naa, ọ naa be ya! Ọ naa, ọ naa be ya!'

Ogadinma danced slowly, smiled as wide as she could, as the girls led the train that finally stopped in front of her father. She knelt before him after the girls had danced away. She shut her eyes briefly when he touched her face. Her mother's unsmiling face flitted into her mind. Had her mother also felt this jittery on her wedding day? Was that why she didn't smile in the photo? She opened her eyes. Her father was smiling. He poured palm wine into a gourd, took a perfunctory sip and pressed the gourd into her hands. 'Take this to the man you have chosen to be your husband,' he said.

Her shoes had filled with grits of sand which bit into her feet with each step she took. She tried to remember what Ifeoma said about pretending she hadn't seen Tobe, how she was supposed to tease other men, flirt and smile, before finally going to Tobe.

As she walked past, men stretched out their hands and begged for the wine.

'Nne, give me the wine and I promise to take care of you.'

'*Nwaanyị ọma*, don't you remember me any more? I made a promise to love you.'

'*Nne*, come to my home and I will make you the happiest woman.'

The compound was filled to the brim with people, all of them dressed in elaborate fineries. The voices teased, playing out their part in the old tradition. She placed one foot after the other, walked down the length of the compound, past smiling faces. It was Kelechi's presence, at the canopy crowded by visitors, that calmed her nerves. Kelechi with his confident smile that seemed to assure her that everything was going to be all right, that she didn't need to worry herself into a knot. He looked like she remembered, and his well-fitted white kaftan made him look more broad-shouldered.

When she finally got to where Tobe sat, she knelt and offered him the gourd. He looked at her, and she worried that he could sense her nervousness. But then he took the gourd and drank from it, and stroked her face with his thumb. Cheers erupted around them. He helped her to her feet, and together they went to her father and knelt before him.

'Hold your wife's hand,' her father told Tobe.

Ogadinma caught a last glimpse of her father's eyes as blessings spilled from his chapped lips:

'You will have six male children, and you will have three female children

You will prosper in all your endeavours, you will never lack

You will raise your children and your children will care for you when you have grown old

No evil mind shall see you, and none shall succeed in their plot against you

You will live in good health, in love, and you will grow old together

Chukwu will never hide his face from you.'

The clans chorused: 'Ise!'

She knew she had finally brought honour to her father's name.

6

They returned to Lagos right after the wedding, one sunny after-noon in March. The roads were deserted. Soldiers toting long guns speckled the streets. It was a Wednesday, and it was as if every-one had packed their chaos and left. This strange, grave orderliness was not the Lagos she had come to know.

Tobe's new gateman, a young dark-skinned boy who looked as if he should be in school, threw open the gates, and then he rushed over to greet them as Tobe rolled to a stop in front of the house. 'Oga, madam! Una welcome o,' he said. His forehead was wide and curved and took up half of his face, and when he bowed in greeting again, Ogadinma thought his skull was shaped like a mango.

'*Ehen*, Kunle, how are you?' Tobe asked him.

Kunle bowed and grinned again. 'I dey fine, sir!'

Ogadinma had been to his house often but the mere expansiveness of the one-storey structure, with its tiled front yard that was wide enough to contain another house, the coconut trees that dotted the sides, the flower beds with blooming, colourful beauties whose names she did not know, still left her dazed.

Tobe slung a hand over her shoulder and led her to the front door. 'We will get the bags later,' he said. Ogadinma was dizzy; she could not yet believe that this had become her home. When she thought of home, it was the flat she lived in with her father. Not this sprawling house, this astonishing marker of wealth.

Tobe opened the door. Trapped dank air rushed out, carrying the smell of dust and paint. Everything was covered in a film of dust – the dining table, the shelves holding the TV, the side tables, the centre table and the flower vase. The same brown film covered the floor of the passage that connected the rooms, the kitchen, the bathroom. Tobe stood in the passage, hands on hips.

'We have so much work to do.'

He pulled her close to his chest, rubbed his hands over her stomach, down between her legs, cupped her breasts. He led her into the connecting room, whispering things but she could not comprehend his sentences because her knees had gone weak and her breath came in gasps. She was thinking, how glorious this feels, when he kissed her and she tasted his wet tongue. The floor was giving away under her feet. They were floating on the bed. He was hovering above her. It was like a dream. But when he pulled up her dress and parted her legs, the memories of Barrister Chima forced themselves into her mind, so sharp. She explored the angles of Tobe's body, running her hands over the length of his back, willing the sad memories away, but they did not leave.

And when Tobe climaxed and collapsed against her breasts, she shut her eyes and wrapped her arms around his body.

PART 2

7

Ogadinma was lounging beside Tobe on the veranda, drinking freshly pressed orange juice and looking out on to the street, when the telephone rang, and Tobe went to get it. Her body still tingled. They had spent the past three days doing nothing but making love and waking up and eating. She had begun to learn the way his body moved, how quick and greedy he was for her. All of this time, she did not know that this was what being married felt like. She had never seen her father with a woman, had never seen her uncle and aunt sharing what she now shared with Tobe. When she thought of marriage, she visualized a mere cordial relationship with emotionally distant people who played the constricting roles of husband and wife, who spent their lives talking about how to find money for children's school fees and rent, how to keep their children well-behaved, who went to church together and slept behind a curtained-off bed. Not what she enjoyed with Tobe. She sipped her juice and sighed as the tangy sweetness trickled down her throat. She skimmed through the pages of Wole Soyinka's *The Trials of Brother Jero*, hardly digesting the words on the page. She had read the play three times, though, and knew the lines by heart. She listened for Tobe's return. She knew that when he was done answering the telephone, he would come from behind and kiss her neck and scoop her into his arms, and they would return to the bedroom, or, if he was impatient, make love in the hallway, or in the kitchen. He was that greedy for her body.

She waited for his return, her body prickling in anticipation. But he spent too long taking the call and she sensed then that something was not right. So she went inside and found him by the telephone, head bowed, one hand holding the handset against his ear. He spoke in a quiet, grim tone. When he put down the telephone, he told her, his voice low, that soldiers had arrested Segun over allegations that he had diverted government money.

Her heart sank into her stomach. She came and sat beside him and thought of what to say to him, and wished she knew how to lift his mood. But she didn't know the right words to say, how to break through this sad veil clouding his eyes. 'They will not see us,' she said, finally.

He muttered something incoherent, grabbed his car keys on the side table, stood and said he needed to go somewhere. He did not tell her where. She waited for him. She imagined he had gone to the army headquarters to plead for Segun's freedom. When he came back hours later, he did not touch the food she served. He did not pull her to him and kiss her neck. He did not answer immediately when she asked for the update on Segun. He stared blankly at the television, and his square face seemed to crumble into folds of anguish.

That night, when he joined her in bed, he stared blankly at the ceiling for a while, lost in thought. So lost was he that he did not hear her the first time when she said, 'Segun will come home soon, I strongly believe it.' She shook his shoulder and repeated the words again before he said, 'I hope so.' And then he held her against his chest, but he did not make any attempts to peel off her nightdress or even kiss her. She waited for him though, nudged him with her body, pressed her lips to his neck, but gave up when he began to snore lightly.

The following day, she was contemplating the grating silence in their home when her father called, the first time since she had moved in with Tobe.

'*I makwa*, it rained yesterday and I put a basin by the side of the TV because the leak from the floor above has worsened,' he began, 'but that stupid landlord is not thinking of repairing things. All he knows is how to increase rent.'

'Tobe's friend was arrested by soldiers yesterday,' she said. 'The soldiers are arresting government contractors and sending them to prison. I am so worried.'

There was a short pause before her father spoke again. 'Nothing will happen to Tobe. Do not fear, i nụ? Nothing will happen to him.' He spoke with so much authority.

'Yes, Papa. They will not see us.'

But she was not reassured. She put down the telephone. The cries of children playing a game of football behind the house filtered in from the window, loud and raucous. She looked around the room; although it was spacious and had windows that ran from floor to ceiling, she felt suffocated. She heard a thud against her wall and went to the veranda to inspect where the noise came from. The rear of the house stood close to the fence, and she could see into the empty plot where the children stood, waiting for her. They had volleyed their ball, again, onto her veranda.

'Aunty, sorry o,' they chorused.

She picked up the limp, dusty ball.

'Dis boys no dey hear word,' said a firm voice from the next compound. A woman leaning on the railing. Her name, Ogadinma would later learn, was Ejiro. Slight and fair, and looking not much older than Ogadinma, she had the intimidating air of someone who went about making sure everyone acted properly. 'Na so dem take dat ball break my window yesterday. Make you no give dem dat ball again,' Ejiro said.

Ogadinma liked her immediately and considered doing as she had said, but the boys were already kneeling, their pleas vigorous.

She tossed the ball over and they beamed and chanted thanks. Soon they were kicking at it again, shouting instructions at each other, the episode already forgotten.

Ejiro shook her head.

'I couldn't do that to them,' Ogadinma said, feeling suddenly apologetic. She switched to Pidgin. 'Dem don beg tire. I go be like bad person if I no give dem de ball.'

Ejiro waved away her apology and retreated into her house. But they met again that afternoon when Ogadinma went to shop for groceries at a store close by. The woman was small, and the skin of her knuckles and her knees were startlingly darker than her face and arms. She should tell her to stop bleaching, but since they barely knew each other, she raked her gaze over Ejiro's body and searched for something kind to say.

'You remind me of Sade Adu,' she said.

'People always say that.' Ejiro laughed. She spoke English with the same musical quality her Pidgin carried. 'What cream are you using? I don't like how dark your skin looks.'

Ogadinma felt stung. 'I use Nku and my skin is just fine.'

But Ejiro ignored her defensiveness. 'Nku? That rubbish cream? Use Tura and see how beautiful you will become. See my skin? You can't be married to a rich man and have your skin looking like those women hawking vegetables under the bridge.'

Ogadinma inhaled deeply, anger rising hotly up her face. She should have uttered a terse reply, but Ejiro had already moved on to another topic, was already picking out things from the shelf and talking about how she loved using only foreign spices and Uncle Sam's rice to cook for her husband.

Later, Ogadinma asked Tobe, 'Am I too dark? *Biko* tell me.' She told him about the encounter with Ejiro.

He laughed. He seemed suddenly happy, so at peace, and Ogadinma was pleased that the dim veil had finally lifted from his face. That evening, when they dined out with Kelechi and Femi, he told them how she had been worked up by what Ejiro said.

'Please don't listen to these Lagos women. Don't let them intimidate you into bleaching your skin,' Kelechi warned.

Soon the conversation switched to Segun. Tobe had visited him in prison and had contributed towards paying up what the soldiers accused Segun of diverting. Ogadinma marvelled at his unquestioning loyalty, how he encouraged Kelechi and Femi to help their friend. She liked their friendship. Since moving to Lagos, she had made no friends of her own. Ejiro, though unpleasantly blunt, seemed honest. And she had kind things to say when they met two days later at the same grocery store.

'I like dis your skirt,' Ejiro said, as she picked through shelves for Uncle Sam's rice and imported spices. 'I have one that looks just like it. Did you buy it from the boutique down the street?'

'My husband gave it to me yesterday. I don't know the shop he bought it from.'

Ejiro gave her a superior smile that seemed to say that Ogadinma was stupid for letting her husband do her shopping for her. 'I know all the happening boutiques in town. The last thing I want is my husband shopping for me. What do these men even know?' she said. 'Please pass me the Maggi liquid seasoning,' gesturing at the slender bottles lined up on the top shelf.

Ogadinma began to explain that Tobe chose what she wore, but she knew that would make her sound dumb. So she said, 'I like your lipstick. Where did you buy it from?'

'My sister sent me a packet from London. That's where all my cosmetics come from,' Ejiro said. 'I saw your husband driving out this morning and wondered if you drive too.'

'No, I don't drive.'

'You should. You are the wife of a big man and shouldn't be seen trekking the streets of Lagos, sweating like a truck-pusher.'

Ogadinma laughed, but Ejiro did not. She was already reaching for another bottle of spice. 'I will ask my husband to teach me,' Ogadinma said.

'There are licensed teachers in town. I know the best driving school in Lagos.'

'Thank you,' Ogadinma said, but she wanted to slap herself for cowering before the woman. And later, she was irritated with Ejiro for making her look like she was incapable of carrying herself like the wife of a big man.

They had just stepped out of the store when they heard the loud cries, the thump of feet, the swirl of dust from down the street. Ogadinma saw the bold lettering on the banners the protesters held over their heads which said, ASSOCIATION OF NIGERIAN STUDENTS, UNIVERSITY OF LAGOS CHAPTER, before she saw their faces.

The students sang in a measured, angry unison. 'We dey vex, yes we dey vex! Food don cost for market. Light we no dey see. Water we no see drink. We want democracy o. Yes, we dey vex!'

People gathered by the roadside to watch the procession. Ejiro clenched her basket tight and said she had to go. 'This is not good at all. These soldiers will now see another excuse to start shooting up everywhere.'

She bade Ogadinma goodbye and hastened to her gate. Ogadinma hurried home too.

The chants continued: 'Today, today, tomorrow no more. If I die today, I will die no more! How many people soldiers wan kill? Dem go kill us tire! How many people soldiers wan kill? Dem go kill us tire!'

From her veranda, Ogadinma watched as the students streamed down the street, hundreds of oily faces twisting and grimacing as they jogged past, chanting. They seemed so fearless, so determined, and she wondered if she would have joined such a protest, to make her voice heard, if she had gained that university admission.

Tobe arrived home shortly after, sweating and mopping his brow, bearing news of the riot. The students had run into a group of soldiers who dispersed them with canisters of tear gas and gunshots. But the students soon regrouped and broke into government buildings, set cars and properties on fire, blocked off major roads.

Tobe loosened his tie. Sharp angles were appearing under his shirt. Until then, Ogadinma hadn't realized how much weight he had lost. She knelt before him, unlaced his shoes and removed them and his socks. He drew a sharp breath as she unbuttoned his shirt, and then he caressed the back of her neck as she rested her head against his soft stomach.

'They almost killed Segun,' he said. 'They beat him like an armed robber.'

She pressed her head against his stomach again. When his breathing had evened, she rose and said, 'Come and eat. I made jollof and fish.'

He stood and hugged her, pressing her head on his chest. Then he followed her to the dining room.

The following morning, the federal government announced that it had shut down the University of Lagos until further notice, and Tobe told Ogadinma that Uncle Ugonna had suggested they move to London until things quietened down.

'I don't think it's a good idea,' he said. 'Because, what if they have flagged my passport? It will look like I am running away.'

'What if they didn't flag your passport?' Ogadinma asked.

'But I don't have anything to hide.'

Now was when she should tell him that everything was going to be all right, that she believed his innocence. But she was shivering with fear; there was no point pretending she wasn't afraid. And this was because she had never seen him restless like this.

After he left for work the following day, she tried to read Chukwuemeka Ike's *Sunset at Dawn* she'd bought the week before, but the words bled into each other and she put the book down. She went to Ejiro's. The house was not as big as hers, although it was tastefully furnished, and the sofas were clad in shimmery red velvet, the TV stretching from one end of the wall to the other.

'I may be travelling to London. I don't know yet. It all depends on my husband,' she told Ejiro as she cupped a bowl of catfish pepper soup. A sweaty bottle of Maltina sat on the stool beside her. The soup was deliciously hot, but her mind was muddied with worry and she could not tell Ejiro what was happening with Tobe, because their friendship was still new and she did not know if she could trust her with such information yet. She put the bowl down and said, 'I have never been to London but I hear it's a beautiful place.'

Ejiro moved to the edge of her seat. The talk about London interested her. She, too, had never been to London, and she would give anything to visit it. 'You are so lucky,' she told Ogadinma, her eyes lit up with childish curiosity. She told Ogadinma about her sister, Magdalene, who once visited London and returned with a British accent and bags filled with designer dresses and shoes. Ejiro wanted to visit London too, but her husband was not interested in travelling at all. She told Ogadinma about the places where her sister shopped in London. And Ogadinma listened, laughed, but her laughter flopped weakly as worry nibbled at her insides. If Ejiro noticed her moodiness, she did not inquire after its cause. Instead, she asked Ogadinma if she wanted more pepper soup, if she wanted to try on her lipsticks, if she wanted to see the new set of shoes and bags she just bought from the boutique down the street. Ogadinma was grateful for the lengths Ejiro went to in order to cheer her up.

But her heart sank again after she returned from Ejiro's. She thought of Kano and felt a disorientating pang as she remembered the trips to her father's shop, the walks down the streets of Sabon Gari, the games she played at the Ado Bayero Square, the lazy rains of April through to July, the deceptive August break of scorching sun that baked the flatlands, and then the sudden return of the rains in September, heavy and fervent, flooding the streets and tearing down small trees and electricity poles and ripping zinc sheets off the roofs of houses, before dusty winds from the Sahara misted up the air in December through to February, howling and howling and covering everything in a film of brown, sucking moisture off everything and anything, until one's skin flaked and cracked and leaves shrank and died. She never liked harmattan, but it was when she and her friend Mary gathered with other girls in the yard for their beauty routines, when they scrubbed their cracked feet with pumice stones and slicked the tender skin with petroleum jelly. She missed those days, those little things that made Kano home, those things she no longer experienced in Lagos.

If the worst happened and she had to leave Lagos, she would prefer Kano, her tiny room that looked out on to the yard. She would prefer to live with her father until the storm was over.

When Tobe came home that afternoon, he was edgy, and even his driving showed his restlessness, because he had barely extinguished the engine before rushing out and heading for the boot. He dragged out a Ghana-Must-Go bag which was so heavy he pulled it along the hallway rather than lift it. In his room, he sank to his knees and unzipped it, revealing piles of notes.

'The Special Committee has summoned me to the Supreme Headquarters,' he said, his voice quavering. He was sweating as he pulled out bundles of twenty-naira notes from the bag. 'They have finally come for me.'

Ogadinma stood by the door, unsure of what to do, to crouch and help him, or to just stand and watch him. She did not know the right thing to say at such a time or how to handle this kind of horror. He had pulled up the mattress and begun to stack the bundles in neat rows on the floor of the bed.

'I will call Aunty Ngozi,' she said, but he did not look up.

Aunty Ngozi came as soon as she heard. 'Where is he?' she said when Ogadinma let her in, her face twisted into a mask of fear. Her roughly tied scarf loosened and floated to the ground. She did not pause to pick it up. She did not even wait to hear Ogadinma's response.

When Ogadinma came inside, she found Aunty Ngozi sitting beside Tobe on the edge of the bed. She was holding his hand, listening as he explained how the soldiers had dropped by his office with a letter summoning him to appear before the Special Committee to account for all the money he received from the previous government, how they accused him of diverting government money and building substandard roads. He spoke too fast. Ogadinma wondered if he feared he would be jailed, because even though he kept telling

Aunty Ngozi that his books were clean, he twisted his hands, sweat pouring down his face and pooling under his arms.

'*Nee anya*, look at me, they will not do anything to you. Do you hear me? I say, as long as God lives in heaven, they will not touch a hair on your head,' Aunty Ngozi told him, her voice firm; she must have sensed that he needed the pep talk to calm his jittery nerves. But Tobe was still restless. He pulled open his bedside cupboard and got out a sheaf of papers, and as he tried to shove them inside his bag, they slipped out of his hands and floated to the floor. Ogadinma staggered as a sharp memory played across her mind, of when she walked into Barrister Chima's office and witnessed the papers floating off Amara's desk. She hurried over and began to pick up the paper, her hands shaking.

'I am going with you to see that Special Committee,' Aunty Ngozi was saying. 'They cannot accuse my brother of a crime he didn't commit. *Mbanụ*! I cannot let that happen.'

'Sister, my lawyer is going to handle this,' he said. Then he turned to Ogadinma. 'Whatever happens, if they take me to jail, don't visit me in jail.'

'They will not put you in jail,' Ogadinma interjected.

'God forbid bad thing!' Aunty Ngozi shouted and snapped her fingers over her head. 'Stop talking nonsense, Tobe. I say, stop talking nonsense!'

But Tobe was now holding Ogadinma by the shoulders, his fingers digging into her arms, his eyes wild like he was possessed by a demon. 'You must not visit, do you understand me?' he continued. 'I saw how they harassed Segun's wife. Those people are animals. Just wait for me. We will sort things out with them. Do you hear me?'

She and Aunty Ngozi followed him out to the car. He pressed her to his body in haste, and she said she would be waiting for his return. But he was already rushing into the car, and Aunty Ngozi was already getting into the passenger side. She stood by as they drove off, and long after they had left, she still stood watching the empty parking lot. Then she went to sit at the veranda to wait for his return. But he did not come home that night.

Ogadinma heard about Tobe's arrest the following morning. She had barely slept the night before, had kept jerking awake each time she heard the honk of a car, the bang on neighbours' gates, the flutter of bats on the roof. She had called Uncle Ugonna's house ten times and no one picked up the phone. She wondered if they had all gone out, if they were still with Tobe at the Supreme Headquarters. She waited for a call back, and when that didn't come, she sat watching the phone for a while, a great annoyance exploding in her chest. Why were they not taking her calls? Why were they not calling back? Perhaps they ignored her because was too young, she was still seventeen. Perhaps they felt she was not old enough to meddle with adult business, too young to comprehend the gravity of what was happening. She was so upset. She considered calling her father but didn't. It was past nine at night and she knew he would be watching *Newsline*, that he would watch *New Masquerade* afterwards, that he would remember the times they watched the show together. She didn't want to spoil that moment with her burden. So, she slept fitfully that night, often waking up to look out of the window, to listen for the call for prayer from the mosque nearby. The world was pitch-black; NEPA had cut off power and it was impossible to see anything outside her window. It was the blackest, most moonless night she had ever witnessed. And when she put her head back on the pillow to catch snatches of sleep, dawn came, and lazy rays streamed through her window, streaking her room gold.

The phone rang. She had been willing for a call, had longed, all night long, for the phone to ring, had worried herself into a nasty headache, wondering what had happened to Tobe. But now her bladder was suddenly filled with urine. She was no longer ready for the news. She inched closer to the phone, dizzy with fear. At the fourth ring, she snatched the handset from the cradle and said 'Hello,' panting. She knew then that the worst had happened because she could hear the measured silence at the other end, the laborious intake of breath, before Aunty Ngozi spoke, her words muffled as though her nose was filled with water.

'*Nne*, they have put my brother in prison,' she said, her voice cracked. And then she began to cry. Slow, hoarse cries that startled Ogadinma. Ogadinma's heart was breaking but she was too shocked by Aunty Ngozi's cries to grieve, too twisted with confusion to think of Tobe. For a moment she said nothing. She stared at the phone. What was she supposed to do – comfort Aunty Ngozi, or cry, too? She had never imagined that a time would come when she would hear Aunty Ngozi cry like that.

Then Aunty Ngozi told her how everything had happened: Tobe and his lawyer appeared before the military tribunal and submitted all the papers showing he completed the road contract, that it was in fact the government that still owed him some money, but the tribunal gave him the option of paying a heavy fine or going to jail. Tobe refused to pay what he did not owe and they took him away. Aunty Ngozi began to sob in huge bursts again, her voice choked and trembling.

'Get your things together,' Aunty Ngozi said after she had gathered herself. 'I am coming to collect you.'

It was after Aunty Ngozi ended the call and Ogadinma sat on the sofa, holding her head in her hands, her fingers pressing the sides of her eyes to calm the beginnings of a throbbing headache, that she understood what Aunty Ngozi meant by 'Get your things together'. There was a subtle authority in that declaration, which made it seem like she had no say in all that was happening.

She went into her room and nearly fell by the bed because her head felt suddenly light, too weak to process all that was happening around her. She pulled out a bag from her wardrobe and began to throw things into it. Her clothes. Underwear. Sandals. Shoes. Scarves. She wished she knew the things to take. She stood in the middle of her room, massaging her temples which had begun to throb again. Then she went into Tobe's room and stood by the door, staring at the bed where he had so carefully stacked the bundles of twenty-naira notes. She wondered if she should take the money too. She was still staring at the bed when she heard the loud honk of a car, and then the screech of metal on concrete as Kunle threw open the gates. Aunty Ngozi knocked on the door moments later, and she went out to get it.

Aunty Ngozi crushed her in her embrace, swung her lightly from side to side. She smelled of Lux soap and talcum powder. 'Do you have everything you need?' Aunty Ngozi asked. Her eyes were swollen and red.

She should ask why Aunty Ngozi had come to collect her, why she shouldn't be allowed to stay in her husband's house, but she said, 'I think I have everything, Aunty.' And then, without thinking about it, she blurted, 'Tobe kept money under his mattress.'

Aunty Ngozi nodded and said, 'He told me to bring all of it.'

They went into Tobe's room, both of them lifted the mattress and then began to stuff the bundles into the carry-all that lay discarded on the floor.

Ogadinma was relieved by the formal precision in the way Aunty Ngozi arranged the money, how she worked mechanically, her hands so steady, as if she hadn't been crying that morning. Once they had packed everything, Aunty Ngozi pulled the bag outside, and Ogadinma got her bag, too. As they stepped outside, she let her eyes linger at the passageway, the rooms and the kitchen, before she locked the door. Aunty Ngozi told Kunle she would return every day to check things at the house.

'Don't let anyone into this compound,' Aunty Ngozi told him, pulling an earlobe with her fingers, in the way that people did when they issued important instructions. 'You dey hear me so?'

'Yes, ma,' Kunle said, standing to attention. And to Ogadinma he said, 'Bye-bye, Aunty.' Ogadinma mumbled a response and got into Aunty Ngozi's car. Ejiro's veranda was empty and the door leading out to it was shut. She wondered if Ejiro was inside, and if she should walk over and tell her that she was leaving.

'I will come back regularly to check the house,' Aunty Ngozi said, breaking into her thoughts. Then she turned the key in the ignition and eased the car onto the deserted road.

As they drove out, Ogadinma kept her gaze on their house. She stared at the smooth white walls, the hulking pillars flanking the entrance, the sleek shape of the railings encircling the veranda, the sofa where she and Tobe often lounged in the evenings to sip freshly pressed juice and nibble on fried plantain. How quickly everything had changed. How easily her life was crumbling. She began to cry.

Aunty Ngozi touched her shoulder. 'Why are you crying, eh? Stop. Everything will be all right,' she said. 'The tyrants must release your husband because he has done nothing wrong. He is not a thief.'

Ogadinma's tears stung her eyes like hot pins. Her nose dripped with snot and her chest was choked with sobs. She didn't stop crying. Not even when Aunty Ngozi begged her to stop. She cried all through the drive, until they pulled up in front of Uncle Ugonna's house and Aunty Ngozi killed the engine and pulled her into her arms.

8

All of the next morning, Ogadinma refused to eat. She turned her face away when Aunty Ngozi brought her a breakfast of hot Milo and sliced bread. She pulled the blanket over her head when Ifeoma brought her a bowl of egusi soup and fufu in the afternoon. She wept silently when Aunty Ngozi insisted she must eat something that night, and when she spooned the spicy beans and plantain porridge into her mouth, she dashed into the bathroom and vomited.

The following morning, Aunty Ngozi felt her neck with the back of her palm, screamed and said Ogadinma had fallen ill to malaria. '*Nekwa anya*, your body is burning,' she said. 'Your husband will be very disappointed if he hears what you are doing to yourself.'

Ogadinma finally acquiesced.

'Milk is very scarce now,' said Aunty Ngozi as she prepared a cup of hot chocolate for Ogadinma. 'Everyone is grinding soybeans to make milk, but I don't like it. I don't think you will like it either. That's why I brought out this tin of Peak Milk, the only one we have left. Please, don't waste it.'

Ogadinma wondered what Tobe had eaten that morning, if he was also given soya milk; if he slept well at all. She had read the big story in *Daily Times*, about how prisoners were squashed together in tiny cells, how they stayed awake because of the fat rats that crawled out of the holes in the walls at night, how the facilities had been run down and prisoners all suffered skin diseases, that they rarely ate, and when they did, they were served portions too small to fill a child's stomach. She stared at her cup of hot chocolate and the fried eggs and sliced bread, the luxuries she still enjoyed which Tobe no longer had, and began to cry. And after she had exhausted herself from crying, she began to eat.

She spoke with her father later. He said he would come to Lagos if she wanted him to. He sounded so calm, his Igbo so crisp, and she remembered years ago when the soldiers punished him for overtaking them at a junction, how he had remained unruffled even as they shoved him around like a petty thief.

'They will let him go because he did nothing wrong,' he told her. 'I believe that he did nothing wrong. These soldiers always like to show their power. Just be strong, i nugo?'

'Yes, Papa.'

'Everything will be all right, i nugo?'

'Yes, Papa.'

But everything was not all right. Aunty Ngozi and Uncle Ugonna said they were speaking with people who knew the state governor, who could help with Tobe's release. Ogadinma woke every day waiting for his return, so they could move back into their house and for everything to be as it was before. But Tobe did not come home that week, or the next, and each time she asked, Uncle Ugonna or Aunty Ngozi would say they were still working on his release. As the weeks passed, she began to wonder if they were really working on it or if they were too preoccupied with their lives. They did not tell her how Tobe was faring, what he ate, if he was doing well, until she asked and asked. And they simply shooed her away with soft, gentle words, as though she was not strong enough, as though she was still a child. And this began to annoy her.

Nnanna had gone to seek admission at the University of Benin, and so Ifeoma doted on Ogadinma. Ifeoma brought her meals, prepared her bath, offered to wash her clothes. And when Ifeoma asked if she needed an extra duvet one night, Ogadinma shook her head and said, 'I am fine like this,' irritated by the excessive gentleness.

That night, she dreamed that Tobe had broken out of prison and as they raced down the street, the soldiers hot on their heels, a house appeared at the junction, and when they ran inside, they resurfaced in her room in Kano. She woke up sweating. Ifeoma was still sleeping, her legs spread open, her wrapper bunched around her waist. Ogadinma pulled down the wrapper and straightened Ifeoma's legs, then got off the bed and went outside.

It was a Saturday and neighbours had gathered outside, cleaning their drains, cutting and clearing their front gardens. The Head of State had declared a compulsory sanitation exercise which must be held on the last Saturday of every month. Uncle Ugonna and Aunty Ngozi were cleaning, too. While Uncle Ugonna shovelled out dirt from the gutter, Aunty Ngozi raked it into a pile. They saw her and dropped their tools, and as though choreographed, began to walk towards her. In all the five weeks since Tobe went to prison, since she came to live with Aunty Ngozi and Uncle Ugonna, they treated her like she had become a fragile thing, and did not let her overwork herself.

'Let me help,' she told Aunty Ngozi.

Aunty Ngozi shook her head. '*Nne*, you need more rest,' she said. 'We are almost done anyway.'

'Yes,' Uncle Ugonna said.

And Ogadinma sat by the door, wanting to work, wanting her husband back, and wondering why the hell were they taking so long to bring him home. But she knew she could never speak to them rudely; speaking to them in that manner was akin to yelling at her father – something she would never be able to do, even in her dreams.

She swiped at the sweat that had beaded her forehead. Lagos made no sense without Tobe by her side. The neighbourhood was too quiet. She did not hear the loud music that always rent the air on weekends, and there was something different about the people, how they went about the sanitation exercise with the eagerness of people numbed by fear. The soldiers had subdued Lagos.

But Uncle Ugonna and Aunty Ngozi didn't seem to mind the atmosphere. They went to work every morning and returned in the evening with no information about Tobe. They would sit in the parlour at nights to watch the news, nor when NEPA had cut the electricity, they listened to Radio Nigeria. When she joined them at church one Sunday, they played a tape in the car. It was Igbo Christian songs. Aunty Ngozi sang with a quavering voice. Uncle Ugonna bopped to the music. Ifeoma was also whispering the tune. Ogadinma watched them. They all seemed to be at peace, and she looked out of the window and wondered how they could be that calm when her world had been rocked to a stop, when Tobe was still in prison and she was not sure what their life would be like when he came home, if he would even come home anytime soon. When she looked at them again, she found Uncle Ugonna watching her from the rear-view mirror.

'Are you all right?' he asked her, looking at her as if he was trying to read her mind.

'Why is my husband still in prison?' she asked him.

Aunty Ngozi turned around to face her, her mouth pinched with irritation, and began to shout. 'So, you think we are all happy that my brother is in prison, eh? So, you think we have all folded our hands and let him suffer in prison, eh?'

Uncle Ugonna touched Aunty Ngozi's shoulders, his eyes darting between the rear-view mirror and the road. 'Don't shout at her. She only asked a question,' he said gently.

'*Rapukene m*, I don't like how this girl has been squeezing her face these days,' Aunty Ngozi told him, her voice breaking. '*Haba*. We have tried everything we can to get Tobe out, but he is still headstrong and has refused to give the soldiers what they want. Tell me, should I now go and kill myself so that Ogadinma will believe that we have been working hard to get him out, eh? Should I just kill myself to please this girl?'

Ogadinma stared at Aunty Ngozi. Her shoulders seemed shrunken and the skin around her neck and her face had become shades darker, the body of someone who toiled in the sun every day. Uncle Ugonna had changed too, his neck thinner and sticking out of his bony shoulders. They had both drastically changed since Tobe went to prison. Ogadinma felt a sudden rush of guilt; she had been so absorbed in her sorrow that she did not see how they grieved. She stared out of the window at passing cars, the trees blending into each other, the dust-stained houses, and wished she knew why Tobe refused to reach an agreement with the soldiers, why he still would not let her visit, if he even thought of her. Then, a thought crept into her mind that he did not think about her, because who would go for many months without bothering to even see his wife or hear her voice? She was overwhelmed with a dizzying rush of sadness. She had never considered the possibility that Tobe would forget her. All this while, she had thought of him, but now it dawned on her that he did not think of her, that he was being too headstrong and making things difficult for everyone.

When they got home, she finished the plate of rice Aunty Ngozi gave her and drank the bottle of Coke Uncle Ugonna offered. Although she ate with relish and tried to smile so that Aunty Ngozi would see that she was no longer squeezing her face, her eyes still tingled with unshed tears when she showered that evening. And when her father called to ask how she was doing, she wanted to say she was not fine, that nothing made sense any more and her heart was still breaking, but she imagined him holding the phone tightly to his ear, listening to her tensed breathing and everything she was not saying. He was all alone in their flat in Kano with no one to keep him company, no one to comfort him in a time of distress. So she did not want to burden him with her troubles.

'I am well, Papa,' she finally said.

He seemed to take forever to respond. She tried to pace her breathing, knowing that he was still listening to the strained silences. 'I will call you again tomorrow to know how you are doing,' he said.

'Thank you, Papa.'

After she ended the call, she went into the bathroom, locked herself inside, sat on the toilet bowl and wept into her palms. She had never felt so helpless in her entire life.

And then she received the tape recorder from Uncle Ugonna on a rainy evening in August, the same day she turned eighteen.

She had forgotten her birthday; she had worried herself into a tight ball of tension, wondering why Tobe did not want to see her, because if Aunty Ngozi and Uncle Ugonna could visit him and return home every time without a scratch on their bodies, then she should be fine, too. She had begun to resent him.

But the tape recorder changed everything. Uncle Ugonna said he had paid a prison warder to sneak it in because Tobe wanted to send her a message on her birthday. Ogadinma stared at the device – a small, black shiny thing whose battery compartment was still sealed in a clear plastic bag. Tobe had remembered her birthday. Her eyes burned with tears. She switched the recorder on and held it against her ear. For a moment, there was only static silence, and then his voice came. He sounded like his old self when he had a cold, and he coughed at intervals as he asked if she was doing well. He said he missed her. He said a day never went by without a thought of her. He said he would come home soon, and no one would separate them again. He talked as though his lungs were lined with thick mucus. Ogadinma's tears blinded her, her slow sobs drowned out all sounds until she couldn't hear every other message the tape carried. And long after the recording had ended, she still held the device close to her ear, and an overwhelming sense of shame rippled through her. She had resented him for the wrong reasons. Then she made up her mind to make Uncle Ugonna take her to Tobe; she would run away if he didn't grant her request.

Ogadinma shifted as far away as she could from the prison warder. The dank emptiness of the room made her feel nervous. She resisted the urge to press her nostrils shut. She had not imagined that the place would smell so thickly of stale urine. She glanced around the room. The blue wall paint had begun to peel, and the edges of the floor were stained a deep brown and coated with dirt. At one end of the room, a warder in a washed-out uniform sat slouched over a table, eating bananas and groundnut. At the other side, visitors sat stiffly, waiting.

Beside her, Uncle Ugonna sat staring at the floor. He looked like he hadn't had a good sleep in many days. When she threatened to run away if he didn't bring her to Tobe, he tried to talk her out of it, and when that failed, he held out his hands to her, and when she did not come to him, he plopped on the parlour sofa with a weary sigh. That night, she wondered if she would have carried out her threats. And now, sitting beside him and waiting for them to be taken to Tobe, she realized she could have gone through with it.

The door was thrown open and a warder in a faded brown khaki uniform, his face creased like crumpled paper, summoned them in a loud voice. 'Oya, make una come,' he said.

Uncle Ugonna stood up first and Ogadinma held tightly to the bag containing the flask of white rice and chicken stew she had brought for Tobe. Uncle Ugonna had said prison food was bad, that he and Aunty Ngozi always brought food during each visit. She clutched the bag close to her chest as they stepped into the search area where an ashen-faced warder stood waiting. The warder took the bag from Ogadinma, peeked inside, and began to shout.

'Who tell you say you fit carry food come here, eh? You think say we no dey give dem food, eh?' His voice carried down the hall.

'We don see your oga,' Uncle Ugonna began to say, just as the warder they had met at the door rushed inside and whispered into the ears of the angry man, who immediately lowered his voice and began to smile. 'Oya, carry your food.' He pushed the bag over to Ogadinma, before he waved them into a smaller, boxy room.

Tobe walked in later. And for a moment, Ogadinma simply stared at him; he looked much taller and this was because he had lost so much weight, the angles of his shoulders visible through his stained shirt.

He held out his arms to her and said, '*Nwunye m*, you shouldn't have come.'

She wrapped her arms around his body. There was a strong smell of urine and something else on him. His arms and legs were riddled with scabs. She suppressed the sudden desire to cry.

'My husband,' she said.

He touched her collarbone, ran a lazy finger along the length of it. 'Look how skinny you have become,' he said.

They sat, and he slung a hand over her shoulders. He chatted with Uncle Ugonna, his voice oddly cheery. She could not believe the state he had been reduced to; that this was Tobe, chubby Tobe, Tobe who walked with extra swagger, who carried himself like a king. She could not believe that this withered, unkempt man was the husband she had married only months ago.

She brought out the flask and he quickly dug into the food and sighed as he scooped up a piece of chicken and chewed. 'You have done well,' he said. 'This is like Christmas Day to me.' And to Uncle Ugonna, he said, 'Every time you come here feels like Christmas Day. Do you know the last time I ate chicken? This morning, we were given spoiled beans they cooked overnight with potash. And I removed twenty-five stones from the small portion they gave me. I don't think they even bothered to wash the beans before cooking it.'

He continued eating, often lifting his head to tell them stories, how a riot had broken out in the prison yesterday, after inmates who had been sentenced to death learned that the former governor who signed the death warrants was now detained in the same prison on charges of corruption. The inmates broke out of their section and stormed to this side and had almost reached the governor's cell before soldiers came and started shooting.

'You should have seen the governor,' Tobe laughed. 'He defecated and peed in his trousers. God saved him yesterday. Those boys would have torn him to shreds with their hands.'

'I heard he was given a twenty-five-year sentence by the military tribunal,' Uncle Ugonna said.

'He's not the only one here. This place is packed full of governors, most of them are still awaiting trial like me. The other day, one of them was beaten blue-black by the inmates and he was told to sleep in the corridor with the rats for one week.' Tobe shook his head. 'This place is a republic of its own. We have our president and the deputy, and even a chief justice. God will punish you the day you cross any of them.'

'I can imagine,' Uncle Ugonna said.

Tobe shook his head and said, 'No, you can't. We even have our own currency. The warders sell new inmates to the Big Ogas of different cells. The Big Ogas are like governors. Each cell has a Big Oga. If you look chubby and rich, they will sell you to the meanest Big Oga in exchange for favours. Those men have their hearts in their backs. *Obi fa dị n'azụ.* They will make you call your family every week to send them money through the warders. God punish you if your family refuse to send the requested sum.'

Uncle Ugonna began to say something but then stopped, his gaze flitting from Ogadinma's face to Tobe's. Her stomach sank. Tobe's arms were patched and scarred, some fading marks riddled his neck, and there was a thin scar on his lower lip. She tried to wish the worrying thoughts away; he couldn't possibly have been a victim, she told herself. If she wished it away, then it would be true.

Tobe stopped eating and turned to look at her. She felt transparent, as though he could look into her heart and see that she had resented him, and so she quickly said, 'I have missed you.'

He cupped her cheek, kneaded the soft skin, then dropped the hand and returned to the food. 'The problem with eating this good food is defecating,' he told Uncle Ugonna later. 'Sometimes we wish we don't defecate at all because the bucket is in the same cell we sleep in. They empty the bucket once every week. Sometimes they forget to do that.'

'When will you come home?' She held him. Her throat was choked with sobs. 'When will they let you go?'

He began to speak but then the warder opened the door and began to shout, 'Oya, make una dey go. Una time don finish!'

Before the warder escorted him out of the room, he hurriedly pulled her into his arms and kissed the top of her head. 'I will come home soon,' he said, his eyes filled with great resolve. 'I promise.'

During the drive home, Ogadinma thought about his promise. She thought about it at night when she stretched out in bed, and again the following morning. Each time she remembered the earnestness in his eyes when he said it, a warm sensation rose in her chest. His words birthed something new, because the weight of sadness pressing down on her shoulders lifted, the lethargy in her joints disappeared, the knot in her stomach unfurled and she could finally think clearly again. She began to cry, but this time the cries cleansed her, as if the tears came from deep inside and washed away all the sorrow. And she believed that Tobe would finally agree to pay what the soldiers demanded. That they would move back into their house and return to how they used to live. Maybe his finances would take a beating, but Tobe would resume running his company and she would convince him to let her learn a trade, so she could contribute to their upkeep, and in no time they would earn back what he had lost. She woke each day waiting for news that Tobe had finally changed his mind.

9

The following week, Ogadinma was in the kitchen cooking ofe egusi with Aunty Ngozi when Uncle Ugonna came home earlier than usual.

'I hope he did not forget to get me the oranges I asked him to buy. You know that man easily forgets things,' Aunty Ngozi said, although her face was stretched in a warm smile.

'I want some o,' Ogadinma told her, stirring the soup and sniffing the air. 'I think I am a little constipated. The oranges will help soften my stomach.'

Aunty Ngozi laughed and went to meet Uncle Ugonna in the passageway. She was glad that Aunty Ngozi was no longer upset with her, that they had returned to the old routine of cooking and chatting and exchanging banter. She stirred the soup, patted the spoon on an open palm and licked. The soup needed a little more salt. And as she reached for the salt shaker, Aunty Ngozi's stifled cry ripped through the still air. Fear jumped and clutched at Ogadinma's knees, and she worried that something bad had happened to Uncle Ugonna at his place of work. She went to the passageway to see them.

'These people are evil. It will not be well with them.' Aunty Ngozi was beating her chest in agony and saying, 'O *Chukwu, o Chukwu*,' over and over, in a voice that seemed on the verge of tears. The end of her wrapper had loosened and trailed to the ground, but she did not bother to retie it.

'*Nne,*' Uncle Ugonna beckoned Ogadinma with a wave of the hand, 'the Deputy Head of State has penalized your husband heavily for taking too long to pay what they demanded. Now, we have to sell the house and his company to be able to meet their demands, or they will punish him further with a harsh sentence. Tobe has agreed to sell everything.'

Ogadinma's heart began to push painfully against her chest. What did he mean by 'sell everything'? She tried to pace her breathing before she spoke, but her chest felt pressed down with something weighty, and she was suddenly dizzy. 'Doesn't he have money in his bank account?' she asked, gasping. 'I thought he brought enough money home to solve this problem.'

Uncle Ugonna wrapped his arms around her and pressed her face against his chest. The egusi soup had begun to burn and a charred, spicy smell began to fill the house. She muttered something to Uncle Ugonna, broke from the embrace and hurried to the kitchen to take the pot down. She had never imagined that they would lose every-thing, that Tobe would come out of prison with nothing to go home to, and this filled her with horror. She had grown up with little and could cope with any circumstance she found herself in. But Tobe without his wealth was an image she had never thought to visualize. She did not know that Tobe. And now this idea of him terrified her.

Uncle Ugonna put the house and the company up for sale, and found them a new, cheap first-floor flat on the outskirts. There was nothing much for Ogadinma to pack; in an hour, she had gathered their bags and the utensils she needed, and before they left, she gave Ejiro her new contact address and phone number. By afternoon, she had settled into her new home. And that weekend, she and Aunty Ngozi went grocery shopping and returned to Uncle Ugonna's house to prepare soups and stew.

'Your husband does not have good friends,' said Aunty Ngozi, who was cutting the ugu leaves into thin slices. 'They all disconnected their phones and refused to reply to all our letters when we reached out to them for help. We don't know where Kelechi is. We would not have sold these things if his friends came to his rescue.' She shook her head. 'He has no real friends.'

Ogadinma continued to pound the pepper and crayfish. She did not feel the need to talk these days. She did not think of Kelechi, who always called Tobe his 'brother'; she did not wonder why Tobe's other friends would turn their backs on him. She did not think of these things, because she was too busy wrapping her mind around their new reality, trying to make sense of the sudden turn of events. Every time she thought of Tobe moving into their dank, new apartment, her heart stopped. She could not imagine him in that small apartment, without his means of livelihood. What would he do when he came home?

'I have found your husband a shop in the Alaba Market,' Aunty Ngozi said. 'My friend Nkiruka has promised to take him under her wing and teach him how to run a cosmetic shop. The business is really booming now. You know your husband is coming home next week, so we must have everything ready for him.'

Ogadinma looked up. She had heard Aunty Ngozi say that Tobe would be coming home next week. Yet she still asked, 'They are going to release him next week?'

Aunty Ngozi said yes, and continued to talk about her plans to help Tobe. Ogadinma's gaze kept drifting to the bags under Aunty Ngozi's eyes, her wrapper which was tied loosely over her chest and exposed the tops of her drooping breasts. No one had been the same since Tobe went to prison. Everyone was waiting for his return, but now Ogadinma was filled with dread.

She wanted to tell Aunty Ngozi that she was afraid of who Tobe would become when he came home, that she feared the loss of his wealth would change him. That the apartment was too small, the walls were peeling, the doors musty, the sofas splitting at the seams, the passageway narrow and dark. That Tobe might not like these changes, and she was worried about living with a man who had lost everything. But she knew that Aunty Ngozi would not like to hear this, that she would expect her to accept their new reality without questions, like a virtuous woman. So she said, 'God knows why everything happened.'

Loud music drifted in from the open window. A party was under way in the next compound. It had been a while since she heard anyone play music so loudly that it felt as though the speakers were placed right outside the kitchen window. Aunty Ngozi began to sing along to the Highlife music, her voice carrying down the passageway. Ogadinma watched her. She had expected Aunty Ngozi to be weighed down with dread as she was, but the older woman was carrying on as if the changes were normal, as if it was a temporary matter and that Tobe would be fine. Ogadinma looked away because guilt had begun to nibble at her insides. For a woman whose husband was finally coming home after much tribulation, she was not enthusiastic enough, and this filled her with guilt. So, she lifted her voice, too, and joined Aunty Ngozi in singing. Although her voice trembled and she was out of tune, she still sang. And for the first time since she moved into the new flat, she began to believe that things would eventually change for good.

Tobe came home one morning in October, the same day Ogadinma was flogged by a soldier. She had gone to shop for groceries and was walking past the bus stop when she heard – *Are you people animals?* – followed by the zipping sounds of horsewhips. The whip landed on her hand, wrapped itself around her arm, and pulled. She screamed. Her skin reddened immediately, and a shock of pain, like a ravenous fire, rose up her arm, her entire body. The soldiers were flogging everyone at the bus stop, ordering them to form an orderly queue.

'Are you deaf?' said a soldier.

'I am just walking past,' she said through tears, nursing her arm.

'Then, hurry up! Abi you carry shit for nyansh?' he replied.

She hastened away; she had to, anyway, because the soldiers were still circling commuters, who obediently formed a straight line. But she kept looking back, shooting the soldiers a hateful gaze, wishing them death by fire.

At the first store, a girl leaned out of the window and announced, 'We no get anything again, make una go!' At the second store further down the street, soldiers worked the padlocked entrance with shears and pliers. She paused. It was too early to have another encounter with another group of soldiers; her arm still stung, like she had been feasted on by giant mosquitoes. But people were gathering up in front of the store, forming a queue, and she heard a man say that soldiers were doing the same thing all over Lagos: breaking into stores belonging to greedy hoarders and selling food provisions to hungry Lagosians. She joined them. A Peugeot 505 soon pulled up and a man in black shorts and a shirt that must have been buttoned in haste, rushed out of it, sweating and panting.

'Sir, please, this is my warehouse,' he said. 'Why are you cutting it open?'

'So, you are one of those people hoarding food in the country and causing scarcity, eh?' said one of the soldiers. He approached the shop owner, clenching his gun and shouting, 'Oya, open this place now. I say, open this place now! And you must sell them at the normal price.'

The man made as if to open the store. 'But, sir, I did not buy them at normal price,' he started to say, and then buckled to the ground when the soldiers jumped him, all of them kicking and shoving and flogging him. The man rolled on the dirt in his bid to avoid the assault.

'I say, open this store now!'

He got up and dusted himself with dignified embarrassment, before he opened up the shop. The soldiers stood around to make sure he sold the items at the set price. When it got to Ogadinma's turn, she did not realize that the man's forehead was bruised from the beating, that he had bled from the nose. His left eye had begun to swell shut, and he breathed heavily as he got the things she needed. She wondered if he was holding back from crying, if he would cry after everyone had gone. He carefully bagged Ogadinma's foodstuffs, and told her the price. He was a small man, with delicate hands and thin shoulders, who looked like he would crumble when hit with blunt force. She was surprised that he was still standing, still attending to people, after all the beating he had endured. She looked around. The soldiers were standing so close, watching every move made. She wanted to tell him sorry, but she paid for her goods, told him, 'Thank you,' and took her bag and left.

She had just set her bag in the kitchen when a knock came at the door. She got it and found Tobe and Uncle Ugonna and Aunty Ngozi, and she threw herself into his arms and held on. 'My husband,' she said.

'*Nwunye m*,' Tobe said, tightening his arms around her. 'My wife. It's so good to see you again.'

She drew back, although she still wanted to hold him. She wished that Aunty Ngozi and Uncle Ugonna were not observing her, because she feared they would see how locking eyes with Tobe made her nervous. It was too disturbing, looking into the eyes which were familiar but different, which seemed veiled with something sombre. He looked subdued.

Inside, Tobe sat on the chair closest to the door and Ogadinma sat beside him. He slung a hand over her shoulder, and she leaned against his neck.

He rubbed her shoulder and said, 'This place is modest.' Then he removed his hand from her shoulder and sat forward, nodding absently as Uncle Ugonna talked about the state of things in Lagos, how difficult it had become to get a moderately priced flat.

Ogadinma followed his gaze. There was nothing modest about the cramped, small space: the peeling paint, the low-hanging ceiling, the white fan that danced with a squeaky sound. For the first few days after she moved in, she woke up at nights sweating. The ceiling of her room was mouldy, the walls lumpy and smeared thinly with chalky white paint that did little to hide the roughness. The kitchen was too narrow, and the toilet was a boxy, small room with a toilet bowl on one side and a cemented space on the other for bathing. Water splashed all over the toilet seat when she scooped from her bucket and upended the bowl over her head. The neighbours' window was so close that she heard their conversations and even the clinking of spoons on plates when they ate their meals. She had wondered how Tobe would feel when he came home. Now he looked at the parlour, at an old rug that wafted a faint, musty smell, the small Philips black-and-white TV sitting on a stool and the telephone Uncle Ugonna had, generously, installed for them. He looked so sad. But Uncle Ugonna chatted so heartily, as if he could not sense that tension had fallen around them, tension that knotted her stomach and filled her bladder with urine.

'With time, things will get better and you will find a better place,' Uncle Ugonna said, as though he sensed Tobe's discomfort.

Tobe nodded absently, then he went and sat at the dining table to eat the ofe akwu and white rice Aunty Ngozi dished up for him.

'My friend Nkiruka has agreed to coach you,' said Aunty Ngozi, her voice oddly enthusiastic; but her darkly lined eyelids did little to hide the drooping arcs under her eyes. 'She is doing so well, especially at this time when people are afraid to import things since the Head of State closed the borders. But Nkiruka knows how to bring in those things. Her brother is a big distributor. I think you should try that line of trade, and with God on our side, everything will pick up quickly.'

Tobe shrugged.

Later, after they had left, he went into the bathroom to bathe, and Ogadinma listened for his sounds, but nothing came. For a long time, he stood in there and did nothing. And she imagined him looking out of the window into the backyard, at the mouldy floor and the cracked walls fluffed with greenish algae, the busted pipes which dripped waste water all over the floor before disappearing into the clogged drain outside. She imagined him cringing at the stench from the next house whose septic tank had apparently filled to bursting. She sighed when he finally started bathing, and when he came out later and headed for his room which she had mopped thoroughly until it smelled of bleach and detergent, she worried about his quietness.

That night, when he pulled her into his arms, he hurriedly tugged at her wrapper and removed his clothes. His hands were unsteady as he parted her legs, his thrusts jerky. He was done in minutes and quickly rolled away from her, as if he desperately wanted some distance.

She wanted him to speak, to condemn the state of the house, to acknowledge how poorly they now lived; she wanted him to shout or cry and articulate his frustration so that the air between them would no longer be so edgy, so that she would be able to exhale.

10

And then Kelechi visited.

'Tobe, my brother!' he said immediately he stepped into the parlour. He sounded flustered, and the new shrillness in his voice surprised Ogadinma. He hugged Tobe, thumped him on the back, swayed.

But in his embrace Tobe was as rigid as a pole. When Kelechi sat on the sofa, he spread his legs open and leaned back, as if to show that he was not worried about the state of the flat. 'How have you been, *nwanne m*? I have been away for a while and have only just returned.'

'I am doing well,' Tobe said stiffly. He sat forward, clasping and unclasping his hands. And he was looking at Kelechi, an open, unabashed look, but Kelechi would not hold the gaze for too long.

There was a moment the two men said nothing to each other, and this made Ogadinma nervous. She felt sweat beading her back, trickling under her arms, her brows. Tobe had hardly spoken to her since he returned, had worn a sombre mien every day. But his face had come alive now. He was sitting a few feet away, looking directly at Kelechi. His eyes dead cold, his jaws suddenly prominent, his nose defiant. She had never seen him that way before. And Kelechi, who sat upright in his carefully ironed blue kaftan, seemed unsettled by Tobe's intense gaze.

Ogadinma muttered something about checking the food on the stove and left. But she did not shut the door leading out to the passageway; she stood behind it to listen to their conversation.

Kelechi spoke for a long time about how he had just returned from abroad, that he got this address from a friend, and that things were so hard, but he was struggling to keep a positive front. The longest Ogadinma had ever heard him speak. And Tobe mumbled in monotones. Often, there would be an awkward lull in their conversation, times when the two friends had run out of stories to fill in the gaping maw in their relationship, and then Kelechi would bring up another topic about the government and the failing economy, and Tobe would respond with silence.

'You call me *brother* but you abandoned me when I needed my brother's help,' Tobe finally said.

There was a moment when the air was so still she could almost hear their tense breaths, before Kelechi said, 'I ran, Tobe. I ran because the Special Committee invited me to account for the works I did for the Anambra State government. Remember the radio station contract I handled? They would have sent me to prison like they did every other contractor and public official. They even froze my bank accounts. But I fled to Ghana, my brother. That's why I wasn't here for you.'

Tobe muttered something, and Kelechi hurriedly responded like a hen pecking at strewn corn, telling Tobe how he had become friends with some senior army officers, that it was these officers who cancelled the warrant for his arrest, who helped remove the hold on his accounts. He talked for so long. And this startled Ogadinma, how Kelechi had become talkative. She pondered his words, looking for signs of lies, of betrayal. All she could sense was his desperation to appease Tobe, the longing to reunite with his old friend. Tobe should see this desire, too. He had to.

There was a shuffle of feet and she hastened into the kitchen. Her beans and plantain porridge was still simmering. She was hungry but her stomach was too queasy, her nerves jumpy.

When she came out later, Tobe was standing at the veranda, looking out on the street below. Kelechi had left. She searched Tobe's face to see how their discussion had gone: his brows were squeezed into rigid lines, his nostrils flaring. She looked down the street, too, wondering if she should start a conversation. A motorcycle rode down the dusty, uneven road, the rider struggling with the handlebars and the two small children propped in front of him, and behind him, a woman with a baby strapped to her back, held fast. She could not look at Tobe's face yet. She felt so conflicted, her chest churning with a painful mix of emotions, a firm loyalty to Tobe and a tiny belief that Kelechi could not just have abandoned Tobe. She had a feeling that Kelechi would return and resolve things with him. Maybe Tobe was still too headstrong because he needed a way to vent; maybe he was projecting his frustration on the only friend he called his brother and would soon heal and everything would return to what it used to be. She searched his face for a sign that said he would get over his anger. She didn't want him to be isolated. She didn't want them to keep living in isolation.

'This place stinks,' Tobe said in a voice so low he might have been talking to himself. He shoved a hand into his pocket. There were tight lines around his mouth and a brash arrogance in the way he kept his distance from the mouldy balustrade, as if he didn't want any contact with it. '*Dike adaa!*' he said, shaking his head, his face contorting into a sad mask as his eyes raked over the dire surroundings. 'A strong man has fallen!'

She had never seen him like that before, never seen this shade of dejection in his eyes, never witnessed him cry out in this manner. He stood there, his shoulders bent as though the weight of the world sat on them. She knew then that he was finally coming to terms with their new reality. She wanted to tell him: listen to me, it is true that you have lost everything, but a *dike*, a strong man, is not judged by how much he has in his bank account, or the material things he has acquired. A strong man is the one who refuses to yield to despair after one fall, because he knows that those things will eat him inside out, erase everything that used to be him, everything that could have kept him going, and fill his empty shell with bitterness.

But she could not say this to him. He looked so impenetrable. With a heavy heart, she returned to the kitchen to stare idly at the pot sitting on the kerosene stove.

In the following days, Tobe opened his shop at Alaba Market. He left home early and returned late. He spoke little at home and lingered in his bedroom, and when she forced a conversation or told a joke, he did not laugh too loud, did not argue too eagerly, and he no longer sang his favourite songs when they came on the radio. Ogadinma measured her steps around him, staying not too far away and coming not too close. She hoped that this moodiness was a passing phase, and so she hovered around him, waiting in vain for the man she had spent the best weeks with, the man who lowered his guard and clung to her in sleep.

One weekend, Ejiro visited. She gave Ogadinma a tub of face cream, a stick of deodorant, some soaps and a set of multicoloured underwear. 'My sister just returned from London. She brought lots of good things and I thought to bring you these.'

Ogadinma took the tub, opened and sniffed it. Her Nku cream had long run out and she had been using Pears Baby Lotion because it was the cheapest she could find at the store down the street. 'You knew exactly what I needed,' she told Ejiro.

If Ejiro was startled by the state of the flat, she did not say it. Instead they sat on the floor, as they had done in her house, and drank the Maltina Ogadinma had dashed out to buy. They talked about everything, about her old neighbourhood, often giggling, Ejiro's voice carrying down the passageway. She told Ogadinma how the small boys had smashed her window yet again with their football, about the new tenants that now lived in Ogadinma's old house, how the woman was so full of herself and didn't respond to Ejiro's greeting.

'I hear her husband is a bank manager,' Ejiro said. 'Maybe that's why she carries herself like one thing like that. But who cares anyway? She no dey feed me, and me I no go ever open dis my mouth greet her ever again. If I ever try am, make my mouth bend!'

Ogadinma laughed, and she was startled by how happy she sounded, how her voice no longer seemed weighed down with worry. It had been a while since she genuinely laughed.

'Hard times no dey last,' Ejiro finally said, as though reading her mind. 'You see dis world, e dey rotate. Sometimes, e go bring good things. Other times, na bad news e carry come. But e go continue dey rotate. So, no even carry face or kill yourself with misery, because things go soon change for una. You dey hear me so?'

Ogadinma said nothing for a long time. She thought about Tobe. He had come home the previous day reeking of beer, stumbling down the passageway. There was something heartbreaking in the way he stumbled, as though he was struggling to be his dignified old self, while this new desolate version battled for control over his mind. She had stood by the door of the bathroom and listened as he vomited, and when he came out and retreated into his room, she went inside and saw that he had puked all over the toilet seat, all over the floor. She cleaned the vomit and mopped the floor with water and detergent, but the smell hung thickly in the flat and did not disperse even after she threw the doors open to let fresh air in.

'My mind strong,' Ogadinma told Ejiro. 'I no dey shake. Na my husband dey worry me. Him no dey happy at all. He no dey even laugh with me sef.'

'No worry. Him go soon calm down. Na him make the money, and na him lose am. So, no surprise say him dey sad. Just stay strong for am. Make him know say him no dey alone. You hear?'

'Thank you, Ejiro.'

After Ejiro left with a promise to visit again, Ogadinma felt gloomy again. It was as if Ejiro sucked away the cheerful air she had brought. She tried to take her mind off things. She sat slumped in the kitchen chair and stared at Buchi Emecheta's *The Joys of Motherhood*, her eyes blurring as she struggled to make out the printed words. So she kept the book, tidied up the parlour and prepared the dinner of yam and tomato sauce. Aunty Ngozi often stopped by to bring them foodstuffs and sometimes she brought them soups prepared with large pieces of meat and azu mangala. They had run out of the delicacies and now she had to prepare yam. She wished she had extra money, or she would have bought some eggs and added them to the sauce, but she had used the last coins she had saved to buy the two bottles of Maltina she and Ejiro drank.

Tobe came home shortly after she had finished cooking, moody as usual, and she smelled the beer on his breath when she hugged him. This filled her with dread. Her husband was disappearing right in front of her eyes and she despaired because she didn't know how to save him. She instinctively wrapped her hands around his waist and refused to let go, not even when he tried to shrug her off. She kissed him, startling herself and him. The dark arcs under his eyes made them look eerily wide, and the skin of his face was rough like the bark of a yam. She kissed him again; the back of her eyes burned with tears and her chest trembled with sobs. Something was breaking inside her, slipping out of her, taking all the strength away. She had assured herself that she would remain strong, but she was crumbling.

Then he pulled her with him to his room. And then he was tugging at her dress, pulling it over her head, removing his shirt and trousers. Her tears blinded her. When he slid inside her, she remembered their first days together, how she had felt an out-of-body feeling, as though the pleasure was too much for her soul to handle that it had to slip out. But he felt different this time. Lean and weightless, his bones digging into her sides, his knees jabbing the side of her thighs as he lifted her waist to meet his swift thrusts. She let her tears flow.

Afterwards he slumped on her chest and didn't move. She wrapped her hands around him. Her body remembered his, even though he felt different. Her body still knew him. She wanted to ask him to quit the drinking, to tell him how much she had missed him, but he was already snoring. She tightened her arms around him and did not let him go, even when sleep came and her eyes drooped shut.

Aunty Ngozi and Uncle Ugonna visited them the following day, on a Sunday, when the air was thick with the smell of spicy goat-meat stew and the clinking of spoons on enamel plates flitted in from the neighbours' flat next door to theirs.

Tobe dragged himself out of his room and plopped on the sofa. He had slept all through the night and woke late in the morning. He said little when they shared a breakfast of pap and akara and said even less when she served fish stew and white rice for lunch. The stew had thin slices of fish and only one large piece, and she had added more pepper because she knew he loved his stew spicy. She gave him the biggest piece of fish but was dismayed when he didn't touch it. He had eaten only half the portion of the rice she served him. She had worried that he was sliding back into the gloomy moods, but she tried to wave it away because she remembered their lovemaking the night before.

And so, when Aunty Ngozi and Uncle Ugonna came, she tried to be chatty, to cover for Tobe who wore a long face. If they noticed his sullen silences, they did not speak about it. Uncle Ugonna said he was filing for retirement from the police force after a soldier beat up an orderly assigned to him. He had reported it to a senior army officer, and the soldier threatened to have him shot.

'These soldiers have taken the country hostage. I can no longer serve in such a system that is rife with such corruption,' he said. 'They can kill anyone and get away with it and nothing will happen.'

Aunty Ngozi clucked her tongue and said, 'This country has gone to the dogs.'

'They don't have human sympathy,' Uncle Ugonna continued. 'That's why I avoid them and everyone who supports them. Those who support them only do so because they also want a taste of that power. They will betray even their blood siblings for power.'

Tobe absently nodded, said, 'Hmm,' and often stared at something on the floor, as though it held more interest than the ongoing conversation.

Ogadinma wished he would speak. The talk about soldiers reminded her of Kelechi's visit. Ogadinma wished Tobe would talk about that; she wished he could say anything, just anything. And when he didn't, she spoke on his behalf, hoping Tobe would see that she was on his side.

'That's how Tobe's best friend, Kelechi, betrayed him. He now mingles with soldiers. Same soldiers that are ruining this country,' she said.

Everyone turned to look at her. Aunty Ngozi asked Tobe when Kelechi visited and he told her, in miserly details, how Kelechi had tried to rekindle their friendship.

'*Tufiakwa!*' Aunty Ngozi snapped her fingers over her head, the clicking sound piercing the still air. 'Thank God you chased him away. That man is not a good person.' She snapped her fingers again.

'He is not a true friend, and you don't need people like that around you,' Uncle Ugonna said.

'Oh, I no longer bother about him at all,' Tobe said. A nerve was throbbing by the side of his head, fat and pulsating, but he smiled in the way that showed he wanted to hide how angry he was. 'I would never have spoken about him if this topic didn't come up.'

He said other things, suddenly chatty, his words piercing, but Ogadinma was no longer listening, because her gaze was focused on the firmness of his jaw, the dark lines appearing on his forehead, each furrowing when he spoke. She knew she had offended him. She wished she could pinch their mouths shut and retrace time and she would never have spoken about Kelechi. Then she tried to hold his gaze, so he would see how sorry she was, so that he would see that she had acknowledged her mistake. But he did not look at her.

After Aunty Ngozi and Uncle Ugonna stood up to leave, Ogadinma followed behind Tobe and escorted them to the yard where they had parked their car. They talked for some minutes by the car, and Tobe even laughed, a genuine laugh that was so bubbly, his shoulders shaking, his chest heaving, and Ogadinma was almost relieved. He stood by as Uncle Ugonna and Aunty Ngozi got into the car and revved the engine, and then he waved as they eased the car onto the busy road and drove off.

He headed for the stairs and Ogadinma followed behind him, fear gripping her chest again. She was panting as she climbed the stairs and had just stepped onto the veranda when a hand grabbed her by the neck, pulling her inside and shoving her against the wall. She was thinking, was it Tobe, before he drove his fist into her face, rattling her teeth. There was a sickening snap of cartilage. Dizzying packets of pain shot up her nose, swallowing her face, rising in swift courses over her body. She screamed. She was falling. She was on fire. She opened her mouth to cry out again, but saw his feet driving into her face before she blacked out.

When she came round, she was still crumpled on the floor. For how long, she did not know. The neighbourhood was crowded with rusty brown roofs and high-tension electric wires she thought were hanging dangerously over some of the houses, the wires kept apart by discarded shoes strung by their laces to keep the wires from jamming together.

It began to rain, hasty splashes that fell in slanting lines, hitting their roof like a hail of pebbles. The door of the parlour was still open and the droplets splattering on the veranda sprayed inside, soaking up the curtains and the rug. She sat on the veranda, in the rain, her body soaked to her chest, her whole body burning and shivering at the same time. The children from the next yard were screaming excitedly, and she could hear them dragging buckets and basins, gathering water from rain troughs, dancing in the rain. She imagined them in little or no clothing, lugging buckets on their heads, as she used to do when she was a small child in Kano. She listened to their voices because she did not want to think, or even begin to think, of the pain licking all over her body. She had feared that this would happen because she had known that he would snap, that he would crack and grow into something else. She had sensed it in the grinding of his jaw, how he walked like one on the edge, how restless he was when she tried to start a conversation. Now the new Tobe had fully emerged and she was no longer sure she could endure this strange man.

Later, she went into the bathroom to shower, and then she leaned against the wall and began to cry. She still wept after she climbed into her bed, even after Lagos went to sleep and only the chirping of the crickets and croak of the toads in open drainages filled the night.

By morning, Tobe was shuffling from the passage to the bathroom, and later, out of the door, and she knew he had left for the market. She swung her feet off the bed and grabbed the mirror on her nightstand. She looked at her reflection: the purpling bump on her jaw, the upper and lower lids of her right eye that were now swollen shut, the dark patch around her throat where his grip had bruised her skin. She tossed the mirror aside and closed her good eye and tried to convince herself that everything was all right, that her eye was fine and she had nothing to worry about. But there was a persistent voice inside of her which whispered that she was not. She opened her eye again and the clock said it was almost noon. In a few hours Tobe would be home. The very idea of sleeping again in the same apartment with him filled her with terror, and she felt a headache coming. Her mind was webbed with utmost fear. She was convinced that he would find another reason to hurt her again. She imagined that next time, he could pin her to the wall and drive his fist into her good eye, over and over, until it erupted into a gooey mess. A tremble began to spread to her whole body.

She went to her wardrobe, pulled out her bag and hastily began to stuff her clothes in. A film of sweat coated her entire body, dripping from her neck, under her breasts, in between her legs. She dragged the bag out of the room and into the passage, then she stopped in front of Tobe's door, pulled it open and rushed inside. She knew he left rolls of naira in the pockets of his trousers for when he desperately needed them.

And she found them. Naira notes bound with rubber bands or folded and shoved down the back pockets of his trousers. She hastily stuffed some into her purse; she did not have the time to count or confirm if they would be enough to pay for her transportation to Kano. She just wanted to get away from the flat as fast as possible.

She stopped at the door. Though she wanted to leave, she still wondered how he would feel when he found her gone, and she briefly imagined him trekking the whole of Lagos, searching for her. She hurried over to the landline and dialled her father's number, because she knew Tobe would call him, but she couldn't reach him. So, she left Tobe a note, informing him that she was going home. She didn't let herself think of the fate of her marriage, if she was bringing shame to her father's name by running from her marriage, if she would return again. She didn't let herself think because her head ached and fear clutched around her ankles. She just wanted to go home.

When she left the flat and shut the door behind her, her feet felt cast in lead and the stairs seemed too fragile, as though they would cave in and trap her for Tobe to find her. She placed one foot after the other, dragging her bag behind her slowly, until she was out of the compound.

She arrived in Kano the next day, in the morning, when mothers were pounding pestles into mortars and banging pots and spoons in the kitchen. She had just walked into the yard when her father appeared in front of their door and called her, 'Ada m.' She stopped at a distance before him, tension and fear swimming in her head until she was dizzy. Running away from Tobe had been the only thing on her mind yesterday; she had not paused to think about what her father would make of her decision. And now he was standing in front of their door, dressed only in a faded wrapper tied at his waist; his chest seemed wider, his face fuller than she remembered, his skin covered with a film of oil. If she had seen him on the streets, she would not have immediately known that this chubby, good-looking man was really her father.

'Ada m,' he said again, spreading his arms open for an embrace, and she walked into his arms and held him in a long hug. He didn't seem surprised to see her and she knew then that Tobe had called and informed him of all that had happened. And she was glad that he didn't seem upset.

'Did you arrive well?' he asked.

'There was a hold-up at Lokoja,' she said. 'We would have been here earlier.'

He moved back a little, stared at her for a while longer. 'You look tired,' he said. He did not say anything about her swollen nose, or the bruising around her eyes.

He led her into the flat lit by a kerosene lamp, the one with the broken handle, whose globe never fitted well. 'Go to your room and rest,' he said. 'I will heat up water for you to take your bath, then you will have breakfast and sleep. I know you are tired after that long journey.'

'Thank you, Papa,' she said. She expected him to say more; she wanted to say more, to break the awkward silences and tell him how heartbroken she was, how she thought she was going to die. But they stood watching each other and he touched her face, caressed her cheek, before turning to walk into the kitchen.

She stood by her door, staring into the room. She heard him fill the kettle with water, and then kerosene fumes sifted into the passage when he lit the stove, making her eyes burn. She looked out of the window, to the entrance of the flat opposite, the flat in which her friend Mary lived with her mother. The floor of the veranda was spotted with grease and the walls were stained a dirty brown, the same brown streaks she noticed when she walked into the yard. The metal railings were rusted, the floor cracked in many places; the yard had aged. Perhaps if her father did not still live here, she would not have believed it was the same place she spent all her childhood. She remembered afternoons spent on their veranda, playing a game of Whot or Ten-Ten with the children of the other flats. But they had all grown and left home, the flats taken over by new families. Everything had changed, and it seemed she had turned out for the worse.

She was still standing by the door, hugging herself, when her father returned to say that he had prepared her bath. 'I will make your tea,' he said. 'Do you want me to fry some eggs also? I still have some eggs left.'

'Does Mary still live here?' she asked instead. She remembered that her father never liked Mary's mother, who ran a beer parlour in front of the yard. He blamed Mary's mother for all the burglaries in the compound because the beer parlour attracted dodgy fellows who lingered around the neighbourhood long after she had closed for the night. Still, her father allowed her to stay friends with Mary, perhaps because their closeness filled in a hollow in Ogadinma's life; it was why she never felt like an only child.

So, when she asked her father where Mary was, he paused before he told her, almost pensively, 'I hear Mary is now studying at the University of Jos. Her mother closed her shop and I hear she relocated to Benin.'

'Do you know their telephone number? Do you know their new address? I want to speak with Mary.'

He shook his head no, slowly, as if to say he was sorry for not remembering to get the new contact information.

Mary was now in a university and that was what mattered; Mary had always wanted to go to university. Ogadinma wanted to say, 'It's okay,' but a quivering started in her stomach and rippled all over her body. Her father wrapped his hands around her and held her against his chest. And she sobbed on his shoulder, choking cries that made her body tremble. After she was exhausted, he led her to the bathroom and urged her to take a shower, then he went to the kitchen to make her some breakfast.

All that morning, Tobe did not ring. The meeting she expected her father to call did not take place; instead, he left for work at around noon, and so she stayed in her room, staring out of the window and listening for the familiar sounds of her childhood. Even those did not come. The children did not play in the yard as they did during her time; they did not play the game of Ten-Ten in the afternoon when they returned from school, and they did not play football or scratch the bottoms off tins of Peak Milk and Milo to build toy cars and trucks. Instead, they trooped into a neighbour's flat to watch Indian films, chattering and making loud commentaries about each scene, about each actor, watching movie after movie, until evening came and they all rushed out and hastily began to do their chores – to sweep the yard and wash the plates and pots and clothes, before their parents returned from work.

Her father returned early in the evening. He rapped on her door before he looked in. '*Nne, kedu?*'

'I am fine, Papa,' she said. 'Good evening, sir.'

'Evening.' He looked around the room, at her bag which was resting by the wall, before his eyes returned to settle on her. 'Please come and help me change this carpet,' he said, and he turned and left.

She knotted a wrapper over her chest, before she went into the parlour. The new roll of carpet stood at a corner and there was a tub of gum and a green brush beside it. The old carpet was cracked in places but it still looked relatively new. 'Are you going to throw this away?' she asked him, pointing to the floor.

He bent and grabbed one end, pulling it up. Dust rose. He coughed and said, 'I'll throw it away. See how it has cracked and faded.' He pulled up the carpet some more. More dust rose. 'You can start from the other end. Be careful so sand won't jump into your eyes.'

They began to remove the old carpet, ripping it off the floor, and piling it right outside their door. Afterwards, he grabbed a broom to sweep the floor and she rushed to take it from him, because it was rude to let an elder do that chore. But he refused, and so she stepped well away from the dusty area so he would not have to sweep around her legs, because that was rude, too. She was startled by the things her father waved away, things he did not mind although he was a man, things others expected that only women must do. She tried to remember Tobe sweeping their flat, or even the rooms of their old house, but she couldn't. She had never seen him lift a broom, had never seen him dust the shelves or wipe down the centre table. He would always wait for her to sweep the parlour before he would go in to switch on the TV. She wondered if he would sweep the rooms now she was away, if he would wash the pots and the plates, if he would cook his own food. She wondered if he missed her too. She did not want to go back to him any more. She wanted to move in with her father and never return to Lagos. But she was still worried about how lonely Tobe would be in that empty, musty flat, how he would have to sleep all by himself now.

'Your uncle, Ugonna, saw your mother,' her father said. 'She also lives in Lagos. She has been living in Lagos all these years.'

Ogadinma stared at him, feeling a pounding in her head. This is what she had wanted: for him to talk about her mother, so that through his stories she would able to see who her mother really was. But he never spoke of her. And she had often resented him for keeping her in the dark. Now, he was ready to talk, as though she had not lived through these years begging for this moment. Why was he raising the topic now that she, herself, had left her marriage? Anger made her hands shake and she wished she could have the courage to tell him to shove the topic.

She smeared sweaty palms on her wrapper. 'How is she?'

He had measured the length of the carpet he needed and was trimming the ends with a pair of scissors. Sweat had beaded on his forehead and was now dripping towards his eyes. He swiped at it. Then he placed the carpet on the floor, checked to see that it fitted, before he raised it and began to apply the gum underneath.

'Ugonna said when he saw her, she pretended she didn't know who he was and he went and spoke to her. She never remarried all these years. Maybe because no one will marry her. Because, tell me, which man in his right senses will leave all these fresh women roaming the streets for a second-hand? I ask you, which man in his right senses will opt for a bend-down-select?' He was suddenly angry, speaking in hasty Igbo, his words rushing out of his mouth, uncontrolled. 'Sometimes, things don't go as we want. Sometimes, we make mistakes, but that is not enough reason to run. We are not cowards. But your mother, she was too headstrong, too stubborn. And where has that landed her, eh, I ask you, where did that land her?'

The reason for the carpet-changing became clear. He spoke for a long time about things he did for her mother, how he set up a business for her, that she began to mingle with women who put silly ideas in her head, that these women were the reason why she fled when war came.

'Now she lives in the smelliest part of Lagos, shrunken and tired and smelling of kai-kai. That's what Ugonna said, she now drowns her sorrows in the locally made brew that stinks like putrid piss.'

'Tobe wanted to kill me, Papa,' Ogadinma said. 'I spoke out of turn, but that is not the reason he would try to kill me. Look at my body. Look at my face.' Her voice was choked with tears.

He was staring at her, a steady, piercing gaze. And then he began to rub his forehead as though he suddenly had a headache. She noticed new things about him: his face was no longer etched with stress lines, his arms rippled with flesh and muscles and his stomach had begun to bulge. Her father had never looked better.

'You think you have endured what others haven't?' he said. 'Many times, your uncle and my mother begged me to take a new wife, but I refused because I knew the new woman would not treat you as her own. I did that for you and made sure you never lacked. And what did you do afterwards? You went outside and brought pregnancy from god-knows-where like Okwy, and killed it under my roof.

'I forgave you even though that sin was unforgivable,' he continued. 'Your aunt Okwy got pregnant at home and we gave her away to an old widower. That is what we do to girls who get pregnant at home. But you, I sent you to Lagos. What happened with your husband is sad, but it has happened, and it is not a reason to run from your home, you hear me?'

She stared at her clasped hands. A vein pulsed by the side of her eye, blood thudded in her ears. Never had she felt such rage. He cared more about her staying married than her safety. She should tell him how she felt, but then she had never been one to throw tantrums; she had never ever confronted her father in a rage, had never learned how to do such. So she nodded, swiped at her eyes, at her running nose. 'Yes, Papa,' she said.

'You must forgive him. Do you understand me?'

'Yes, Papa. I have heard you.'

There was a moment when he said nothing. He reached out and gently wiped the tears streaming down her face, and then fondled her jaw and smiled. Although she still felt rage in her bones, something softened in her. It was the way he rubbed her jaw, the way he looked into her eyes. He had always done that since she was a child, always knew how to win her over with just a touch, a smile. 'Go and wash your face,' he said. 'Tomorrow, we are going to Lagos to see your husband.'

The sun was bright and hot the morning they arrived in Lagos, a searing, blistering heat that burned the soles of her sandals. They were drenched in sweat by the time they got to the flat.

Tobe answered the door. 'Ọgọ m nnọọ,' he told her father. 'Welcome, my in-law. Please come inside.' Then he moved away so that her father entered first, before he turned to Ogadinma. 'Nwunye m, how are you?' he asked her.

'I am well,' she said, searching his face to see if he had missed her and regretted what he did. He ought to. But he looked better than she remembered: there was an extra glow on his skin, and his cheeks seemed fuller.

He took her bag, and with the other hand, he clasped her. His blue shirt smelled of a familiar cheap scent. She slipped out of his embrace and entered the parlour to find his uncle Ekene, who she would later learn had come from the village, and Uncle Ugonna and Aunty Ngozi.

She greeted the men, and then Aunty Ngozi, who gave her a sullen once-over before saying in a crusty, irritated voice, 'Ehen, welcome,' before heading out for the passage.

Ogadinma followed her, and she began to pace her breath because she knew that Aunty Ngozi was angry with her.

'I thought you had sense,' Aunty Ngozi said, immediately they were out of hearing distance. 'Tell me, Ogadinma, tell me, did I make a mistake introducing you to my brother, eh, I ask you, did I make a mistake? So, at your age, you do not know how to keep things within your family, eh? You ran to Kano to call your father. Now that you have called him, and our uncle Ekene has been invited, what has happened? Have they killed Tobe now? Did you hear them shouting at him? *Ọ dịka ị maghị ihe?*'

She talked for a long time, repeating things she had said before, her face puffy from shouting. Ogadinma did not hear much of what she said because she was no longer listening. Instead she thought of Ifeoma and her penchant for embarrassing her mother in the presence of everyone, how Aunty Ngozi never berated Ifeoma for her rudeness. And now the same Aunty Ngozi was shouting at her, her voice carrying out of the room, into the parlour, into the neighbourhood. She was silent for so long that Aunty Ngozi soon realized that she was not going to say anything, that shouting would not make her feel remorse.

'All I am saying is that you must learn to keep your family problems within the family.' Aunty Ngozi softened her voice. 'There will not be a next time. I have spoken with your husband and he has assured me that this will not happen again. Still, it is wiser to keep things in the family. Do you hear me?'

Only then did Ogadinma look up to meet her eyes. 'I hear you, Aunty,' she said.

Aunty Ngozi sighed and nodded, then she left the room and went to join the men in the parlour. But she returned shortly after to say that the men wanted to speak to her.

When she went into the parlour, her father looked grave, Uncle Ugonna stared at his clasped hands and Tobe sat, hugging his midsection, as if he'd suddenly caught a cold. Uncle Ugonna waved her to a chair and spoke first.

'*Nne*, we have heard everything that happened, but we want you to calm your spirit. What happened between you and your husband was sad, but you do not burn down your house to kill a rat. You will not let anger destroy the bond that holds you together, do you hear me?'

She nodded.

Tobe's uncle Ekene said, 'And for our brother Tobe.' He gave Tobe a long, searing look. 'Our people say it is not always wise to judge a man in the presence of his wife, but you have caused this woman so much pain – just look at her, *negodụnụ iru ya*. What were you planning to do to her? Redesign her features? I don't know how you are going to make this up to her, but you must.'

Tobe stared at the floor between his spread feet as his uncle spoke. He was upset, but this did not deter Ekene. 'You are angry because we are correcting you in your wife's presence, *eh kwa*?' Ekene continued, 'Let me tell you: we are your family. And if we fail to tell you your sins to your face, people will mock us. So, we will tell you the truth: you have behaved like a madman and it is the family that bears the shame because the madman does not comprehend the concept of shame.'

When the men said she could go, Tobe stood up. '*Nwunye m*, come,' he said. She walked towards him and he wrapped his hands around her body, pressing her so close, until she could hear the frantic heartbeats under his chest.

That night, they shared the plate of the ofe onugbu and fufu Aunty Ngozi had brought. Tobe ate most of the food, moulding his fufu into large balls which he dipped into the bowl of soup, scooping up pieces of fish and meat before swallowing, and she could see his throat bulge as the fufu travelled down. The silence unsettled her. She looked up often to examine his face and wished he would talk about the bruises on her face, that he would apologize for what he had done to her.

When she checked the mirror earlier, the swelling around her left eye had lessened, leaving only a purplish patch underneath and the redness in her eye. Her jaw still ached, her head still pounded. She wanted him to talk about what had happened between them, but Tobe was absorbed with eating, with licking the soup, with chewing the pieces of meat and fish. His chewing irritated her, the bulging of his cheeks, the smacking of his lips, how he licked his fingers and ate merrily like nothing had gone wrong between them. Only after he was done, after he had washed his hands, popped a toothpick into his mouth and leaned back on his seat, throwing his arms out, in the familiar way he often did when he had a good meal, did he speak to her.

'That useless Muslim Head of State is so concerned about recognizing the Sahrawi Arab Democratic Republic as an independent territory, but fails to see that there is hunger in the land. People can't even buy essential commodities in the market.' He clucked his tongue. 'What is that thing they said about poor priorities? These soldiers are so daft!'

'I want to go downstairs and buy some Panadol,' she said. 'My head hurts.'

For a moment, he looked flustered. 'There is money in the drawer. Take some and buy the Panadol. Also buy me a bottle of Harp.'

Ogadinma nodded and stood up. Although their families had resolved the issue, she expected him to speak about it.

When she returned, she found him sitting in the dark. The lantern had died down. She picked it up from where it sat on the table, held it close to her ear and shook it. She only heard the rustle of wick in the metal encasement. It had run out of kerosene. And so, she took it to the kitchen and refilled it and returned to find Tobe snoring, his head cocked at an awkward angle. She noticed new things about him, how he was gradually filling out, his stomach softly pushing again under the thin fabric of his shirt.

She shook his shoulder. '*Di m,*' she called him softly. 'I am back.'

He muttered something, perhaps the ruminations from a dream, and woke up. He looked at her with bleary eyes, then pulled her to him so that she sat on his lap.

'*Nwunye m,*' he said. He touched her face, ran a thumb along the patch under her eyes, her lightly swollen jaw, her chin, her neck. The rims of his eyes looked engorged. He kissed her, pushed his hands under her blouse. She felt a mix of emotions, the urge to melt against him, and to shove him so hard he would bang his head against the wall.

He led her to his room. She shut her eyes and could feel the wetness dripping down the sides of her eyes as he slid inside her, and when he began to gasp and jerk and buck above her, his head buried against her neck, she held him. It was the only thing she could do, because she knew then that he would never apologize, that he would never speak about what had happened between them. She knew that she must have to accept that this was who Tobe really was.

Still, she worried about the wrinkle in their relationship, because even though she struggled to push it away from her mind, there was that small yet troubling feeling that he would hurt her again, that he would never regret hurting her.

She was thinking about this the following afternoon when a knock came to her door and when she got it, she found Ejiro grinning and holding up a bag.

'I brought the Maltina today,' Ejiro shouted, laughing, but her laughter quickly died when she saw Ogadinma's face. 'Jesus Christ! Did he do this to you?'

She let Ejiro inside and shut the door. 'It is nothing.'

'What is nothing? Have you looked at yourself in the mirror, Ogadinma? I almost didn't recognize you. Jesus, this man wants to kill you.'

'You don't have to worry about this. It is nothing,' Ogadinma said again, feeling defensive.

'What do you mean by *it is nothing*? Any man who can do this to his wife is capable of murder.'

Ogadinma was upset, and though she didn't know half of what Tobe was capable of, she said, 'My husband is not capable of murder, in Jesus' name! Please, stop blowing things out of proportion.'

Ejiro was silent for a long time, and when she spoke again, her voice came out almost in whispers, dripping with concern. 'Have you told your people?'

Ogadinma shrugged. She looked down the street, perhaps because she couldn't hold Ejiro's gaze, so she wouldn't spill everything. 'You don't have to worry about this. Let's talk about something else, abeg. How you dey?'

'I think you should tell your father.'

Ogadinma sighed. 'He already knows.'

'He has seen your face?'

'I ran to him and he brought me back here.'

Ejiro's lips slackened. 'I am so sorry, Ogadinma.'

'See, they have warned him. Everything has been settled.'

'That was what my sister told us before her husband eventually killed her.'

Ogadinma looked at her.

'Odion, that was her name. We didn't know she was dead until her twin saw her in a dream. When we got to her house, her husband had already packed his things and fled. He buried her inside their bedroom.' She touched Ogadinma's shoulder, shifting her so that they stared into each other's eyes. 'See, once a man beats you like this, he never stops. He may stop for a while and apologize and promise never to do it again, but he will do it again and again, until he kills you.'

'So, what do you want me to do, eh? He is my husband. He won't do it again,' Ogadinma snapped. But worry nibbled at her mind. She turned back to stare out at the street, at the dusty road where okada riders manoeuvred round deep potholes the size of large basins. She could not remember the last time she was this hopeless. She turned to Ejiro who was still watching her keenly. 'This will not happen again,' she repeated.

Ejiro stared at her. 'Wetin you do am?'

'I put mouth for wetin no be my business. He come vex.'

Ejiro stood back, her eyes widening in their sockets, and when she spoke, it was in a melodious Pidgin, as if she didn't want her anger stiffened by the antiquated civility of the English language. 'Na only talk you talk and he come beat you like this? You sure say na human being you dey marry so? God forbid bad thing!'

'Ejiro—'

'Abeg, leave me. Abi you nor dey see your face? See how dis man take redesign your fine face for you? Him dey very wicked. That man no like you at all!'

Ogadinma said nothing.

'I swear, my mother go kill any man wey try dis nonsense on top her pikin body. She go kill dat man kpam kpam! After Odion die, my mama swear she go scatter the life of any man wey try her children again. My husband know already. Him know say na six feet underground dey wait for am if him ever touch my body.'

Ogadinma kept her gaze on the railings. She took a deep breath, hoping the urge to cry would pass. But it did not, not even when she began to breathe through her mouth.

'I am very worried for you,' Ejiro said. 'You are like my sister and I am very worried for you.'

'Ejiro,' she said, her voice hoarse. 'It was nothing.' And then the tears came. Her shoulders shook. Her chest heaved. Snot dripped from her nose and she swiped at it with an end of her wrapper. Ejiro held her hand and patted her back until she stopped crying.

11

One November morning, when the dusty wind from the Sahara was already misting the air, Ogadinma woke early to prepare Tobe's breakfast. She tossed diced onions into hot oil and the stench rose in the air, churning her stomach. She hadn't slept well the night before. She had woken up four times to urinate but still felt an unusual pressing on her bladder afterwards, and just when she drifted into deep sleep, sunlight streamed through the window and the shrill ring of the telephone rankled the air. Her head was pounding.

She poured diced tomatoes into the pan and was stirring the sauce when Tobe appeared at the door and said he was going to get some things from Aunty Ngozi.

'I am pregnant,' she blurted out. 'It is three weeks and my period has not come.'

Tobe looked surprised. He stared at her face and then at her stomach, as if he wanted to say something but did not know how to begin. She resumed stirring the sauce, making slow circular motions with the spoon, wondering if the news pleased him. There was still the queasiness in her stomach, but she also felt a warm rush of satisfaction, because all this time she had feared something had gone wrong with her womb, that she might never get pregnant and he would take her to a hospital and find out that she once had an abortion. Now she finally felt complete.

He came up behind her, threw his hands around her and pulled her against him, his flaccid penis pressed against her buttocks. He kissed the back of her neck, the side of her face, and began to sing an Igbo song of praise.

'*Chineke m oo, I meela onyenwe m oo…*'

'This pregnancy is a sign of good things to come,' he said as he sang, as he swayed with her, his words muffled against her neck.

She had been upset with him for a while. Now he was playful again, he was the old Tobe again. He wanted them to eat from the same plate and watch the TV together. Afterwards, he ran his tongue along her lips, her nose. She kissed him slowly at first, and then she was prying his lips open and plunging her tongue into the waiting warmth. He tasted of toothpaste. He bunched her nightdress around her waist and pulled off her underwear. She was thinking, was this all a dream, before his wet tongue worked its way down her belly to the fold between her legs. She thrust against his mouth. A scream spilled out of her, and Tobe pressed the flat of his palm over her mouth, saying, 'Baby, the neighbours will hear you.' He had never called her *baby*.

The scraping of pots from the neighbours' flat woke her. The world was buried under a blanket of darkness, the street illuminated only by dots of electric bulbs, and from her window came the distant sounds of Afrobeat music. She rose from her bed. Her back ached. Cold winds billowed the curtains, carrying the smell of roasted yam from the neighbours' flat. Tobe opened the door and walked in; he was still naked.

'Did you rise well?' he asked, sitting beside her. 'You drifted off and I didn't want to disturb you.'

His eyes rested on her body, and she pulled her wrapper to her chest and knotted it under her arm. She was shy. 'I am sorry I overslept,' she said. 'I should go and prepare your dinner.'

'I think I should tell my sister to get us a housegirl,' he said. 'You need someone now you are pregnant. You don't need to stress yourself too much any more.'

She touched his face; his skin under her fingers was smooth and fleshy. He was filling out in the right places. 'I think I am fine by myself,' she said.

'You need the help,' he insisted, 'maybe not immediately. But I will tell my sister to start looking.' And she found it foolishly exciting that he cared that much about her welfare, even though she didn't need the help. She didn't get any help when they lived in the big house.

Later, they sat on the veranda and ate jollof rice and fish. Tobe scooped his rice, ate contentedly, as if they were lounging in the expansive balcony of their old house. He told her about his plans to expand his shop, how he was already making contacts with prospective customers coming from distant places like Aba and Uyo.

'Our child will be very smart,' she said out of the blue. And he nodded and agreed with her.

'He will be very smart.'

They spent more evenings like this, idling outside and making small talk. Sometimes, too, when electricity had been restored, they cuddled before the TV. He was no longer moody, he had stories to share, and sang when his favourite songs came on the radio.

Aunty Ngozi and Uncle Ugonna dropped by one evening, carrying gifts of beverages, a flask filled with nkwobi and a keg of palm wine. Tobe shook Uncle Ugonna's hand firmly, but Uncle Ugonna waved away his thanks and asked Ogadinma to get them some mugs. Then they sat on the veranda and talked about the recent events in the country, dipping their fingers into bowls of spicy nkwobi and sipping the fresh-smelling palm wine.

'Have I told you that my wife is pregnant?' Tobe said, and Aunty Ngozi jumped up and began a little dance. She swung her arms, she swayed her waist, she stomped her feet as she sang an Igbo song, before she scooped Ogadinma in both fleshy arms and swung her round and round.

'*Ehen*, that is what I am talking about!' she laughed.

Uncle Ugonna cocked his head dramatically and gazed at her flat belly, as if she was suddenly transparent so he could see into her womb. 'Our son is on the way,' he said. He thumped Tobe's back. 'The one who will inherit your name is on the way!'

'*Nne*, you must not stress yourself at this time, *i nu*?' Aunty Ngozi said afterwards. 'You know you are always working, always cleaning something and sweeping and washing. You need to calm down *kita*, so that you and your baby will not be stressed out. You hear me?'

'Your aunt speaks the truth,' Uncle Ugonna said.

'What she needs is a housegirl,' Tobe said. 'You have to help us get one.'

Aunty Ngozi nodded and said, 'I will speak to my friend Nkiruka. She knows where to get good girls.'

Ogadinma thanked her and wished, yet again, that Tobe would stop fussing about this. There was nothing much to do in the house anyway, and a housegirl would be an extra mouth to feed, an extra burden on Tobe's income. She wished she was working too. She had spoken with him about selling akara by the roadside and he vehemently rejected the idea, said it was his job to provide and care for her and she must never bring up that matter again.

She cleared the bowls and mugs and took them to the kitchen to wash. She looked out of the window. Her neighbours were carrying on with their daily activities. There were too many people in the yard; the house was a three-storey building with eight flats, but some of the occupants shared their flats with other families, splitting rents. Every morning, they would hang wet clothes on the railings, from the top floor to the ground floor, and even on the fence. Ogadinma had never seen that many clothes hung out to dry at the same time. It was why the walls of the building had become discoloured, and the floor of the yard was often wet, the edges of the walls overgrown with moss. On humid evenings when the mouldy smells hung heavy, she would shut the back windows to keep the air out, leaving only the windows of the parlour open because they looked out on to the street. And there were too many children in the yard. When it rained, they all trooped out to dance and fetch water. Today, they had divided themselves into groups; while the girls played a game of *suweh*, the boys kicked at a limp football, and some others, who weren't interested in the games, rode on skateboards built from wood and discarded wheel bearings. Ogadinma rubbed her flat stomach and wondered if her child would one day play with the children in the yard.

Two mothers chatted on the veranda opposite hers, their eyes glued to her window. Her first reflex was to duck but then she didn't; the mosquito netting was built such that neighbours couldn't see into her flat. She always heard when the women gossiped or fought, especially Mama Femi and Mama Iyabo, whose shouting matches and frequent brawls had become a familiar drama. 'You stole my palm oil, you petty thief. You will not go out and work like other women,' Mama Femi said the other day, her voice tearing across the yard. And Mama Iyabo shouted back, 'I did not steal your palm oil, you cheap prostitute!' Mama Iyabo hooted and clapped and soon they grabbed at each other's blouses, tearing off their wrappers, till neighbours came and pulled them apart.

Today, Mama Iyabo and Mama Tochi fixed their gazes at Ogadinma's window.

'Does that one ever come out of that flat?' said Mama Tochi. She squeezed her mouth into a pout and gestured at Ogadinma's flat. 'Since she and that her proud husband moved into this yard, they never associate with anyone.'

'Ah, you have noticed them too?' said Mama Iyabo. 'I greeted the stupid man the other day and he looked at me as if I was nothing. The very stupid man. Who does he even think he is?'

'I hear he used to be a big man.'

'But now he is sharing this yard with us, *abi no be so*? Why is he carrying shoulder for everybody? Is he feeding anyone in this yard? And that his wife that always acts as if she lives in a mansion, is it not this same yard we are all managing?' Mama Iyabo hissed through her browned, widely spaced teeth.

'I wonder o,' Mama Tochi said, and re-knotted her worn wrapper under her arm. 'It is that his skinny wife I pity. The skinny thing that carries her shoulder like she is one queen like that. She never comes out to greet anybody. Abi she don greet you before? Because she has never said a word to me since they came here.'

'What will I do with her greeting?' Mama Iyabo said. 'She should carry it and feed herself, maybe it will give her the flesh she desperately needs.' And they both tipped their heads back and laughed.

Ogadinma bent over the sink and began to wash the plates, her mind raking over the past as she tried to remember her communications with the women in the yard, especially Mama Iyabo. The first time Ogadinma met her on the stairs, they greeted and sized each other up. In the set of Mama Iyabo's shoulders, her thick arms that bulged inside her faded lacy blouse, her wide, flaring nostrils, Ogadinma sensed that Mama Iyabo had been a fighter all her life, the kind of girl who beat up the boys on her street, who never backed down from a fight, who was feared by her mates. Ogadinma had wondered how Mama Iyabo saw her, but she could not tell, because the woman spoke at length and in a space of ten minutes had rendered mini-biographies of all the women in the yard: whose husband was sleeping with househelps, whose husband fathered her neighbours' children, which woman was a cheap prostitute, which one begged to feed her seven children because her bus driver husband spent all his money on the girls at the motor park; which woman must be avoided because she was a terrible gossip. On and on Mama Iyabo went, her mouth running like a burst pipe. Ogadinma had nodded all through and then muttered something about checking what she had left on the stove, before extricating herself from the gossip and fleeing into the confines of her flat. When they met the next time at the store and Mama Iyabo had nice things to say about her dress, Ogadinma, guessing that the praise was a launch pad into another round of long-winded gossip, thanked her and fled. She knew that Mama Iyabo was not pleased that she was avoiding her, because she remembered the stern set of the woman's shoulders, and the cold stare and measured words when they walked past each other the next time. Mama Iyabo never smiled at her again.

Tobe's laughter floated from the veranda, hearty and loud, and she could almost imagine his shoulders quivering, his chest heaving. This was how he laughed before things changed; this was how he laughed that first time she met him in Uncle Ugonna's house, that day he praised her soup. Ogadinma smiled, surprised at the acuteness of her memory. Things were almost as they used to be, as they were supposed to be.

She lifted her blouse and touched her flat belly and remembered the first time she got pregnant, how she had raced up and down the stairs, and had drunk lime until her throat burned. She became overwhelmed with grief; she had not wanted her first pregnancy. Now she had a second chance and she relished the idea of her belly pushing under her clothes.

In the following weeks, she stared down at her stomach often, counting the days until her baby arrived. When she showered, she did not scrub the area around her belly as vigorously as she did other parts of her body; instead she rubbed palm over it and rinsed it off with water. She was doing that one morning when Tobe opened the door and joined her. He saw what she was doing and smiled. She giggled. He took the sponge and began to scrub her back, and after he was done, she scrubbed his, too. They shared the bowl, taking turns to scoop water from the tall bucket and upend over their heads. They bathed silently, bodies pressing against each other in the boxy bathroom, splashing water all over the toilet seat. And she thought, this is perfect, this is a new beginning.

By late December, her pregnancy had elevated and pushed out softly under her clothes, the bump visible enough for the neighbours to see. The women greeted her with much enthusiasm and they watched her with keen interest when she hung clothes to dry on her clothesline.

Nothing seemed to change at home. The days were peaceful and routine. Tobe left early for his shop and came home early in the evening. And sometimes, on the days he made good sales, he brought home roasted plantain and groundnut. They spent Christmas in

Lagos, although she had wanted to travel to her home town to spend the holiday with her father and her grandmother. But she called her father often and he filled her in on the happenings in the village: the daughter of the clan who had got married, the family that lost their grandmother, how Christmas was different without her.

By January, Tobe brought fewer and fewer gifts home. She was in the kitchen preparing a meal of egusi soup and garri when he came home one evening, lugging a bag of roasted chicken. She could smell the smoky spiciness and could tell he bought it from the roadside seller who roasted the chickens on a wide wire gauze set atop a barrel filled with hot charcoal. Tobe had taken her to the barbecue spot once. That day, when they came home, her clothes and hair smelled of smoke; she still smelled even after she had showered.

'I will add some in the soup,' she said, taking the bag from him.

He shoved his hands into the pockets of his white kaftan, the one she had washed the previous day and ironed with light spray starch until it was crisp and smooth. 'Nwunye m, I think I am going to close that cosmetic shop,' he said.

She placed the bag on the table. 'Why?'

'Because it is no longer profitable.' He sounded desperate. 'I still have cartons of expensive creams and soaps no one wants. Everyone is buying Stella Pomade and Lux. I have to look for something better to do. I have decided to sell off the remaining goods to my neighbours and use the money for something else.'

This was not a good thing, she knew at once. 'What do you want to do?' she asked.

'I will be joining Ifeanyi,' he said.

'Who is Ifeanyi?'

'He is my friend at the market.' Tobe moved closer, tensed lines appearing on his forehead. 'Ifeanyi used to sell cosmetics but he now runs a booming tiles business, and he has promised to introduce me into the business. He is a good friend.'

She wanted to ask why he never brought this friend home, but it was not the best time to ask this, and so she said, 'When will you start?'

'Next week.' He held her by the shoulders, looked down at her belly and asked if the baby was already kicking. She gave a forced laugh and said it was too early. And as he kissed her, she wondered why he was only just telling her about this new friend and why he would trust someone who had never visited their home.

Nnanna came the following day, in the afternoon, carrying a green food flask, the one Aunty Ngozi always filled with soup and nkwọbi. A few months had passed, and he had suddenly morphed into a more mature man.

'My favourite cousin,' Nnanna said, wrapping his hands around her.

'Am I really your favourite cousin?' she teased him and punched him lightly on the shoulder. 'I haven't seen you in many months and you don't even call.'

'*Nne*, it is school o. I would have come home after the first semester, but I had a lot of things to sort out in town, especially accommodation. Getting a good house in Benin is a difficult thing.'

'What about the hostel?'

He laughed. 'If you want to know how wicked people can be, then move into a hostel. Do you know many of us had to bathe outside because some students defecate on the floor, and some even go to the extent of splattering the walls with shit? I couldn't survive one semester in there.'

'That's terrible.'

He stood back and peered at her belly. '*Nekwa*, you don't even look like you are pregnant. Where is this pregnancy everyone is talking about? I can't even see it.'

She laughed and punched his chest playfully.

'So, how are you holding up here?' he asked.

She grinned and said, 'Everything is fine now. We are doing very well.'

He held her gaze, worry wrinkling his brow. 'Are you sure you are holding up well, Ogadinma?'

She turned away and began to unscrew the flask and found it was filled with onugbu soup. She knew that Nnanna was watching her silently, that he had heard about Tobe's violence, and perhaps had come to talk it over with her. And she was not comfortable with discussing that any more; what happened had happened and she wanted to leave it behind her. When she turned around, he was watching her. And he looked sad, his brows still creased with concern.

'We are doing well, Nnanna,' she said quickly. 'Tell me, how is this new place you moved into?'

There was a moment when they both stared at each other. She smiled and nodded reassuringly. 'We are doing fine, Nnanna. Please tell me everything about your new place.'

He sighed, and said, 'It's a BQ, and I share it with a friend.'

'A friend?'

He looked away, grinned. 'I... Well, she is my friend.'

'Hmmm! You are living with a girl.' She laughed. 'What is her name?'

'Ada.' His eyes crinkled at the corners. 'She is so brilliant, so smart. She just graduated from my school.'

'She graduated already? Is she older than you?'

'By just five years. I don't care that she is older.'

She smoothed her dress with the flat of her palms. There were too many things swirling around in her head. She was grateful that he did not insist on talking about her situation, and she also envied his schooling – that he was lucky to get university admission and live with whoever he chose, wherever he chose. 'I am just thinking, how did you get money to pay for a BQ?'

'I got a job in a bank as a clerk. They accepted me with my WAEC certificate.'

'This is good news, Nnanna.'

'They have promised to convert me into a full staff member after I have graduated. Ada and I will get a better house when this happens.'

'You love her, don't you?'

He nodded before he said, 'Yes.'

'She must love you too. Who wouldn't?' He had always been a good-looking boy. Once, when she still lived with them, the neighbour's daughters came over to borrow his textbooks and they giggled and fidgeted around him, and he had been too distracted to notice. But he now knew how appealing he was; she could tell from his finely ironed clothes, the sculpting of his hairline and the fullness of his well-groomed beard.

He talked about other things, his studies and his love for Benin and Ifeoma, who had just gotten admission into the University of Lagos. She could hear the grating *kroo-kroo-kroo* sounds from Mama Iyabo's flat, where someone was scraping the burned part of a pot.

'When you meet Ada, she will tell you I am the best thing to ever happen to her,' Nnanna said suddenly.

She hissed and said, 'You are so full of yourself.'

They began to laugh, and she was overcome with a renewed and pleasant bonding with him, the kind she had always wanted to have with Ifeoma.

Tobe started his apprenticeship at Ifeanyi's shop the following week, on a Monday morning, and came back that evening, grinning. Tiles trading was simple, he said, and he could learn all the tricks in less than a month. There wasn't much profit in retailing, but it was better than running a cosmetic shop, because the buyers were mostly business establishments and the rich who came from distant places, and he could sell out a truckload of tiles in two weeks. He left every morning for Ifeanyi's shop and returned in the evening, bristling with new ideas about the trade. It was the happiest Ogadinma had seen him in a while, and she wished she could do something magical and make this success permanent so that he would recover all he had lost.

In the following weeks, he said Ifeanyi wanted them to team up and import a consignment of tiles from Italy, that Ifeanyi had made a connection with manufacturers willing to form a long-term business relationship with them. They would sell off the consignment the week it touched down at the Lagos port, and prepare for another trip. Tobe worked out the mathematics as he told Ogadinma this, and when he lifted his head from his pen and paper, his eyes shone, his lips stretched wide in a smile. He would make forty per cent profit if he invested all the money he had, and this would be after expenses had been deducted. He leaned back on the sofa, his gaze focused on the ceiling, a hand stroking his jaw as he spoke. Ogadinma watched his lips move. Couldn't he see that it was risky to put all his money into a new venture? That it was more frightening particularly because this new friend he had made had never visited their home? The thought played across her mind as Tobe talked on and on about this new venture. He said he should have thought about this tile trade a long time ago. He and Aunty Ngozi would have not wasted all the funds he ploughed into the cosmetic shop.

Ifeanyi visited them on a Sunday, at past seven in the evening, when the orange sun still shone as though it had forgotten when to give way to night.

Ogadinma had just set the table for dinner. She dished him some garri and ofe onugbu. Ifeanyi was seated opposite her and his eyes settled on her body as he moulded his garri into large balls, even as he dipped them into the bowl of soup and swallowed, his throat visibly bulging, the shrunken nut that was his Adam's Apple quivering as the bolus travelled down his throat.

'*Nne*, you cook so well,' he said, licking his fingers.

She smiled and said thank you and bowed over her food. A smarter man would know to keep his eyes away from his friend's wife, but not Ifeanyi. It irked her that Tobe didn't notice these things, that he could consider someone like Ifeanyi a friend.

'I like that you are eating good food in my house,' Tobe told Ifeanyi later, 'but you must marry a wife this Christmas or I will ban you from coming to my house.'

And Ifeanyi laughed, a cackling, exaggerated sound that flopped around the room. 'Ha, my brother, you know I would have married if I saw the right woman.'

'So, you are telling me that of all these Lagos girls you have been sneaking with, you have not seen a single one good enough to settle down with?'

Ifeanyi laughed again, his voice awkwardly loud. 'Nna, leave those things roving on the streets. When I am ready, I will travel to my village and find me a ripe fruit that has not been sucked by every mouth. These ones here are not wife material.'

Ogadinma looked up from her plate and found Ifeanyi watching. He smiled. His eyes had the same glassy quality as those of hyenas she had once seen in Sabon Gari Market in Kano, tethered to heavy chains by tamers who used them for paid performances. Her father had said hyenas were cunning, intelligent animals that skulked around, stealing other animals' meals. She bowed over her plate and continued to eat.

Long after she had cleared the table, Ogadinma couldn't shake the unsettling feeling about Ifeanyi; it was in the way he looked at her, the oily smile he gave Tobe when they huddled together discussing important things. After he had left, Tobe switched on the TV and sang along to 'Love Me Adure' on NTA, his voice so loud, so irritatingly discordant, that Ogadinma sighed in relief when the orange electric bulb suddenly dimmed, the beam much lower than a smoky kerosene lamp, before the lights went off.

'Do you want to sit outside a bit and enjoy the fresh air?' she asked him. 'This place is getting hot.'

He headed for the veranda and she followed behind him. His shirt was stretched smooth over his body, his shoulders wide, and he walked with a bounce in his heels, proud. After he settled on a stool, she pulled one close beside him and sat, the two of them looking out to the street which was so dark that, save for the occasional cars speeding past with their headlights on full beam, people would bump into each other in the dark.

'You are travelling with Ifeanyi?' she asked him quietly.

'No. I discussed it with him, and he said it is better he goes alone this time, this way we will incur fewer expenses. I may join him on the next trip,' he said.

And something sank in her stomach, but she gave him a forced smile as he placed his hand on her knee and began to knead it softly.

'I am happy he even agreed to do this with me. Many people would prefer that I buy from them after they had imported the tiles, at a retail price. Ifeanyi is a great friend.'

She nodded and gazed out to the street. How should she tell him about her distrust for Ifeanyi without offending him? 'Do you trust him?' she asked him slowly, and when he turned and looked at her, she quickly added, 'I am asking because I care.'

'I trust him,' he said, seeming irritable. 'Before he closed his cosmetic shop, he gave me some of his goods and was patient until I had sold the last bar of soap before asking me to pay up. Many people wouldn't be that patient. If there is someone I could trust with my life, it is Ifeanyi.'

She nodded and tried to believe him. Perhaps she had judged Ifeanyi too harshly, had mistaken his ungainly openness for mischief. But there was still that throbbing doubt that pricked her skin. She was thinking too much about this friendship, and it was so because she still remembered how Kelechi betrayed Tobe.

Tobe gave her a look, an expression that made her uncomfortable, and so she hurriedly said, 'The night is so dark. I haven't seen any moon in many days now.'

The change of topic seemed to lift his mood a bit. He leaned back on his seat, his tone softer when he spoke again. 'Maybe we should go inside. You know these Lagos mosquitoes, they will soon begin to feast on our bodies.'

12

They were having dinner the following week, on Good Friday, when things started to go wrong. Tobe had just finished eating his onugbu soup and fufu when the telephone rang. Ogadinma went to answer it. The frantic voice at the other end said he wanted to speak with Tobe, and when he took the phone, he sat first, listening to the voice, and then he jerked to his feet and shouted, 'God forbid it! What are you telling me, Ofoma? What kind of nonsense are you telling me?' He dropped the phone and rushed out of the parlour. Ogadinma watched him. She knew that something bad had happened and that it had something to do with Ifeanyi. She wanted to go to Tobe and ask what it was, but she could not. She was too frightened to go to him. She could hear him shuffling in the room, pulling open cupboards, grabbing his car keys, and when he emerged, he dashed out of the door and didn't even look in her direction. And when he returned an hour later, he did not respond to her greeting. He went into the parlour and sat down.

She stood by the door for a while, wringing her hands. When she entered the room later, she found him crumpled on his favourite seat, dolefully staring at the TV. She sat next to him and felt the urge to do things with her hands, to smooth her skirt, to reach out and scratch her suddenly itching back, to hold him. She wanted to do something but did not know what to do because he seemed impenetrable, his face crumpled into folds of tensed lines. And that was what terrified her: the angry set of his face.

'What happened, *Di m?*' she finally asked him.

He stared at her. For a long time he just looked at her. It didn't seem like he was going to answer her question, and she felt fear, like hot pins, stinging the back of her eyes, clamping its fingers around her throat. She did not know what he was thinking, why he was looking at her like that, if what happened had something to do with her. She had begun to rearrange herself on her seat, shifting and smoothing her dress nervously, when he eventually spoke.

'Why have things been going wrong since we married?' he asked.

She opened and closed her mouth, and felt something wither insider her. 'I don't understand what you mean, my husband.'

'Ifeanyi has ruined me,' he said.

Ha! she thought, she was right about Ifeanyi after all. But she could not say this to Tobe, and besides, it was the worst time to say such a thing to anyone.

A nerve pulsed by the side of his head. And then, he began to laugh, like one who was on the verge of losing his mind. 'I emptied my bank account and he fled with my money, his brother's money, and even what he borrowed from his bank. I hear he ran to Germany.'

The room had grown chilly, her skin flushed with bumps. She threw her arms around him; she did not know what else to do. He sat stiffly at first, and then he held her. They stayed that way for a long time, the warmth sifting from the thin fabric of his t-shirt, shielding her from the cold.

'Why is this happening to me?' he muttered, almost to himself.

'Don't give up, my husband,' she said.

He slipped away from her embrace. The lights went off at that time and she went to get the kerosene lamp. When she returned, he sat crumpled on his seat, his head buried in his hands. He looked like a sack of stringy clothes. Tobe, whose boxy shoulders swallowed her frame when he hugged her, now looked like a tired bag of skin and bones sinking into a corner of the sofa.

'God, why is this happening to me?' he muttered into his hands.

'Why must everything crumble again after everything I went through, why?'

Ogadinma went and sat beside him. What was a wife supposed to do at such a time? Pray? Hold him and weep and everything would magically be all right? She reached for his hand; it lay limp in hers. He did not want the touch of her skin. He stood up and went into his room. She heard the click of the door and knew he wanted to be alone by himself.

She went into her room and crawled under her sheet, listened for his sounds, but the sturdy wall separating their rooms was unyielding. Later, he opened the door and went into the parlour. The lights had returned, and her room was brightly lit. She sat up. She hoped he would come over and they would hold and comfort each other. She hoped the telephone would ring and he would get a call saying Ifeanyi had been caught and his money retrieved. She waited for the miracle to happen, just one miracle, but the only thing that came were his cries. Deep, rumbling sobs that didn't stop, that seemed to shake his whole body, that seemed to shake the very foundations of the house. He did not stop crying, and she tried not to imagine him crouching on the floor of the parlour, his arms wrapped around his midsection as his heart broke. She did not think of her own eyes that had filled with tears. Instead she pulled the sheets over her head and willed for sleep to come.

In the following days, Tobe spent most of his time at home. He would wake up in the morning and loiter from room to room, or he would stay in bed until past ten in the morning before he showered and left.

Food began to disappear from the cupboard. He left little money on the table, amounts that were never enough to make a full breakfast. And so, she began to substitute iced fish for meat, and tin tomatoes for the fresh, expensive ones. She bought cups of local rice instead of foreign rice, and she would pour the grains onto a tray, set it on her lap and pick out stones. The cooked rice was always too puffy and stuck to the stew like fufu to soup.

But Ogadinma did not yield to despair, not even when Tobe gradually became verbally abusive. He found every excuse to complain about the things she did, the ones she did not do well. 'Does it mean that you can't properly scrub the floors? Just *negodinụ* everywhere, see how dusty this passageway is and you said you scrubbed it?' he said one morning. 'Are you sure you sucked your mother's breasts well? *Nekwa anya*, you have to be smart because this nonsense you are doing is itching my body.'

Ogadinma watched the wall gecko run across the wall. A wasp flew in from the door leading to the back of their flat. 'I will clean the floors again, my husband,' she said, slowly. She did not look at Tobe when she said this, because she feared that it would anger him further.

Lunch that day was local rice and fish stew. The stew was watery, and the fish sliced so thinly it was the size of her two fingers pressed together. Tobe gaped at the helping in his bowl. She scooped the stew onto her rice, eating silently. She was certain that the fish tasted good, but Tobe was glaring down at it.

'What is this nonsense?' he asked.

She did not need to look at the bowl because she was eating the same thing, but she looked. 'Rice and fish stew,' she said.

Tobe was staring pointedly at her, then he scooped a portion of the stew, lifted the spoon higher above the bowl and tipped it, so that the stew trickled down, like red water speckled with bits of pepper and onions, into the bowl. 'So, this is how your people taught you how to make stew, eh?' He scooped the stew again, raised the spoon and let it drip. It spattered on the edge of the bowl, on the table, on his white shirt, on his trousers. A bad sign.

Fear clutched around her ankles and wrists and made her hands shake. She could sense the rage building inside him, turning his eyes dark, but she didn't know what he was going to do to her. It would be better if she saw him draw up his fists, at least that way she would know to shield her face with her arms, and if she fell, she would curl into a tight ball and protect her baby. She was reaching for a table towel when he slapped the bowl with the back of his hand, like a bat to a tennis ball, and the bowl flew off the table, towards her; the stew spilled from the bowl and hit her smack on the chest. Hot, spicy stew splashed on her body, on her face, and even jumped into her eyes, before the bowl clattered to the floor and cracked. She screamed and jumped off her seat, grabbing her face, her eyes. She was temporarily blind and as she made to rush into the bathroom, to get some water to soothe her eyes and chest, she ran into the door and bumped her head against the wall. Excruciating pain rose in swift courses around her head. Her eyes were on fire. Her chest was burning. She found her way into the bathroom and sank her head into the bucket of water. When she stood up again, she still felt the unbearable needles of pain pricking her eyes, like grits of sand rubbing against her tender eyeballs. She was sobbing, throaty cries that shook her body. She walked blindly into the kitchen and reached for the salt shaker. She thought of her father and how he would make her lick a pinch of salt whenever pepper got into her eyes. It didn't take all the pain away, but the burning sensation on her tongue took away the irritation in her eyes.

When she returned to the parlour, Tobe was glaring at the news report on TV, the picture grainy as though it was filmed under a heavy rainfall. She wished he would turn around and look at her, so he could see how red her eyes were, how the area around her eyes was swollen. But he did not look, not even when she lingered cleaning the table, the carpet. She hovered by him.

'Let me make you some garri and egusi soup,' she said. 'We still have some soup left and it is very fresh.'

He ignored her and went over to the telephone. 'Sister? Have you finished cooking?' Tobe said into the mouthpiece. 'No, I haven't eaten since morning. I don't know the nonsense this idiot cooked today.' He glared in her direction and she bowed her head, and silently left.

Aunty Ngozi came later, clutching two large flasks. She was dressed in a yellow sequinned wrapper over a white lace blouse with puffy sleeves, and a gold ichafu wrapped in layers atop her head. She had just returned from church. She pulled Ogadinma to the kitchen after she had served Tobe the ofe akwu and white rice she had brought.

'Nne, what happened?' she asked, her voice quavering with concern. 'Why didn't you give your husband food?'

Words frothed in Ogadinma's chest, her throat was squeezing and when she opened her mouth to speak, the first thing that surged out of her mouth were choking sobs.

Aunty Ngozi held her, saying, 'O zugo, stop crying. Your husband is going through the most difficult moment.'

Ogadinma swiped at her face, breathing fast. 'He threw a bowl of hot stew at me.'

Aunty Ngozi blanched, then mellowed. 'He has lost everything again. So, don't be upset that he takes out his frustrations on you; that is the burden we women have to bear, you hear me?'

'So, I must continue to endure this abuse even though I am pregnant with our child?' She sniffed into the hem of her dress.

Aunty Ngozi held her, whispering familiar things about endurance and forgiveness, and Ogadinma muttered an excuse and returned to her room.

She crawled into bed, her mind muddled by grief, and for a long time 'this idiot' played across her mind, formed a loop and haunted her. If anyone had told her that there would come a time when Tobe would assault her so viciously and dismiss her as an idiot, she would have said they were high on cheap drugs.

And in the following days, she woke each morning, frightened by the mere presence of Tobe. Fear calcified in her stomach and, like a stone, it jumped each time his eyes met hers, each time he opened his mouth to speak. She looked out of the window often and wondered why people still laughed. Sometimes, after Tobe had left in the morning, the thought of running away would come to her mind, but her knees melted as the thought flashed by, because she knew, even her body knew, that she could never run; there was no place to run to, there was no one to run to. She knew that even if she ran to her father, he would always bring her back to Tobe.

13

Ogadinma visited Ejiro one morning. 'I want your mother to help me do something about Tobe,' and then added quickly, 'but I don't want him to die. Can she help me?'

Ejiro did not ask questions, perhaps because she had been waiting for this day. Perhaps, too, because she saw the tired lines around Ogadinma's eyes, the thinness of her neck, how edgy she had become. She went over to the telephone to call her mother. She called Ogadinma her 'best friend' and said, 'Mama, do quick o before dat man go kill am for me.'

It warmed Ogadinma's heart that Ejiro was her succour. She even smiled when Ejiro rubbed her belly, when she brought out the bottles of Maltina and bowls of hot jollof rice, and they sat on the floor of the room and ate and chatted. Ogadinma felt something lifting off her chest, off her shoulders, a dead weight that had refused to let her breathe well for so long. She was grateful that Ejiro did not ask what happened this time, that they talked instead about the new proud neighbour, the happenings in Lagos and Ejiro's sister's latest trip to London.

After that visit, she became less edgy and did not shiver when Tobe glared at her. And the following week, when Ejiro visited and handed her a black vial and said she should pour the contents into Tobe's soup, she hugged Ejiro and suppressed the urge to dissolve into a fit of joyful tears.

'It will not kill him, abi? I just want him to be kind to me,' Ogadinma said.

'It will not kill him, and it will not make him sick. Trust me,' Ejiro said.

'So what will it do to him?'

'It will humble him by force.'

Ogadinma stuffed the vial into her pocket without looking too long at it. Perhaps it was one of those potions she had heard about which turned violent men into submissive husbands. She certainly wanted Tobe to be less violent, to be humbled. The thought amused her, the idea of Tobe washing her clothes and underwear and mopping the floors. She smiled a small sardonic smile. She would finally breathe well and no longer cower under Tobe's gaze. She might not let him cook her meals, because she wasn't so sure about his cooking skills, but she would make him do all other domestic chores.

When Tobe came home that evening, her hand shook a little as she emptied the contents into his bowl of onugbu soup. It did not smell, which was comforting, and when she served him the food, he barely looked at her before he pulled the bowl for hand-washing close and began to wash his hands.

She returned to the kitchen. She was suddenly unsure. She had made a big mistake. She was so sure that Tobe would fall down and die, and so she wanted to run out of the flat before that happened, but her feet had stayed glued to the floor. Blood thudded in her ears, drowning out all sounds, so that she did not hear when he called her name later until he bounded into the kitchen, his face contorted in anger.

'Have you gone deaf, or did you not hear me calling?'

She was sweating. She swiped at her face and looked at him. Nothing seemed to have changed, not his manner. Not his anger. 'I am sorry, my husband,' she said. 'I do not feel very well.'

He stared at her, his brow crumpled with worry, before he said, 'Go and clear the table. I have finished eating.'

As she removed the plates, her mind was slowed with confusion. Had the potion worked at all? Tobe returned to watch the TV. He leaned back on the sofa, his legs stretched out on the table before him. This was not the demeanour of a man who had been humbled; a submissive husband would not ask his wife to clear the table. He was still very much in control, and as though to emphasize this, he turned around and told her, 'Get me a toothpick,' his voice bristling with familiar authority.

Ogadinma's heart sank; the power balance would never be skewed in her favour. She would never breathe well. She would never stand straight. After she returned to her room, she curled against her pillow and began to cry.

She was drifting to sleep, when Tobe came to her door and told her to come to his room. She knew he wanted sex; that had become the routine for them ever since Ifeanyi fled with his money. When she got to his room, he was already undressed. He reached for her body, he pulled himself on top of her. She lay so still, so tensed. She closed her eyes and began to count. She had only counted to ten when Tobe grunted. She opened her eyes and saw that he was holding his limp penis in confusion. Even she was confused. This had never happened before. In ten seconds, he would only just be beginning. But he was done in ten seconds and both of them were so stunned by this that they stared at each other, their mouths gaping in shock, before he rolled off her body and told her to return to her room.

Ejiro called her the following morning. 'Did you do it?' she asked, her voice barely above a whisper. 'I thought you were going to tell me how it all went down yesterday.'

Ogadinma told her about the ten-second incident, how flustered he had been, that he lowered his head when he told her to return to her room. The ten-second incident happened again this morning and he couldn't even look her in the face. Later, he had sat in the parlour, shrunken like a defeathered cock, staring dolefully at the TV. 'Him don humble by force,' Ogadinma said.

And for the first time since things fell apart, she found in that experience a stirring wicked pleasure.

. . .

Uncle Ugonna and Aunty Ngozi came the following week, when she was cooking. She could hear them clearly because the passage door was open and because they did not keep their voices low.

'This thing is getting out of hand,' Uncle Ugonna was saying. 'An elder cannot sit by and watch a tethered goat go into labour. That's why we have come, because this situation is getting out of hand, and it is time we did something about it.'

Tobe grunted and said, 'But, do you all think I have done nothing about my situation? Do you think it gives me joy that I have lost everything?'

'We are not saying you are happy with it. We are only saying we have not done everything we are supposed to do, that's why we have come,' Aunty Ngozi said. She spoke like she had water in her nose. 'My friend Nkiruka knows this powerful preacher called Onye Ekpere who performs wondrous miracles. Nkiruka wants us to go to him.'

Tobe muttered something. Ogadinma inched closer to the door so she could hear them clearly. She did not like the idea of going to Onye Ekpere because the miracle workers in Kano always blamed family members for the misfortunes that befell a miracle seeker.

Aunty Ngozi said Nkiruka's husband would have been deported from Italy had Onye Ekpere not unearthed the rusty padlocks and pieces of red cloth buried in their village home.

'We have to meet this man because this thing that is happening to you is spiritual attack,' Uncle Ugonna said.

Tobe mumbled in agreement. Feet shuffled and Ogadinma hurried back into the kitchen. Aunty Ngozi entered later, smiling.

'*Nne, kedụ?* How are you and our baby?' She caressed Ogadinma's belly, making slow circular motions.

'We are well, Aunty.'

'We are taking Tobe to a preacher. My friend Nkiruka tells me that the man, Onye Ekpere, can haunt Ifeanyi with prayers and force him to return what he stole.'

Ogadinma had never been bothered about going to miracle workers because her father never allowed such nonsense in his house, but now it was about to happen in her house. Uncle Ugonna blamed Tobe's misfortunes on 'spiritual attack', and Ogadinma's heart sank. She knew things could quickly escalate with the matter of the spirits. As a child in Kano, she heard about preachers who blamed women for the misfortunes that befell their men, how they put these women through series of rigorous cleansing ceremonies. She could never imagine going through such emotional and physical turmoil. The thought worried her, but she shook the feeling away and told Aunty Ngozi that it was a good idea. She was not sure why she said that. Maybe it was because of the seriousness with which Aunty Ngozi had delivered the message, or because she knew that everyone would frown if she protested against the idea.

And Aunty Ngozi was pleased that she was okay with it, because she smiled and rubbed Ogadinma's belly again, before saying, 'I'll give Nkiruka a call. She will book the appointment on our behalf.'

But when Aunty Ngozi came the following morning, a Bible tucked under her arm and a black scarf knotted tightly over her head, she said Ogadinma must join them to see Onye Ekpere, that the preacher had demanded so.

'Why is that necessary?' Tobe looked about to change his mind. 'I thought it was only to pray for me?'

'Nkiruka said it is even a good idea because any spiritual attack against you can also easily affect your wife. And we don't want that.'

Ogadinma took her time pulling on her dress. She was no longer sure about this. She thought about calling her father, but that would mean speaking with him with Tobe and Aunty Ngozi watching and listening to their conversation.

Tying her scarf at the base of her neck, she joined them in the parlour and they all filed out to the front of the yard where Tobe's car was parked. The car sputtered a few times, shuddered and died. He gripped the wheel with one hand and turned the key again, his back arched, tense. The engine cranked, coughed, before it started. He leaned back and sighed. Even Aunty Ngozi exhaled as he revved the engine.

'*I makwa*, people come all the way from Uyo and Calabar and Onitsha to see Onye Ekpere,' Aunty Ngozi continued after they eased onto the road. 'If not for Nkiruka, we would not have been able to meet with him so soon. I hear people book him months in advance. Did you bring the three bottles of Goya Olive Oil with you?'

'Yes, I have them in my bag,' Tobe said.

'And the two bags of salt and two packets of Lux soap?'

Tobe gripped the wheel tight. 'What does he do with these things anyway? I thought he is praying to God? What does he need soap and salt for?'

'Because that's how he does his prayers. He will use the salt to prepare Holy Water for you. He uses the Lux to wash his hands before and after praying for you.'

'Why would he need to wash his hands, and why this particular brand of soap?'

'You are asking too many questions, and this shows you have too many doubts,' Aunty Ngozi snapped. 'That is not good at all. It means you don't have faith in what we are going to do today, and if you don't have faith, how then will your miracle manifest, eh, I ask you? How can your prayers cross the ceiling and travel to God in heaven if you are so doubtful?'

'So, it's now a crime to ask questions?'

They drove in silence the rest of the trip. Thirty minutes later, they pulled up in front of an unpainted bungalow at the end of a cramped market street. The banner plastered on the wall of the house said, BREAKOUT MIRACLE MINISTRY INTERNATIONAL. OPERATION KILL YOUR ENEMIES! Aunty Ngozi led them inside the large hall packed with dusty camp chairs. Two women in loose-fitting dresses sat at one side of the hall, their faces set in sad lines of piety. Aunty Ngozi waved, and they waved back, before she sat. Ogadinma sat between Tobe and Aunty Ngozi.

Ogadinma glanced at the hall. The place did not look like a church at all; except for the same garish banner pinned to the wall of a raised platform she assumed was the altar, there was nothing indicating that it was a place of worship. Not the cracked floor filled with sand, nor the bare walls that had yet to be plastered. A wrinkled old man came in later, and for a moment, Ogadinma thought he was also a miracle seeker, until the women stood to greet him, their heads bowed slightly in reverence. He moved from chair to chair, shaking hands, exchanging greetings, hugging the women. When he got to their side, Aunty Ngozi dramatically bent on one knee to greet him, gripping his hand with both of hers. 'Good morning, Man of God!' she said in a loud voice. 'God bless you, sir!'

'Please don't kneel for me,' Onye Ekpere said, helping her to her feet. 'You only kneel for God.' He pointed a shaky finger at the ceiling. 'All praises should go to him. I am just his servant.' There was a hint of a smile by the side of his lips, but it quickly disappeared when he turned to Ogadinma.

She was startled. 'Good morning, sir,' she said, slowly.

But Onye Ekpere did not respond to the greeting. Instead he asked for her name, and when she told him, he said, 'And this is your husband?' He did not look at Tobe when he said this.

Ogadinma cast a quick glance at Tobe's face, before bobbing her head.

'But I was not talking about him.' He pointed a finger in Tobe's direction. 'I am talking to this other man standing by your right side. He said he is your husband and I ask you to confirm: is this man your husband?'

Ogadinma looked around them, felt her stomach lurch upwards to her chest, painfully. She had been so engrossed with the state of the church, with observing Onye Ekpere, that she pushed her initial worry about preachers away from her mind. Now, it had crept back; she had been targeted. She looked at Tobe and then Aunty Ngozi; they both were visibly unsettled. They both believed Onye Ekpere. 'Which man, sir?' she asked him, her voice choked with fear.

'He has been with you all your life. He is the reason for your troubles because he is very jealous and wants you all to himself.'

Aunty Ngozi shouted, 'O *Chukwu, O Chukwu!*'

Tobe stood back, as though he was suddenly afraid of Ogadinma.

Ogadinma had begun to shiver, and when she spoke, she hardly heard herself. 'I don't know who you are talking about, sir.' She looked at Tobe and begged him with her eyes not to desert her. But he stood well away from her, shifting so far, as if she was suddenly infected with a strange disease.

Onye Ekpere broke into an Igbo song, his voice rumbling, '*Ike o, ike niie bụ nke ya. Ike o, ike niile bụ nke Chukwu.*' He danced, clapped, his thin frame swaying to the rhythm of the song. Aunty Ngozi and Tobe joined in, and even the other women on the other side.

He ended the song abruptly and invited them into an inner room by the side of the altar, which was bare, the floor cracked and dusty, the walls riddled with holes. Tobe still stood well away from Ogadinma. Aunty Ngozi, too. Onye Ekpere poured some water into a blue basin, tore open one of the soaps, and began to wash his hands. For a long time, he scrubbed, muttering, before he rinsed off the lather and wiped his hands dry with a kerchief he retrieved from his pocket.

'*Bịa ebe a,*' he told Ogadinma, pointing at the centre of the room. 'Come here.'

She went to him. She felt like she was caught in a bad dream, that this strange drama playing out before her was a nightmare. As she stood before him, she thought of her father and his aversion to organized religion, how he would have sneered at this bizarre spectacle. 'I do not have any spiritual husband,' she protested.

But Onye Ekpere burst out in another song, his hands stretched out to the ceiling as he invited the Holy Spirit. 'Yes, Father, I hear you, Father! Jesus, send us your Holy Spirit!' He trembled, flailed, like a drunk stumbling his way in the dark. He broke into a sputter of tongues, incoherent jabber that would have been funny to Ogadinma on any other day. Aunty Ngozi was calling on Jesus and the Holy Spirit. Tobe sang slowly.

Onye Ekpere laid a bony hand on her head, pressing down with so much force. 'What is your name?' he asked her.

She tried to shake off his hand but he pressed tightly, and she fleetingly wondered why he couldn't magically sniff out her name as he had done with her supposed spiritual husband. 'Ogadinma Okafo,' she said.

And the man jerked forward and backward, spasmodic movements as though he was zapped with electric shocks, his hand still gripping her head. 'Abba Father! I apply the axe of fire upon any chain binding Ogadinma Okafo in the name of Jesus!'

'Amen!' Tobe and Aunty Ngozi chorused.

'You satanic manipulation going on in her life, destroying everything she touches, destroying the life and businesses of the people close to her, I command you to cease now in the name of Jesus!'

Tobe's 'Amen!' reached for the ceiling.

'You forces of witchcraft assigned to manipulate Ogadinma Okafo out of her destiny, come out now in the name of Jesus!'

'Amen!'

He shoved her forward and backward, as he chanted, 'I command you to come out now in the name of Jesus!'

'Amen!'

'I break you, satanic forces! I command you to come out now!'

'Amen!'

'Come out! Come out!'

'Amen!'

Ogadinma willed herself to stay still, but Onye Ekpere clenched her face with one hand, and grabbed the back of her head with the other. She could not escape him. She could not breathe well. And so, she fought him, and he fought back: shoving her, dragging her. She feared her neck would snap. She feared for her baby.

'Please, let me go,' she begged.

Aunty Ngozi and Tobe were chanting and thumping their hands, their voices fevered and loud. Onye Ekpere tightened his grip on her face. She folded her arms around her stomach, as strength left her knees, and she crumpled to the floor.

When she opened her eyes later, she was lying on the dusty floor. She hastily rubbed a hand over her belly. Something fluttered in her stomach, and she clamped her hands around it, relieved. Onye Ekpere stood at one corner of the room, speaking with Aunty Ngozi and Tobe. He talked in a low voice, his words measured, cutting and swift. Marine spirit. Spiritual husband. Prayer and fasting. That she was the reason for Tobe's misfortunes. But there was a solution. She must stay in the church for seven days for intensive prayer and fasting, to sever her relationship with the marine world.

'She doesn't like swimming,' Tobe blurted. He looked at her, his gaze filled with rage. 'I remember she told me that, before we married, that she hates water. I asked her why and she said she feared she would drown each time she looked into large bodies of water.'

Onye Ekpere shut his eyes and smiled, shaking his head from side to side, as though he was communicating with otherworldly voices. 'That is the spirit husband's influence on her. She knows he would take her away if she so much as swims.'

Ogadinma wanted to speak up, but what was the point? Tobe was watching her with eyes that said she was the reason for his misfortunes, and Aunty Ngozi was swiping at her tears, her gaze full of contempt.

'I want my father.' She began to cry. 'Take me back to my father, please.'

'Don't listen to her, it is the divisive spirit husband speaking through her,' Onye Ekpere told them.

'When do you want to begin the prayers?' Tobe asked.

'We can begin tomorrow,' he said.

'Can we leave her here?' Aunty Ngozi said. 'There is no need taking her home with us now that we know where our troubles are coming from.' Tobe was frowning. 'Please, let us leave her here,' she continued. 'We will provide everything she needs and come for her when the deliverance is done.'

Ogadinma stood up. She wanted to insist that they should take her back to her father, but then she remembered that he expected her to endure whatever came out of this marriage. He was the reason for her suffering, because if he had taken her back the first time, there would not have been any need for this. 'I want to go home. There is nothing wrong with me. Take me home with you, please,' she begged Tobe.

But Onye Ekpere approached her. 'There is everything wrong with you. Shut up! I felt it immediately I saw you. I see the forces manipulating you. *Mana, n'aha* Jesus, that spirit will be cast out! Because there is no other power greater than His name. You must be set free of this evil spirit, so your husband can be free.'

'Amen!' Aunty Ngozi said, her voice thundering down the hall.

Onye Ekpere placed his bony hands on Ogadinma's head. His skin was ashy and cracked, as though he had never applied pomade on his body all his life. Ogadinma looked at Tobe; he was looking at her, too, and conveying all the hatred his mouth could never speak. And she knew then that nothing she said would ever change their minds about her.

And so, when Onye Ekpere said, 'We will break the chains of darkness in your life and you will be set free. Say Amen!' she swiped at her tears, stared at the floor and mumbled, 'Amen.'

Tobe and Aunty Ngozi left and returned hours later with a change of clothes and underwear. Afterwards Onye Ekpere showed her to a small room at the back of the compound. The bed was thin and short, and there was a small table and chair beside the door. The window was a hole in the wall covered with a dirty brown curtain. She stared at the bed, at the stained sheet and the dusty floor, and wondered how many people had slept on it, if they were all women like her brought here for deliverance. She kept her bag on the table, wiped the chair with a hand and swiped the dust against her dress. Then she sat and bowed her head over the table and fell into a blank, grateful sleep.

14

Onye Ekpere knocked on her door at night, when her skin had become clammy and large mosquitoes buzzed against her ears. She had splayed a wrapper on the bed and covered the pillow with her blouse, and was teetering between sleep and wakefulness, when he came. At first, when she opened her eyes, she panicked at how low the ceiling hung, the walls that were too narrow, and the small window that barely let in air and light.

Onye Ekpere came with two women. The porch light was dim, so she could not make out the expression on their faces. 'Come with us. It is time to begin your cleansing,' he said, and turned and left. The women followed meekly behind him, their backs slightly bowed, their long gowns flapping against their legs in the light wind.

The sky was starless on that night and even the moon did not come out to play, and so Ogadinma squinted as she picked the path that led to the church. Her grandmother once told her that spirits, both good and bad, came out on nights like this, that they whistled in the wind and rustled with the leaves and you could tell they were close when you felt your head swell and your skin prickle and fill out with goosebumps. She hastened down the short path, and almost sighed in relief when she walked inside the church lit by bright fluorescent lamps.

Onye Ekpere was standing by the pulpit with the two women who were now singing and thumping their hands. 'Ogadinma Okafo, come forward,' said the man, pointing to a spot on the floor. And she went there and stood. He got down from the platform and as he approached her, he spoke, his words measured. 'We are going to war,' he said, 'and to win this battle, you will present yourself to the Lord as the day you came into this world.' He paused. 'Take off your clothes.'

She drew a sharp breath. 'Sir?'

'Asị m, yipụ akwa gị.' He approached her, his gaze piercing. 'Pull off your clothes. Or do you not know that God answers the prayers of naked people faster? That He then sees you have stripped yourself of your pride and arrogance, and are standing before Him, naked and true, like the day you were born, when you knew not your left from your right?'

His hair was a mess of uncombed tufts that had locked themselves into unruly kinks. He cared little about his physical appearance: his skin was flaky, his nose stubby with grey tufts, and his lips were chapped and peeling when it was not even harmattan yet. And as he began to wag a finger in her face, flashing browned teeth as he spoke to her, she saw the clump of dirt under his nails. He was the most unattractive man she had ever seen. And anyone who could go to these lengths to make himself repulsive should never be meddled with.

She pulled off her dress and her underwear. She began to cup her breasts, to cover her nakedness with her small arms, but then she left her hands at her sides.

Onye Ekpere began to pray and the women joined him, chanting songs and 'Amens'. Ogadinma stared at the round clock perching on the wall of the altar; it was a few minutes past midnight. The night was cold, swift winds came in from the windows, biting and chilling. Minutes stretched into hours. Onye Ekpere and the women circled her like hunters with prey, shouting words and songs, stomping their feet. She sang in a small voice. Perhaps if she sang along they would realize that nothing was wrong with her. She sang for a long time, until her voice was hoarse.

When Onye Ekpere laid a hand on her head, and said, 'I command you to get out!' she imagined her chest shattering and a full human being, maybe a man as big as Tobe, jumping out of her body. She sank on her knees and began to cry again.

The women helped her to her feet later and pulled on her dress and underwear. It was past four in the morning and Onye Ekpere still looked alert, as though he was ready for another prayer marathon. 'We will continue again tomorrow,' he said.

Back in her room, Ogadinma crumpled on the bed. She was too tired to cry, too exhausted to think. She curled on her side, but just as she shut her eyes, a knock came to her door. When she opened it, she found Onye Ekpere standing before it.

'*Kedụ*,' he said. 'How are you?'

He walked in.

'Please shut the door and come,' he said. 'I have come to perfect today's prayers else all we have done will be a waste. Do you understand me?'

She pondered his words for some seconds, searched his face for signs of what was coming. But the fixed smile on his face did not change, and so she could not read him. 'What do you mean by "perfecting" the prayers?'

'You see, this spiritual husband needs more than just prayers to scare him out.'

'I don't understand.'

He shut his eyes, swung his head from side to side; he had entered another spiritual realm. When he opened his eyes again, they looked milky and wet. 'You have to take off your clothes and I will pray for you, again, just the two of us, to perfect today's prayer.'

She took a step back. 'I can't do that, sir.'

'That is what the Spirit of God says I must do. And if we don't accomplish it, if I don't confirm that it has been accomplished, your husband will not come for you.'

'I can't do it, sir,' she whispered.

'But you must. You cannot say no to the Spirit. You are not even worthy to speak to the Spirit.' He let the words sink in. 'Your husband will not take you back until I have confirmed to him that everything is all right with you. Do you understand what I am saying?'

Ogadinma nodded and pulled off her dress.

'Lie on the bed,' Onye Ekpere said.

She stretched out on the bed and shut her eyes. She did not think about how odd it was that she was naked and alone in a room with Onye Ekpere, her body splayed out before him like a sacrifice, her stomach queasy with dread. She took a deep breath and waited for the prayers to begin, but then she heard the rustling of clothing, opened her eyes and saw him taking off his clothes. She sat up.

'What are you doing?'

'Shhhh!'

'No, sir. I will not let you do this!'

'The Spirit of the Lord is here and you must not spoil this moment for the Lord!'

'Please, leave me alone.'

'Shut your mouth!' his voice thundered, shaking the room. He stood before her, old and wrinkled, his entire body rough like the bark of a dogonyaro tree. 'You will not spoil the Lord's work. How dare you challenge the Spirit? How dare you?'

The rumples in his navel quivered as he approached her, and his penis stuck out like a thumb from the folds of shrunken skin. Tears, stinging and hot, trickled down the sides of her eyes as he climbed the bed and half-stretched atop her, so he would not press too hard on her protruding belly. She averted her face when he looked down at her. His curdled breath was harsh against her neck as he muttered prayers.

'Jesus, as my body touches hers, may the yoke of the marine husband in her be broken! I say, may the yoke be broken!' he chanted.

She did not say 'Amen'. Instead, she let her mind rake over her past, before Tobe came into the picture, when all she ever wanted was to go to school.

. . .

She did everything Onye Ekpere asked her to. She went for the midnight prayers and stripped naked before the women. She sang with them, and at the end of prayers, the women helped her with her dress. And back in her room, she dutifully stripped off again for Onye Ekpere to perfect his prayers.

She did not think of Tobe. She did not let her mind wander too far into her past. Deep hollows soon appeared under her eyes. She did not ask for food when none was left at her door, and when she ate, she took too long to chew, as though it hurt to eat. Morning melded into afternoon, and noon bled into night, bringing her horrors, horrors she resigned her body to.

And it was why on that last morning, when Onye Ekpere lifted her legs, stroked himself and thrust into her, she did not resist him. She had feared that this would happen on the first day, even in the following days when he left streaks of wetness on her thigh. She shut her eyes. She imagined her body slipping out from under him and fleeing from this place, to somewhere so far away from here, somewhere safe. She returned to her room and Kano, locked herself in her small room that looked into the compound, until the horror was over, before she came back to this room. Afterwards, he wiped the stickiness from her body with a white cloth and dropped it on her lap.

'I will shave your head, your armpit and your pubic hair. When you leave here, you will make sure to bury the hair and this cloth in a bush around your house, are you hearing me? It is the final process of severing your relationship with your spirit husband.' A pause. 'Are you even listening to me?'

She did not respond, and he did not prod her. She sat there, her eyes lingering on the door, as he shaved her hair.

Tobe and Aunty Ngozi came later in the morning, after Ogadinma had showered and changed into a new dress. She was sitting on the only chair in Onye Ekpere's private meeting room when they walked in. Tobe stopped in his stride. Aunty Ngozi's mouth drooped open.

'He says I am fine now,' she told them, looking from Tobe to Aunty Ngozi. 'He shaved my head, too,' she said, as though they had not seen that already.

Onye Ekpere entered later. 'Everything you touch now will be going smoothly, like driving on a well-paved road,' he said.

And Tobe and Aunty Ngozi shouted, 'Amen!'

'Kneel before the Lord,' he said, and to Ogadinma, he said, 'Kneel beside your husband and hold his hand.'

And she went and knelt. When Tobe held her hand, she felt how soft the palm was, like he had never had to do any hard work with his hands, like he had people who did things for him and took the blame for his failures.

As Onye Ekpere began to sing, Tobe's eyes were shut tight in concentration. He had not changed at all; the sleeves of his shirt were rolled to the elbows and revealed the muscles which rippled under the fitting fabric and his cheeks bulged as he sang along with Onye Ekpere. He had not missed a meal. He had carried on like nothing had happened, while she suffered.

She gazed out of the window as they drove home, half-listening to their conversation.

'He really is a powerful Man of God,' Tobe said. 'He sees things.'

'I told you,' Aunty Ngozi beamed. 'People come from all over to see him.' She turned around to look at Ogadinma. 'I know every-thing went well?'

'Yes.' Ogadinma briefly held her gaze, and searched for signs that Aunty Ngozi knew what Onye Ekpere did to women. She ought to know about the rape; her friend must have told her what the man did to women. But Aunty Ngozi had already turned her attention to Tobe, her manner brusque. 'Ah, did I tell you what happened at Papa Ugonna's office the other day?' she said to him in a hurried voice that suggested she did not want to dwell on the matter concerning the preacher.

Ogadinma should ask her about it. The tension in the car was tilted in her favour; they were all nervous around her, neither holding her gaze for too long, as if they were hounded by the fear of the guilty, especially Aunty Ngozi. She should confront Aunty Ngozi, ask what she knew about the preacher, if she knew what he did to women. But she sank back, sighed. What was the point, though? This would only make matters worse. As a girl, she saw what happened to girls who spoke up about their rape, how their parents punished and blamed them and everyone isolated and treated them like things cursed by the gods. Her initial bravado deserted her, left her feeling hollow.

Later, she brought out the white cloth from her pocket and unwrapped it. A musty smell rose from it. She ran a finger over the clump of hair.

'What is that?' Aunty Ngozi wore a puzzled look.

Ogadinma folded the cloth and returned it to her pocket. 'My hair. Onye Ekpere said I must bury it in a bush.' And she turned away.

She was certain Aunty Ngozi was still watching her, that Tobe's eyes darted to her in the rear-view mirror, but she didn't look at them.

15

Ogadinma rubbed her belly as her baby moved and didn't bother about the chaos around her: Tobe had encountered another misfortune. He had borrowed money from Aunty Ngozi to import powdered milk from Cotonou, a product whose importation had been banned by the military government. She had told him it was a bad idea, but as usual, he did what he wanted. And on the morning he travelled to Cotonou, she sat in her bed and stared at the moving form of her baby. It was no longer the fluttering or the slight pokes below her navel; her baby was moving, shifting and distorting the shape of her belly. Sometimes, the movements went on for minutes, as if a rat went up her butt, sliding from one side to the other.

This had become her favourite pastime, the activity that kept her mind away from the trauma she had endured. Her due date was near and the idea that she would soon breastfeed her baby cleansed her mind of dark thoughts and filled her with renewed strength.

Then Tobe came home in the evening, sweating and panting.

'My consignment has been impounded,' he told her after she let him in. She looked at him. There was so much she wanted to say to him, things she knew would set the house on fire and cause him to harm her again. So she held her tongue. As he rushed into the parlour, she knew he was going to call Aunty Ngozi.

'Sister, something terrible has happened,' she heard him say.

She went inside and found him hunched over the telephone as he told Aunty Ngozi everything that had happened: he had bought the cartons of milk and chartered a truck to ship them to Lagos. At the border, they were accosted by immigration officers and soldiers who took money from him before they let them pass. But they ran into trouble at Badagry when another set of soldiers demanded more money, and when he couldn't give them the amount requested, they towed the truck to their office.

'I don't have such money, Sister,' he said. He rubbed his face. 'Could you help me raise the amount? I must get the truck soon before it gets lost. I hear they hold secret auctions at their office.'

He held the phone against his ear for a long time, and then he put it down and stood up. 'I am going out,' he said.

He did not tell Ogadinma where he was going, and she did not ask. She did not feel sorry for him. Rage, instead, rose to her chest.

He did not come home that night, and when she sat down to have dinner all by herself, she had a steaming bowl of nsala soup filled with large pieces of meat and mangala fish. She drank a sweating bottle of Maltina, and picked her teeth with a toothpick. Then she leaned back on her chair, rubbed her satisfyingly full stomach, and thought of all those times she had served him large portions and ate very little. She wished she could go back in time and do things differently. She read The Joys of Motherhood again, without any interruption, and the words did not smudge this time. That night, she sang as she showered, and when she lay down to sleep, she ignored the irritating, tender part of herself that told her to call Ugonna's home and ask if they knew about Tobe's whereabouts. This new misfortune was entirely his fault, and so she felt no compassion for him. She felt no need to carry any emotional burden on his behalf.

But it was only when she woke in the morning that she became fully concerned about his sudden disappearance. And so, by noon, when he had yet to come home or call, she went to search for him at Uncle Ugonna's house.

Uncle Ugonna was eating when she arrived.

'Ha, Ogadinma, this one you and your belly came to see us. I hope you woke well?' he asked.

'Good afternoon, Uncle,' she greeted him.

'*Afulu m gi*. Come and sit down.' He waved her over to the empty chair opposite him, pushed his plate aside and wiped his mouth with the back of his hand. 'You have come because of the problems your husband is having,' he said.

'He hasn't come home since last night.'

'I know. He and your aunt have been working to get the truck from the soldiers. They came home very late last night, that's why he slept here.'

'Have they recovered the truck?'

A tight smile appeared on Uncle Ugonna's face and he shook his head. 'Even after they paid what the officers asked for. You know, the country is getting filled with criminals all over again, like it was during Shagari. Yes, you impounded the banned goods. Why are you then requesting for money from the owners? And when they paid the amount you requested, why are you still refusing to keep your end of the bargain?' He made a clucking sound. '*Mana*, let me ask you o, do you even put your family in the hands of God? Do you pray at all?'

'Uncle, what I don't understand is why everyone must hold me responsible for Tobe's decisions.'

'What do you mean?'

She had spoken too hotly, and her words had come out too rashly. She took a deep breath and said, 'Tobe is too stubborn.'

Uncle Ugonna moved closer to the end of his seat. 'What did he do?'

'He makes too many bad decisions. All of this would not have happened if he listened to me.'

And then she told him everything, how Tobe had ignored her worries about Ifeanyi, how he had dismissed her caution against going to Cotonou.

Uncle Ugonna arched his head to an angle, in a way to show he was considering her words. 'He made a mistake,' he said finally. 'I will speak to him.'

'Uncle, you must not tell him I complained to you.'

'I know how to talk to him, don't worry. A man cannot claim he knows it all. That's why we marry and start a family, so we have people who become part of us and even influence our decisions.'

Tobe and Aunty Ngozi came in then, both drenched in sweat. Ogadinma greeted them but Tobe ignored her and Aunty Ngozi only grunted and went into her room, muttering something about taking a shower.

'My in-law,' Uncle Ugonna said. 'How did it go?'

Tobe sat beside Uncle Ugonna, and Ogadinma decided to give them some privacy.

As she left the room, she heard Tobe say the officers had refused to release the truck until they paid extra money.

She did talk to him when he emerged later and did not hasten to meet up with his strides when they trekked to the junction to board a bus home. He gazed out of the window all through the ride. When they got home, she climbed the stairs behind him, watching his tense back, how he took the stairs two at a time. She had just stepped into the parlour when he locked the door with the key, before whipping around to face her. Sweaty patches had appeared under his arms, staining his white t-shirt brown.

'What did you tell your uncle about me?' he asked her.

She swallowed. 'Eh?'

He approached her slowly, menacingly. 'I said, what did you tell your uncle about me and my business?'

'I didn't tell him anything,' she said. She backed away from him, but was soon pinned against the wall.

'So, you are lying to me to my face?' he was saying.

He grabbed her by the neck, slammed her back against the wall. Pain shot up her waist. His hands tightened around her throat. She kicked out. He was speaking in a sputter of Igbo. She could not breathe. She was thinking of how she could protect her baby, before her eyes drifted shut.

When she came round shortly after, Tobe's fists were slamming into her face, against her neck, her chest. She curled on the floor, she held her stomach. Perhaps if she held it tighter, only her body would be hurt and her baby would be all right. Tobe was still punching, kicking and swearing. The pain was raw, pulsing. A fire, burning and licking, started in her waist. Warm wetness rushed down from between her legs, before she shut her eyes.

When she woke up, there was a breathing fire all around her. Tobe was looking down at her. He was crying, his mouth moving in speech, but she could not hear him. She could not reach for her belly because her hands seemed as if they were restrained by vice grips. She could not feel the movement of her baby. She could not feel anything at all. A woman in white appeared and pulled Tobe away.

Then she was moving. There was the squeaky sound from the contraption carrying her. Tobe was walking with her, looking down at her, tears streaming down his face, plopping on her body. She was wheeled into a brightly lit room and nurses lifted her and placed her on a softer bed whose sheet was as thick as a tarpaulin. She could not move, she could only feel. A nurse, wielding a syringe, shot the contents into the IV hanging from the pole attached to her bed. Her mind grew foggy, as if she was trapped on the streets of Kano at the peak of harmattan, when dust swirled in a thick breeze, veiling everything in a gauze of dust, until you could not see the person standing just a few feet from you. And then she blacked out.

She woke from a deep sleep. The room was narrow, the walls painted blue, and the low-hanging ceiling was a blinding white. Her body felt sore and strange at the same time. Thankfully, the window was wide open, and she stared outside at the sky that wore the purest colour of blue.

A nurse came inside carrying a bundle wrapped in a blue-and-white blanket. '*Ị mụlụ ife ogonogo*, a baby with a penis.' She smiled. 'You have a baby boy.' She approached the bed. 'Do you want to hold him? He is asleep now.'

She looked at the woman and the baby she was holding. How did she give birth and didn't know when it happened? It was only then it occurred to her to feel her stomach. 'I have a son?'

The nurse smiled again and placed the bundle on her chest, turning him so that Ogadinma could stare at his face without having to lift her head off the pillows. For a long time, she looked at the puffy face with the pink gums, the perfect chin and the ears that were shades darker than his body, proof that he would grow to be as dark as her or his father. She waited for the warmth that was supposed to flood her chest and stomach, the beginning of the bond between mother and child. But she felt nothing.

'I will put him in his cot,' the nurse said, taking the baby as if she knew that Ogadinma wanted some distance from it.

'How did I give birth to him?' she asked the nurse, who gave her a sad, tight smile, and placed the baby in his cot, before coming to her bedside.

'You had an operation,' she said. 'It was urgent, and thank God, you and the baby are safe.' She made to touch Ogadinma, but then put her hand down. 'I will leave you to rest now.'

Tobe and Aunty Ngozi arrived shortly afterwards. Aunty Ngozi dropped the bag she was carrying and rushed to her bedside. 'You are awake. Thank God,' she said. '*Kedu?*'

Ogadinma did not respond. Nor did she look at Tobe, who came and sat by her bedside and held her hand. Instead, she stared out of the window, at the azure sky and the migrating birds dotting the blue like splotches of charcoal on a bright cloth.

'I am so sorry, *Nwunye m,*' Tobe said, his voice cracking. 'It was the work of the devil. I am so sorry.'

'I want to sleep,' Ogadinma said. She was startled by the calm in her voice. It was what she always wanted to be: fearless. 'Please go. I want to sleep,' she said.

16

Ogadinma's body began to fail her the day she came home. Just as she entered the flat, her son nestled in her arms, something cracked inside her and the ground shifted under her feet. Tobe caught her before she slumped to the ground and Aunty Ngozi snatched the baby from her arms.

'I think she is tired,' Aunty Ngozi said. 'She lost so much blood and water. Please carry her to her room so she can rest.'

Ogadinma shivered under her blanket. She did not want to go out of her room, and later, did not want to sit in the same space with Tobe. She shifted away when he was close by and did not meet his eyes when he looked at her. She could no longer endure him. Disgust. It had begun right when he walked into her hospital ward, and had worsened since she came home. Because this time, his mere presence, even the thought of sitting close to him, filled her with revulsion.

On the morning Aunty Ngozi brought them a housegirl called Mercy, she screamed when she found Ogadinma shivering in the corner while her son's high-pitched cry tore through the room.

'Your body is hot,' she said. 'We have to take you back to the hospital.'

'I am fine,' Ogadinma said. She swiped at the sweat that beaded her face, and then went and scooped the baby from his cot. She held him to her chest; she still did not feel any pull towards him. When Tobe decided they would name him Ebuka, after his late father, she did not care about that choice. Instead, she worried about the emptiness that sat inside her belly, how her sleep was often interrupted by the boy's loud cries. The night before, she had wondered what would happen if she threw him against the wall, and had thought, perhaps, she felt this way because she was also in a lot of pain. Her stitches were healing slowly, and her nipples had chafed and bled when he suckled. The thought of breastfeeding him made her want to cry and cry, because he always latched on her nipples like vice grips, causing unbearable pain to ripple all over her body in rapid waves.

Aunty Ngozi took the baby from her and rocked him until he slept. Mercy hovered by the door and asked Ogadinma if she had any clothes that needed washing.

'Go and prepare the nsala soup things,' Aunty Ngozi told Mercy.

'That girl looks malnourished,' Ogadinma told Aunty Ngozi.

'I am more worried about you,' Aunty Ngozi said. 'You are still avoiding your husband. What happened has happened, and it will not happen again. But it is not the reason you will be squeezing your face all the time.'

Ogadinma looked away. She knew Aunty Ngozi was trying to appear supportive. She could tell from how often Aunty Ngozi visited, the way she cleaned the house and asked Ogadinma what she wanted to eat, if she rested well. But Ogadinma also knew that Aunty Ngozi was also doing these things because of Tobe, to make up for his shortcomings.

Aunty Ngozi sat beside her. 'I know this period has been difficult for you. It has also been difficult for all of us. But look at the good side, you have given your husband a son. And this son brought light to this family, or didn't you know that it was on that day he was born that your husband's goods were released, eh?' She touched Ogadinma's shoulder.

Ogadinma looked at her, at the hand resting on her shoulder. 'My son was cut out of my body,' she said.

'I know, *nne*. But *biko*, stop squeezing your face. Your son is still suckling and he can tell that everything is not all right, that's why he cries all the time,' she said.

Aunty Ngozi squeezed her shoulder. There were tired bags under her eyes, and her face was ashy, as though she had not rubbed pomade in many days. Ogadinma wanted to hug her, but she didn't. She knew that Aunty Ngozi was cajoling her, to get her to forgive Tobe. This cajoling was very subtle, the kind that made her feel like she was overreacting for being angry with Tobe. It was why they all let Tobe hurt her again and again. She stood up and said, 'Aunty, I am tired. I want to sleep,' and went to the parlour to stretch out on the sofa.

In the following weeks, she would sit in the parlour and wear a wavering smile when her neighbours came by to see her son and tell her how handsome he was, how he had her nose and lips, that he would grow up to become the most beautiful boy, that she and Tobe must buy horsewhips to chase all the girls away, because this pretty boy who looked like his mother, with his fine face and long limbs, would become the toast of the neighbourhood. The neighbours came every day bearing gifts of baby soaps and towels and cream and lotions. Mama Iyabo brought a large blue basin and a sachet of Omo detergent, and she held Ebuka in her arms, her cheeks stretched in the most genuine smile. 'Your pikin fine well-well like you,' she told Ogadinma. 'You don give your husband male pikin, now you go get peace of mind. Even if you born ten girls join on-top, e no matter again, because you don pay the price wey you owe your husband.' She stayed a little longer, cradling Ebuka in her arms as she told her own story, how she had given her husband five girls, but his people were not contented, and one day, her husband moved out of their flat and she later learned that he married another woman and was living with her in Ketu, that the woman had given her husband two sons. Mama Iyabo smiled as she said this, although her eyes had glazed over with pain. 'You dey lucky,' she told Ogadinma. 'But make you no waste time to born another one. Just do quick kpam-kpam born all the children wey your husband want, so you go kuku rest.'

Ogadinma did not like that advice. She could not yet wrap her mind around the idea of sleeping with Tobe. She could not even talk to him. He came home often, bringing her gifts of new wrappers, new sets of shoes and bags, a golden ichafu which crackled when he brought it out from the packet.

'*Negodị*, see. Isn't it beautiful?' he told her that evening. 'Look at the design. I saw it today and knew it would suit your perfectly!' He laughed nervously, seeming unsure of how to navigate the thicket that had grown between them. He sat beside her for some seconds, both saying nothing.

'Thank you,' she finally said.

'You don't have to thank me, *Nwunye m*.' He sounded high and elated. 'There is this gown I saw at the boutique down the road. I will go now and buy it. You will like it.'

She simply nodded.

Relief made him seem breathless, and he looked as though he wanted to sink on his knees in thanks to her for bringing down the bristly wall. He held her hand and kissed it, and then, like an excited worshipper eager to please and appease, he hurried off to get the gift for the gods.

After he left, Ogadinma went into the bathroom. The house smelled of baby soap and powder and Dettol. Ebuka woke up and began to cry. Aunty Ngozi sang for him, '*Onye tili nwa na-ebe akwa*,' her voice carrying down the passageway. She was still singing when Tobe returned with the dress. He splayed it out on the bed, and stood, hands akimbo, smiling, like one would when one had done a good job and expected to be praised for it.

'It is beautiful, *ọ kwa ya*?' he asked Ogadinma.

There was an awkward pause, before Aunty Ngozi hurriedly said, '*Eh, ọ maka*. It is so beautiful.'

'Thank you,' Ogadinma told him.

When he made to hold her hand, she shifted away from his reach.

Tobe drove her to the hospital on the day Ebuka turned three months old. Ogadinma kept her gaze fixed on the windscreen as they drove to the hospital. Tobe was talking to her, but she was not looking at him. He had gotten another batch of powdered milk, he said, but this time he bought it from an importer because it was becoming too risky to import these things. He was thinking of venturing into the fabric business because there were no laws banning the sales of fabric and it was a pretty good business.

'Nwunye m.' He touched her knee. 'You must forgive me. I love you too much, that's why it hurts when you do these things that itch my body. Do you hear me?'

When she turned to look at him, she did not smile or nod; she simply looked at him, at the stern lines criss-crossing his forehead, the bulging cheeks and the face riddled with blackheads and stubble. He no longer had any neck to speak of. He seemed so huge. His stomach sat on his lap, pushing against the buttons of his shirt, much bigger than it used to look. She felt the urge to scrub the spot on her knee where his hand had rested. She no longer loved him.

The following morning, after Tobe had showered and left and Mercy had strapped Ebuka to her back with a wrapper, singing him a sweet lullaby, she went to Tobe's door and pushed it open. For a moment, she stood by the door, glancing around the room, at the bed whose sheets were rumpled, at the ceiling which was still mouldy. She did not know what she was looking for or why she was standing there. She went inside and sat on his bed. Tobe had not asked to have sex since Ebuka was born and she dreaded the day he would. She dreaded what would happen when he stretched over her, if she would puke all over him, or shove him away and scream and scream until the neighbours banged on their door.

She pulled open a drawer. Inside were two stacks of naira notes strung with rubber bands. She took a stack, gazed at the mint crispiness. Sweat pooled under her arms. Her mind was cluttered with confusion. She took the remaining stack. And then she quickly left the room, shutting the door with a bang behind her.

Mercy had laid Ebuka out on the bed when she returned. 'I will go and wash his clothes now, Aunty,' Mercy said. Ogadinma noticed that she had filled out, that her cheeks had become fuller.

After the girl left, she got her bag from the wardrobe. She hastily stuffed her clothes and the money into the bag. Her hands shook. Her ears were drumming. She carried the bag out into the passage.

Mercy was lugging the basin full of baby clothes into the bathroom when she saw her. 'Aunty?' the girl said, almost a question.

'I am going somewhere,' she told the girl. 'Please take care of him. His food is in his warmer.'

Mercy did not respond, her mouth only hung open. Ogadinma's legs carried her faster out of the house. She willed for her nerves to calm, but she could not feel calm. Her entire body was shaking, and it did not stop until she had gotten out of the compound and hurried to the junction.

The queue moved too slowly. Soldiers hung around, wielding guns. And when one of them turned to look at her, his fingers gripping a horsetail whip, she held her breath and placed one foot after the other, until she got into the bus. She did not know where she was going, where she wanted to go, but she sat and kept her head down, until the bus eased onto the road and rolled away.

PART 3

17

Ogadinma and her father had visited Aunty Okwy once after her hasty wedding. She still remembered how Aunty Okwy knelt in the front yard dirt, begging to be taken home. Her father had insisted on the marriage and swore to throw her out into the streets if she refused to stay with her new husband. Many years had passed, and Ogadinma was going to see Aunty Okwy again.

The screeching of the grinding machines in the nearby store alarmed her, as did the large well beside the gate. Small children leaned dangerously by the mouth of the well, pulling up water with a rubber pouch and emptying it into their buckets.

She knocked on the door she remembered belonged to Aunty Okwy. The yard was divided into two rows of rooms sitting opposite each other, and the two out-kitchens at the end of each row were so small that neighbours stacked their stoves and tripods by the entrance. Ogadinma was startled by the sharp cry of 'Onye di?' before Aunty Okwy threw open the door, saw her and frowned.

'This one you came to my house today, I hope you didn't bring news of death?' she said, one hand balanced on her waist, the other knotting the wrapper under her arm.

'Good afternoon, Aunty.'

'Why are you here, Ogadinma?'

'Can I come inside, Aunty? Please.'

There was something different about Aunty Okwy. Ogadinma noticed right away her roughly strung isi-owu hairstyle, the thinness of her neck and the dark patches on her cheeks. Eight years had passed, and Aunty Okwy looked twenty years older. She sized up Ogadinma, before holding out her arms, and Ogadinma walked into the embrace and buried her face against Aunty Okwy's neck. Although many things had changed about her, Ogadinma still remembered her smell, the way Aunty Okwy's arms wrapped around her body, and the soft comforting rub of her fingers on the small of her back. She suddenly felt like a small child seeking comfort in her aunt's embrace. And this filled her with peace, weights lifted off her shoulders and her tense nerves calmed. This peace was unfamiliar and uplifting.

Aunty Okwy was clear-eyed when she broke the hug. She led Ogadinma into the room, which was small and dark, even in the afternoon. It took a moment for Ogadinma's eyes to adjust to the poor light. The room was split by a brown curtain into a sleeping area and a parlour. Ogadinma sat on a plastic chair. Aunty Okwy sat on the only sofa facing a table which held a small TV. She did not remember noticing this arrangement of things years ago, perhaps because the curtain was pulled down to hide the sleeping area.

'I heard when you got married. I also heard when you gave birth to your son. You should be breastfeeding your son.'

'I left Tobe.'

'You left your son.' Aunty Okwy clucked her tongue. 'You aren't so different from your mother, *mgbo*?' Although Aunty Okwy's voice was filled with rebuke, Ogadinma was pleased to see there was no rage in her eyes.

'Aunty, where is your daughter?'

'Nonye? She is fetching water at the well with her mates.'

'Oh. I saw the kids. I didn't see her.'

'You didn't recognize her because you don't even know her.'

Ogadinma swallowed. She did not know if Aunty Okwy had had other children since the first pregnancy. Her father rarely talked about her and Uncle Ugonna never mentioned her. Aunty Okwy had long become a taboo in their village home; even her grandmother hardly mentioned the only daughter she had.

'You didn't go to your father,' Aunty Okwy said.

'When Tobe beat me up the first time, Papa took me back to him.'

Aunty Okwy scoffed. 'I would be surprised if he didn't. Your father, Osita, is a terrible and wicked man.'

Ogadinma was startled by the anger in her voice. Her father was strict – yes, she agreed, but wickedness was an attribute she could never reconcile with him.

'Neenu m, look at me. Who would believe that this was what I would turn out to be? Ugonna could not even change your father's mind. Perhaps what your mother did to him destroyed him beyond measure, because I have never seen such a wicked, narrow-minded and stubborn human. He refused to let me stay with Mama and Mama does his bidding because he is the first son. I fukwa your father, it will not be well with that man. That's why he can't keep a woman. I hear how he sneaks around with them, how he even sleeps with other men's wives, but he can't get himself a wife because he knows no woman will ever endure his stubbornness.'

Ogadinma was too shaken to speak. The initial comfort she felt peeled away and the new Aunty Okwy emerged before her: her face was a contortion of emotions as she talked. Her calves tightening, her hands balling into fists. Her body was a knot of old hurt. Ogadinma wanted to reach over and pinch Aunty Okwy's mouth shut, but she knew she never could. She looked around the room as Aunty Okwy raved. At the narrow bed which was not large enough to fit two people, but which Aunty Okwy shared night after night, year after year, with an old widower, their sweaty bodies pressing together on humid nights, while their child, or children, slept on the floor of the 'parlour', separated from their parents by a dark curtain. This, perhaps, was why Aunty Okwy was so aggrieved. And Ogadinma understood this pain, because if this was what it meant to be married, then it was better to be single. For the first time, Ogadinma was grateful that she had had the abortion, that she had been flogged, because she shivered as she listened to Aunty Okwy's sputter of angry words. This would have been her life, what her father would have done to her, too, if she hadn't chosen the easy way out.

'You can't stay here,' Aunty Okwy finally said.

Ogadinma sank to her knees. 'Aunty, please.'

'My husband is a hunter. He will be back next week. He won't let you stay here because, *negodịnụ*, our two children sleep on a mat on this floor. We move the plastic chairs every night to make space for them, so, where will you sleep? There is no space at all.'

'Aunty, *biko*, I don't know where to go.'

A small boy in stained knickers and shirt appeared at the door. He climbed into Aunty Okwy's lap and pointed at Ogadinma. 'Mummy, *kedụ onye bụ ife a*, who is this? Why is she kneeling?' he asked, his Igbo so crisp and rural, Ogadinma tried to tell how old he was, how someone so tiny could speak so clearly.

'This is your cousin, Ogadinma,' Aunty Okwy told the boy, her face melting into a warm smile. 'Ogadinma, meet Chukwuemeka, my second child. He is four years old.'

Ogadinma sat back on her seat. 'Chukwuemeka, *kedụ*?'

The boy grinned at Ogadinma, jumped off his mother's lap and dashed out of the room.

'You can only stay here for a few days, four or five, but you must leave before my husband comes home. I don't want his trouble,' Aunty Okwy said afterwards.

A shudder of gratitude tugged her. That was enough time to decide the next step. 'Thank you, Aunty.'

'So, what are you going to do when I eventually kick you out, eh? Will you go back to your father, or your husband? Better go back to your husband. Your father will never take you in.'

Ogadinma rubbed a hand over her dust-coated ankle. My father is a kind man, she said to herself. My father is a kind, disciplined man who doesn't tolerate nonsense. Aunty Okwy was watching her with sad eyes. 'My father is not these things you say.'

'If you think so, then why are you here?'

Ogadinma looked out of the partly open door. The children were playing, their voices loud and lusty and melding with the grinding sounds of the machines in the mill. She tried to imagine how her father would react if he heard that she had run away again, but she could not. Perhaps she couldn't because she didn't want to smudge his character; she didn't want what Aunty Okwy said to be true.

'You must go to your husband, kneel before him and beg him to take you back. Look at your blouse, it is stained with breast milk. Your son needs you.'

Ogadinma glanced down at the wetness. 'I can't go back, Aunty.'

'But you must because you have no option. If you were a boy, you could sleep in an uncompleted building, under the bridge, any place at all, and no man or boy would violate you. But you are a woman. Everything with a penis between its legs will want to break you.'

Ogadinma began to protest but Nonye pulled open the curtain and walked inside. She was a near copy of her mother; her skin was the shiniest and darkest Ogadinma had ever seen, and when she smiled, her white teeth gleamed against the dark gums. Ogadinma thought she was the most beautiful girl in the world.

'I hear you are my cousin,' Nonye said, inching closer. She touched Ogadinma's cheek, laughed and wrapped her small arms around Ogadinma's neck.

Ogadinma went to bed early. In the middle of the night, she was woken by the chanting and prayers from a nearby church. Nonye and Chukwuemeka did not stir on their portion of the mat. The loud voices filled the night. She shivered, remembering Onye Ekpere and the women and wondered if another woman was being subjected to the same practice.

The prayers were repeated every night, and Ogadinma stayed awake each time, thinking about her next plan. On the third night, she counted her money. She had only spent enough to pay for her transport here. She still had plenty left and, if she guarded it zealously, she could be secure for a few months before she ran out.

· · ·

She returned to Lagos on the fourth day. Aunty Okwy and her children came with her to the junction. The winds were swift that morning and the air was heavy with red dust. Like it was in the village, everything was buried under a layer of red dust, and it was so heavy that Nonye's skin assumed a sleek earthy tone, her white blouse stained at the neck with splotches of reddish brown, the same shade of brown that clung to her hairline.

'Will you come again?' she asked, clutching Ogadinma's hand.

'Yes.' Ogadinma smiled through tear-glazed eyes, and bent to wrap her arms around the girl.

'She will come back,' Aunty Okwy told Nonye, and to Ogadinma she said, 'Go well.'

'Bye-bye,' Nonye and Chukwuemeka said in unison. And they all stood by the roadside, waving, until Ogadinma got on a bus.

Her bus coughed to a stop at Jibowu Park, and she boarded a smaller bus and jumped off at Ejiro's gate. Her heart made frantic hops when the gateman let her in. When Ejiro opened the door and said, 'Ogadinma, what happened, my sister?' her knees melted and Ejiro lurched forward and held her. She seemed so strong, Ejiro, or maybe it was her striking confidence in herself, or because she had a powerful mother who would rush to protect her when called. 'What happened, my sister?' Ejiro repeated. Ogadinma wanted to tell her everything, how Tobe had almost killed her this time, how her son was cut out of her body, how she had become repulsed by Tobe, that she had nowhere else to go. She wanted to tell Ejiro that she was the only person in the whole world who would understand why she had left, who would never ask her to return to her abuser. But when she opened her mouth to speak, cries surged up her throat, her knees finally gave way under her and she and Ejiro sank to the floor. Ejiro held her, muttering comforting words, until she stopped crying.

'You should have come immediately, but I am happy you are here now,' Ejiro said after she had showed her to a room with a bathroom. 'Shower and rest. I will bring you some food, okay?'

She nodded and blinked rapidly to keep more tears from falling. Later, she stood under the warm shower for a long time, letting the water wash pain and fatigue from her body. After she stepped out of the shower and changed into a new dress, Ejiro entered with a tray of food and bottles of Maltina.

'You will stay here until we find you a good apartment. I know someone who can help us get a place sharp-sharp.'

'What about your husband? Will he let me stay?'

Ejiro clucked her tongue, a dismissive sound. 'I will speak with him in the evening. He is hardly at home anyway. He won't mind.'

'Don't tell him everything.' Ogadinma vaguely remembered him, a small-boned man who often drove out in the early mornings and came home late at night. She was sure they had never met, but there was that small worry that he might recognize her, that he knew Tobe.

'Don't worry. I know what to tell him.'

She nodded and looked down at her jollof rice and tried to remember the last time she had a plate filled with this much meat. Ejiro had brought a plate for herself, too, and they sat, eating and talking. Ejiro told her about the fertility herbalist she was seeing, that she would have to adopt children if she didn't get pregnant anytime soon. She spoke about these things with a casualness that was strange to Ogadinma, and did not for once mention her husband in her stream of sentences. And this intrigued and confused Ogadinma, that a married woman would speak with such authority without attributing every decision she made to her husband.

'Your own child will come,' she told Ejiro. She was going to add, 'I will gladly get pregnant for you if you want,' but she didn't because she knew it could come off as insensitive and unnecessary.

'Do you miss your son?'

She told Ejiro about her son, and described his fine features, his small lips, how in the early weeks he had rejected even simple things like water and baby formula. She wondered what he was eating now. She could not keep the swirling thoughts from coming in, the images of her son swaddled up in his cot, him sucking her breasts, his eyes puffy and shut, his fingers bunched into dainty fists. She said she missed him.

In the morning, Ogadinma listened for Ejiro's husband's movements and only came out after he had left. They would sit out and talk all morning, watch TV and pore through fashion magazines by afternoon, and prepare dinner together in the evening. Then she returned to her room to stare out of the window at the busy street and the speeding cars, until sleep came.

By the following week, Ejiro had found an agent and in two days, the agent found her a one-room apartment in Ketu. He brought a man who posed as her brother living abroad because landlords did not rent apartments to single women.

Ejiro drove her to the house at the end of that week after she had paid the rent. Though the apartment was small and neighbours could see into her room if she left her door open, she liked the rural tranquillity, the smell of food in the air and the occasional cries of children playing in the yard. It reminded her of her childhood home. Perhaps she liked it more because it was the first place she could call her own.

Ejiro gave her an unused mattress, a small TV, a transistor radio, a set of bed sheets, a stove, two cooking pots, a set of plates and spoons, and even a bucket for bathing and a gallon to store drinking water.

Outside by the car, she hugged Ejiro. They rocked each other back and forth, and Ogadinma wished they could come back together in the next life, this time as sisters. Maybe twins. Ejiro folded some naira notes into her hand. She stood by, waving as Ejiro drove out, then she walked into her room and locked the door.

That night, she dreamed she was walking down their street in Kano when she saw her father coming towards her. Then the road caved in and swallowed him. She couldn't move. She couldn't scream. She woke up shivering. She did not know what the dream meant. Her body was suffused with sweat and wouldn't stop trembling until dawn came. And as the first ray of light streaked in from her windows, she rushed to the NITEL office down the street to call him.

'Papa,' she said when he picked up the phone, 'Papa, it is me, Ogadinma.' There was a heavy silence. Then he spoke in a gravelly voice, the voice she had never heard before in her entire life, croaky and cold.

'Do not ever call this line again,' he said. 'I am not your father.'

18

Ogadinma sat on the bench by her door, a plate of bread and akara resting on her lap. Small children who looked no more than five years old sat by her feet, watching keenly. On the other side of the yard, mothers were in the out-kitchen, pounding things in mortars. Older children hunched over basins filled with plates or clothes. The yard was awash with morning activities.

She returned her gaze to the children; they were waiting patiently for her to share the food.

The week she moved into the yard, their mothers pulled them close when she walked by, but by the following week, the children began to hang around her doorstep. One morning, as she ate a breakfast of bread and akara and the children came around, she shared the food with them. She did the same thing the following morning. Soon, the mothers began to raise their voices when they exchanged greetings with her, and older children kept buckets of water by her door, their silent way of welcoming her.

Now, she reached into her plate and began to share the breakfast. 'Aunty, thank you,' each child said.

Just then, one of the fathers ran out of his room, shouting in Yoruba, a transistor radio pressed against his ear. Everyone turned to look at him. Ogadinma strained to understand what he was saying; the language was still strange to her ears, and she could only make out the word 'Coup! Coup!' in his sputter of animated speech. He dashed out of the gate and everyone followed.

Outside, a crowd was thickening, excited men and women dancing and chanting and pouring down the street. And it was only then that she learned that the Head of State and the Deputy had been overthrown and another soldier had installed himself as the new Head of State.

One of the mothers, Mama Kunle, came and stood beside her. 'God don hear our prayer,' the woman said, her eyes lightened by the smile that stretched her tribal-marked cheeks.

'What if the new person come worse pass the old one?' Ogadinma asked her, remembering her father's words about soldiers being nothing but thugs, remembering Tobe's experience, too. 'I no trust dis people. All of dem na de same.'

'At least we go see food chop,' Mama Kunle said.

Later in her room, she heard the cries of a baby. A neighbour at the back had given birth to a baby girl who cried often, shrill sounds that rang out without end every night. She cried like Ebuka. Newborns in Lagos cried with the same accent. She pictured Aunty Ngozi bathing Ebuka, singing him Igbo lullabies, creaming his body with Pears Baby Lotion, pouring generous amounts of powder on his groin before wrapping him up with a nappy. And something tugged and pulled her heart painfully. The new feeling warmed and worried her; all those days with Ebuka, she had felt no pull towards him. Now, it hurt when she thought of him, when she remembered how he suckled. And she did not know what to make of these feelings.

It had been three months since she left Tobe and her son. She was still dependent on handouts Ejiro often gave, her future as hazy as the air in harmattan. She had not been able to keep a job since she moved into the apartment. A stint at a restaurant which she left after a leery man slapped her bottom. A poorly paid cleaning job at a bank which she hated because the staff and visitors always peed on the toilet seat and did not flush their shit. She thought she had found the perfect job at a local supermarket, but then burglars struck one night and cleaned out the store. A month had passed since her last job and she had yet to wrap her mind around her situation. People who could afford it were quitting the country in droves, packing their things and leaving with their families, not minding the flattering advert begging Nigerians to stop *checking out*.

She turned on the TV. The news of the coup was already making headlines. Journalists poured into the streets to interview excited Nigerians who praised the new Head of State for rescuing Nigeria from the former dictator. A familiar face appeared on the screen. Kelechi. He had not changed at all. He grinned widely as he talked about how he was pleased with the new military government. The camera panned over his business place, a construction company in the eastern city of Aba, the address printed in bold black ink. He was still talking about the state of affairs in the country but she could no longer hear him. Instead, she was looking at his face, at the soft lines creasing his brows, how animated he looked. This was how she would always remember him: pleasant face, warm smile, a welcoming demeanour. How nice it would be to see him again. Her mind was muddled by uncertainties. She should have nothing to do with him, not after what happened between him and Tobe. She should not have anything to do with anyone who knew Tobe. She turned off the TV and went to stand by the window, looked down at the compound which had now filled out with noisy children. Baba Kola, the house caretaker, came out of his room and yelled at the children in a sputter of Yoruba, and they all quietened down, only for a moment, before their voices rose again. In a few months she would run out of money and she would no longer be able to afford this place. And for how long would she depend on Ejiro? She turned away from the window. What should matter to her was how to pay her rent and buy her own food, nothing else. And if there was one more person she could reach out to for financial assistance, it was Kelechi. So she made up her mind to find him.

She arrived in the east the following morning. The nearer they got to Aba, the more uncertain she became. Had she made a mistake going on this long trip? What if Kelechi was no longer in town?

Kelesco Engineering Company was twenty minutes away, the lady at the motor park had said, but it took an hour to get there. A truck had died along Factory Road, and so the bus had to take a longer route. She was nervous. She wondered how Kelechi would react, why she had even come. She let her gaze dwell on the hawkers, the okada riders meandering through the hold-ups at breakneck speed, the loud bus drivers following each other bumper-to-bumper. Men stopped at roadsides to unzip their trousers and piss into open drains. Women hung on the backs of trucks, pressed between mounds of vegetables and yams. She had read in the papers that Aba was the *Japan of Africa*, the home for craftsmen and women who made near copies of every designer item shipped from abroad, created beauties from scraps and sewed clothes better than Italian designers. But this was a different Aba she was seeing; this was a cluster of chaos.

A man and a woman were quarrelling on the bus. The woman, her jheri-curled hair drenched in glossy finish, sat stiffly away and kept tossing his hand each time he tried to sling it over her shoulder.

'I am so sorry, Achalugo,' the man was saying, his voice low, 'I have chased her away. She will never come back again. I promise.'

But the woman turned to him and began to shout. 'Bịa, Okenna, stay away from me. Why are you harassing me inside this bus? I don't want you again. Leave me alone, *ahn, ahn!* What is your problem?'

The public rejection apparently stung because other passengers gasped, and the man cussed under his breath and said she should be grateful he even looked at her. And she tipped her head back and began to laugh.

'You think because of this thing you have between your legs every woman must bend over and eat your shit? *Taa, gbafuo* here *ọsịsọ!* I said, get out of here, my friend! Get out of here!' She clapped in his face.

The bus rolled to a stop and he got off, still swearing under his breath. Ogadinma came down at the next junction.

As she trekked the short distance to Kelechi's company, she thought about the woman and her boldness. She had not seen the woman's face clearly, but she remembered the raised shoulders, how she sent the man scurrying away like a wounded rat. She fleetingly wished she had clapped and cheered for her when the man got down.

She still thought of the woman when she walked into Kelechi's company. Inside, the secretary, a cantankerous middle-aged woman in an ancient blouse and faded skirt, gave Ogadinma a dirty look after she asked to see Kelechi. Ogadinma suppressed the urge to run a hand over her shirt, to check if her cleavage was exposed. She had felt this way that day she walked into the barrister's office and his receptionist sized her up. But then she remembered the woman on the bus, and so she stood straighter, pushed her chest out, and she held the secretary's gaze.

'Sit over there,' the woman finally said.

And she went and sat on the bench. The woman made her wait for an hour, lazed around the office, spoke with other visitors, walked outside to chat with them for long minutes. But Ogadinma was not going to leave; she had nowhere to go, after all. Another hour passed before the woman directed her to the connecting door. And Ogadinma arched her neck and said, 'Thank you,' to the woman in a grating tone. She did not pause to see the darts the woman shot her.

When she knocked and a booming voice invited her in, her knees suddenly weakened and her stomach began to make nervous gurgling sounds. Kelechi was seated behind the huge desk, the shelf behind him stacked with books.

'Good afternoon, Kelechi,' she said, hovering by the door.

He looked up. 'Ogadinma?'

He came around the table, shut the door and pulled her into his arms. She leaned against him ever so slightly, before breaking the hug.

'*Nne*, how are you?' he asked. 'I can't believe this is you. You came to see me? My God, I can't believe this. Please come and sit.'

Kelechi sounded like he really cared about her. It was the way he spoke, the way he held her. It filled her with hope.

'I have left Tobe,' she blurted out.

He stood back, watched her with concern in his eyes. But he did not ask why she had left Tobe, why their marriage failed, if

Tobe hurt her. He did not ask why she had come to see him, or even how she learned of his address. He instead asked if she had had any meal yet.

'The last meal I had was in Lagos yesterday,' she told him.

'We will go to my house and I will get you something to eat,' he told her. He returned to his desk and began to gather his books. He pressed a red knob on his table and the shrill ring of the bell reverberated around the walls. Moments later, a young boy, not more than twenty, walked in. He greeted Ogadinma with a slight bow, and Kelechi told him to take Ogadinma to his house.

'It is not far away from here,' Kelechi told her. 'Just five minutes' walk. I will clear up my schedule and join you shortly.'

The boy walked like there was fire under his feet as he hurried down the street, leading the way to a gated estate where a crumpled-faced security man sat. The man let them in without asking questions.

The compound was wide. Two cars sat in the parking lot beside the large house whose windows ran from floor to ceiling, with an elaborate tiled terrace that glistened like ice blocks.

He led her into the living room and offered her a seat by the wide TV. He went into a connecting room and returned with a tray holding a bottle of water and a rinsed glass cup. When he made to open the bottle, she stopped him. 'Thank you,' she said.

He flashed a quick grin and hurried out of the house.

Alone in the house, she became nervous. She stood and began to pace the parlour. She wished she could do something with her hands. There were no photo albums close by, not even a magazine to keep her busy. There was a gold-framed photo of Kelechi and a woman hanging from the wall. She looked at the woman, her wide smile and full lips smeared with red lipstick. Without being told, she knew this woman was his wife, and this was because the blue of her puffy-sleeved blouse matched his blue shirt, and her red ichafu was the same colour as his hat. This was a replica of her and Tobe's wedding photo, the same kind that could be found in the homes of every married Igbo couple.

She went over to the TV and switched it on. She had just tuned in to NTA and returned to her seat when Kelechi came in, clutching a bag emblazoned with the name of a restaurant.

She spoke immediately. 'Hello, Kelechi. You haven't changed one bit.'

He sat down and laughed. 'I don't know what to say.'

The room was wide and had enough space for small children to play a game of catch, but she felt stifled. She was sitting less than a foot from him and heard every breath he took, saw every rise and fall of his chest. She could not think of anything except the small space between them. This was the first time in a long time she had been alone with a man who was not her relative, and this realization caused panic to build up in her chest. Perhaps it was so because she had always liked him. Perhaps, too, because there was a budding, fearless part of herself asking her to move closer and touch his thigh. She took a deep breath, wrung her hands together, and said, 'Tobe said you betrayed him, and he punished me for it.'

The question threw him off his stride, and he seemed to take a while to gather himself together before he spoke again. He answered hastily, explained why he didn't come to Tobe's help. She watched the workings of his mouth. Although she didn't want to talk about Tobe, she realized she had been longing to have this conversation, because all this while, she still held onto her strongheaded belief that he could not have abandoned his friend. She needed to look at his face and hear his own side of the story, to prepare her mind for what was to come: if he would help her, or if Tobe was right all along.

'How are you?' he finally asked. 'Are you doing all right?'

She lifted her glass, tilted it and took a long drink, and all the while she thought of how to respond to this question. 'I saw you in the news, that's how I got to learn your address.'

'Oh.'

'You like this new government.'

'Yes, they are my friends and I believe they will be better than the other tyrants,' he said, and smiled.

She remembered the smile; it was the same way he smiled when he looked people in the eye. It was what had interested her about him that first time she met him at the bar. He talked about meeting the present Head of State in Minna before the coup, that this new regime would benefit companies like his own, and there wouldn't be a need to witch-hunt hard-working Nigerians. As he talked, she looked at the photograph on the wall behind him, how wide the woman in blue was smiling, her lips rouged with the brightest shade of red she had ever seen. How liberating it would be to wear such colour, to wear whatever she wanted to wear. To do whatever she wanted to do. 'I have missed you,' she suddenly said.

He opened and closed his mouth, and before he could speak, she moved closer and kissed him. She did not think, did not even pause to consider, of what she was doing. They watched each other. Her heart thudded furiously, and her underarms began to tingle. He was just staring at her with surprise in his eyes, their lips still pressed together. And when she began to pull away, embarrassed by her action, he clasped his arms around her, prodded her lips open and finally shut his eyes. He kissed like he had always been hungry for her mouth. And then he was pushing his hands under her shirt, his breath coming in short gasps.

Everything moved quickly afterwards. She had always accorded a certain reverence to lovemaking, like it was something to be celebrated, to be languorously enjoyed with a husband. But this need was different; this was a mindless, unadulterated display of lust, and she could not think of anything else except for him to calm the tremor building between her legs. When he finally swelled inside her and held her face in both palms, his face contorted in pleasure-pain, she threw her head back and sighed.

He rolled off her body and curled tightly into her back and slept, holding her closely, his limp satisfaction pressed against her buttocks. She listened to his deep breathing, and then the light snores, before she slipped out of bed. His lips were half-parted. In sleep, he looked so much younger. She thought of Tobe, how he would nap with his arms crossed over her body, holding her tightly to himself. Something jumped and clutched at her throat. She went into the bathroom. She stared at her reflection in the mirror, at the slight gauntness of her face, the collarbones that had become prominent, how thin she now looked.

She stepped into the tub and washed herself. Then she went back into the room, climbed into the space beside Kelechi and collapsed into a dreamless sleep.

He drove her to a hotel that night when the town had gone quiet, and the streets were deserted and dark. He held her hand and steered the wheel with the other. When they got to the hotel at Ekenna, the lonely private area she would later learn was carved out for the big men of the city, he slowed almost to a crawl; the road was riddled with speed bumps. At the hotel, the receptionist, a girl who seemed barely awake as they checked in, did not stare too long at them.

All of the night, she slept and did not stir, even when he sneaked out before the break of dawn. By mid-morning, when she woke, she found his note. He wanted her to stay for a week, and he had covered the payment of the room. He also enclosed a cheque addressed to her. She pulled out the slim sheet inside and stared at the figures, unsure at first if her eyes were deceiving her with the excess zeroes, before she sank back in bed, holding the cheque to her chest, and wondering what to do with all that money. She sighed. Now she had the capital she needed to start a trade or pay to learn a craft. She should be happy. She waited for her chest to be flooded with joy, for contentment to settle into her stomach and her bones. But all she felt deep down was a blooming shame, a sense that she had become a kept woman, that she had moved from her father's house to Tobe's and now had become a thing of pleasure for Kelechi. She stood and went to the window to gaze outside at the passing cars on the busy street below, and tried, valiantly, to free her mind of the dampening thoughts.

19

Kelechi came every night at the close of work, when the hotel bar was deserted and the lady at the reception worked with only one eye open. They stayed in the room, lying in bed tired after they had sex. The bed squeaked too loud. She would steel herself as he moved feverishly above her, hoping that her stiffness would reduce the creaking of the bed. It did not.

She often berated herself after he had left: why hadn't she asked if he was married? Why hadn't she asked about the woman in the photograph? Many things had changed since she came to Aba; the future no longer looked hazy. And she was filled with a new sense of recklessness; she felt it in her belly, in her chest, even in the way she walked, which was refreshing.

She began to go on walks around the neighbourhood. She would trek to Okigwe Road to linger at boutiques and cosmetic stores. She found the trek an easy one even though she did not know the city well. All she needed was to keep on the major roads; there weren't many of them. The path from her hotel led to Okigwe Road and northwards to the junction linking Brass Street and Faulks Road – the route to the famous Ariaria Market. The trip to the market, since she took a bus, should have been all of fifteen minutes, but it took an hour. The roadsides were littered with dirt and decay from giant waste-buckets that hadn't been emptied, drainages uncovered and filled with muddy water, clogged with plastic bags, breeding mosquitoes.

She looked out of the window all through the trip. Aba was a city of storey buildings – two, three, four and even five storeys that had no elevators, like the houses in Lagos, and most floors were taken up by churches, each one occupying a flat, their loudspeakers perching precariously on the walls, blaring out sermons and songs. Aba was a city of noise.

Though she returned to the hotel the first day, her feet muddied, her toenails clumped with dirt, she continued the aimless wanderings. The Power Line section of the market was occupied by cobblers who made replicas of every designer shoe and bag and belt they laid their hands on or saw in magazines. The industry had blossomed after the Biafran War, she learned. Those who survived the war rebuilt the ravaged market. They made with hands and local tools near-copies of designer items with leather bought from tanneries in Kano. But looking at each piece, she could see the crude finishing, the gaudy representations; these men were creating cheap imitations of the luxuries many residents could not afford. She wondered how it could be if they didn't need to make these copies, if they made beautiful bags and shoes of their own design, instead of indulging these enervating obsessions.

It was during one of these walks that she found Oma, a hairdresser, who had laughter clinging to the ends of her sentences. Oma talked with her hands and eyes and had a waiting smile for everyone who walked into her salon. Ogadinma marvelled at how one person could have that much energy, a light in a dull room. She did not know much about Oma, but she liked the woman's laughter, how she made everyone who walked in feel indebted, so that even if they did not get their hair braided or permed or their face made up, they bought a compact powder or a lipstick before leaving.

Oma's salon became one of her favourite places, in part because nearly every girl who worked there looked her age. Onyedika, the slim girl who washed and braided Ogadinma's hair into neat, tiny cornrows, said she was studying at the nearby polytechnic on weekends. She was learning how to manage big businesses because she hoped to open her own salon once she had saved enough money, and in a few years, if she worked hard enough, she would open a chain of stores in the city. She talked as she braided Ogadinma's hair, and her eyes danced with the certainty of one who was determined to achieve set goals.

'What do you do?' she asked Ogadinma. 'You are married?'

'No, no.' Ogadinma shook her head. 'I don't do anything for now, but I will start something soon.'

'It is good for a woman to learn a skill or a trade, so she can earn her own money – my mum taught me that,' said Onyedika. 'My father wanted her to be a housewife. One day, she borrowed money from her cousin and bought plenty of foodstuffs, a table and some coolers. The following morning, after my father had left for work, she cooked the food and set the table by the roadside and started her own food stall. When my father heard what she had done, he was so angry, but he couldn't stop her because she threatened to go back to her parents.'

'Your mother is a very strong woman,' Ogadinma said.

Onyedika nodded and continued her story. 'You see, eh, years later, when my dad suffered financial problems, it was my mother that cared for us, paid our school fees, and even paid my father's hospital bills. For over twelve years, she carried our family on her shoulders. Just imagine what would have happened to us if she didn't have her own money.' Onyedika slicked pomade over a section of hair and began to braid it, her oily fingers working swiftly. 'It is good to learn a trade.'

'Yes,' Ogadinma said.

A light began to grow inside Ogadinma after her chat with Onyedika. She told Kelechi that she was going back to Lagos. They had just showered in the narrow bathroom and he was towelling his body when she said this.

'What are you hurrying to do?' The towel slipped to the floor.

She stared at his nakedness, how beautiful he looked even when upset. 'I have to go back to Lagos. My rent has almost expired. I have to figure out what to do with myself now.'

'You are leaving because you are tired of me?'

'And you are married?' she blurted out.

A pause. 'You saw the photo.'

'Are you married?' she asked again.

'Yes. She went to America to have our son.'

She wanted to feel anger, but she felt nothing. And it was because she already knew, because she did not care that he was married. 'I will take the next bus to Lagos tomorrow morning,' she told him instead.

'Please, stay a little longer.'

'No, I can't.'

He watched as she slipped on her dress, as she gathered her braids into a bunch at her nape. And she wondered what he was thinking. But most of all, she liked that she was not angry that he belonged to someone else. She liked the kind of woman she was becoming.

'I know a place you can stay. You don't have to pay rent,' he finally said.

She stared at him. 'Where is this place?'

'It belongs to a friend who lives abroad and visits only once in every two years. I will speak with him.' He opened his arms. 'Come here.'

She watched him dubiously.

'Please.'

She went to him and he held her tightly, his breath warm against her neck.

He still held her when he dozed off into sleep.

She arrived at the duplex in Falomo the following evening. She was sweaty, and her body itched. At the gate, a guard stepped out of the tiny room attached to the gate to ask what she wanted and when she gave him her name, he returned to the room to telephone his oga.

The trip to Lagos was tedious. They had gotten to Berger in Lagos at three in the afternoon, but it took another four hours to get to this area of the city. Kelechi had tried to persuade her to take a flight from Enugu, but she refused. She liked travelling by road because it gave her time to think, to plan, a luxury she was sure a forty-five-minute flight would deny her. But travelling by road left her disoriented and she slept through most of the long trip back to Lagos.

The guard returned and opened the gate. 'Aunty, welcome,' he said. 'Come inside.' He helped with her bag and led her to the quarters at the back of the big house. The area was swept clean and the manicured hedges sat in the garden like blocks of leaves. A tall tank stood at one side of the compound and a huge power-generating plant sat at the other end. He opened the door and gave her the keys to the apartment and then he said he would return to his post.

'Wetin be your name,' she asked him.

'Deji. Na me be the only Deji for this area,' he said, flashing a browned-toothed smile.

'Thank you, Oga Deji.'

'Wetin come be your own name?' he asked.

'Ogadinma.'

'Welcome, Aunty,' he said and left.

She walked into the apartment. There were two sofas and a TV. The floor was tiled, and so were the two connecting bedrooms. The width of the bathroom was as wide as her arms stretched out, and the moderately sized kitchen came complete with a gas cooker, pots and pans and plates and spoons and cups; she didn't need to buy anything at all, and the utensils had never been used. Later, she would think of what to do with her things in the Ketu apartment.

She sat down. Her bag still stood by the door. She heard the ding of a bell, and children from the neighbouring compounds burst out in the familiar songs of gratitude to the power company, chanting, 'Up NEPA!' She got up and flipped the switch on the wall and light flooded into the parlour. And this lifted her mood. She brought her bag inside, shut the door. She stripped off her clothes, stepped into the shower and sponged her body of sweat and stress. Then she stood under the shower, watching as the dust coating the floor washed down the drain, until only a clear, soapy water remained.

20

She telephoned Ejiro. 'Are you happy?' Ejiro asked after she had explained all that had happened.

'Sometimes, this place feels like a prison. I miss all the noise in Ketu, but I am learning to like it. How are you?'

'My husband is going to London for his postgraduate degree and he wants us to go together,' Ejiro said.

A pause. 'You are leaving.'

'I will always call you, I promise,' Ejiro spoke hastily. 'Listen to me, you will never be alone. Do you hear me? I will call every week to know how you are doing.'

As they talked, Ogadinma's gaze kept drifting to the window facing the backyard. She was listening to Ejiro's stream of promises and it felt as if she was helplessly watching as her dear friend was snatched from her, forever. After she put down the phone, she sat and stared at the backyard. She had been living in the apartment for two days, but she could not consider it her home. Her clothes were still packed neatly in her bag. The silence in the yard unnerved her.

The fluorescent light bulb blinked and went off, and the children in the nearby compound cried out in frustration. Then they trooped outside to play, their screams and laughter carrying into the neighbourhood. She walked out of the yard to watch the children kick at a football, their dusty legs stirring up sand, their laughter lusty when they scored a goal.

A week later, while she was wiping dust off the countertops in the kitchen, a knock came to her door and when she got it, she found Kelechi standing before her. Her heart skipped.

'Kelechi, did anything happen?'

'Come on *nne*, I came to see you.' He laughed. She stood aside to let him pass, but he pulled her into his arms and began to kiss her face, running his lips along her neck, her shoulder.

'You didn't tell me you were coming,' she said.

'I have missed you.' He reached for her again, cupped her breasts. 'Oh I have missed you.'

She stood stiffly in his embrace, as something boiled in her belly, rose to her chest and filled her mouth with a sour taste. She had been so immersed in sorrow since Ejiro moved to London that she had completely forgotten about Kelechi. But now he was standing here with her, kissing her, touching her. She had left what they shared in Aba and had come back to Lagos a different person. She did not want to repeat that lust, because that was what it was. And now she did not know how to tell him this without hurting him, how to be true to herself without making yet another daunting sacrifice. She ever so slightly slipped away from his embrace. 'I don't want to do this any more,' she said. The words came out too harsh, and she wished she had spoken more kindly.

His face crumbled. 'What?'

She sat down and buried her face in her palms. He came and sat beside her and removed her hands so he could look her directly in the eyes. 'Why are you talking like this, Ogadinma?'

She wanted to turn her face away so she wouldn't see the confusion in his eyes and feel sorry for him. And yet, she still wanted to draw a line in the sand and mark their boundaries.

'I will not become your property. This is not why I left Tobe,' she told him.

'But Ogadinma, I haven't treated you like that.'

'You didn't tell me you were coming.'

'I only wanted to surprise you.'

'You can't just want to surprise me, Kelechi. This reminds me so much of living with Tobe. He was domineering and made decisions concerning me without consulting me, and expected me to dance to his tune. I am learning to stand on my own. I would rather be shot, be done with all of this, than return to that life, ever again.'

'I am sorry. I should have called you before coming here.'

'We can only be friends, Kelechi, nothing more.'

'What are you saying to me, Ogadinma? Look at me in the eye and tell me what you mean.'

But she did not look at him. She stood and went to the window, looked out at the empty backyard and wished he was not so polite. She wished he would make a careless comment, so she would have a reason to send him away, so she would not have to feel like a terrible human being.

'We can only be friends and nothing more,' she said softly.

He bowed his head and stared at the space between his parted feet. For a long time he stayed that way, and she wondered what he was thinking. When he lifted his head again, he smiled through pained eyes. 'You are an interesting woman, Ogadinma.'

'I just don't want to be committed in any relationship. Not at this time. I am still trying to find myself.'

'Can I still call you?'

She finally came and sat beside him. 'Yes, please call anytime you want.'

He nodded, smiled, but the skin of his face appeared so tight that the smile looked painful.

'Do you want some jollof rice? I also have cold water in the fridge.'

'Yes, thank you.'

She called Nnanna the following week. It seemed like a lifetime since they last spoke. She had woken that morning, yearning to speak with him. She dialled Nnanna's office and left him a message, and then she went into the room to hang her clothes in the wardrobe. For the first time since she moved into the apartment, it began to feel like home.

21

N nanna and Ifeoma appeared at her door the following morning. 'Nnanna. Ifeoma. *Kedu*? Please come inside,' she said.

Nnanna walked in, but Ifeoma remained outside. 'So, it is true? I can't even believe this.'

It had been more than a year and Ifeoma had put on weight. She no longer had any neck, so to speak, and her hips were now wider, her breasts fuller. Ogadinma was so surprised by the changes that, for a moment, she did not notice that the disgust on her cousin's face was directed at her.

'Please come inside, Ifeoma,' she said.

Ifeoma came inside. Nnanna had already taken up the seat by the TV. He had filled out: his face, half-swallowed by a beard, was fuller and toned, and his arms rippled with muscles. Ifeoma went to sit beside him. Side by side, they looked different. Like Coke and Fanta, they looked nothing like siblings.

'I have drinks in the fridge,' she told them.

'We don't want anything,' Ifeoma said. 'We didn't come here to drink.'

Ogadinma stood back. 'So, what did you come here to do?'

'Why did you dump your son like your mother did you?'

Ogadinma folded her arms across her chest. 'I see you have come to judge me.'

'That is not why we have come,' Nnanna began to speak.

'Hold on. My comment is directed at Ifeoma.' Ogadinma turned to face her cousin. 'I will advise that you watch your mouth, you hear me? I do not live in your father's house any more. You will watch how you talk to me.'

'Ogadinma, please sit down,' Nnanna said. 'Stop shouting.'

Ifeoma stood up. 'No, let her insult me. I came to her – what do I even call this place? Her boyfriend's house? – that's why she can talk to me like that. Your mates are working hard to keep their marriages, but you have been so blinded by privilege you think it is an easy world out there. That's why you were heartless enough to leave your son and move into another man's house,' Ifeoma spat.

Ogadinma turned to Nnanna. 'I called you and you brought this uncouth girl to insult me?'

'Yes, I am uncouth—'

'Ifeoma, sit down and shut your mouth or get out of this place.' Nnanna stood up.

Ifeoma was still speaking. 'It seems you have lost your mind, you shameless and heartless woman!'

'It is not my fault that you look so miserable, Ifeoma. So, do not pile your frustrations on me.'

'You are very stupid for mocking me—'

'That's it, go home!'

Nnanna pulled Ifeoma by the hand, dragging her out of the house, but she was still shouting. 'That thing you are looking for, you will get it. Ọ kwa nwoke ahụ na-agụ gị, you will soon get tired of those men and crawl back to Tobe, then he will teach you a lesson, you disgrace of a woman!' Ifeoma's words rang long after she had left the compound.

Ogadinma sat, shaken. Nnanna returned some minutes later.

'I didn't know she would do that. I am sorry.' He came to sit beside her. 'I am still in shock, Ogadinma. I can't believe you left everything behind.'

She swiped at her tears, upset with herself that she let Ifeoma make her feel small. For a moment, she wished she could refuse allegiance to her family. But erasing them would be like peeling skin from flesh, meat from bones, the most painful death.

'You shouldn't have left your son like that,' Nnanna was saying. 'You left that little boy. I don't think you understand what you have done.'

'I understand, because my mother did it.' She drew in a breath. 'I used to resent my mother for leaving, but I don't any more. I don't know why she left, but if she experienced a quarter of the horror your uncle put me through, then I am glad she did.'

'He loved you too much.'

She shook her head and stared at her hands. There was an irritating pulse by the side of her head. How ignorant you are, she thought, how stupidly ignorant. She didn't respond to that comment because she knew that if she did, she would hurt him with harsh words, and he might never visit her again. She wanted him to visit again.

'How is your girlfriend?' she asked him instead.

He gave her a forced smile, and then he took a while before he answered, perhaps because he understood that she was not yet ready to talk about Tobe, that talking about him would cause them to say hurtful things to each other. 'Ada is fine,' he finally said. 'She has an offer from an advertising firm here in Lagos as a creative director.'

'That is good news.'

'I am going to marry her.'

'I would be mad if you didn't.' She rubbed his shoulder and stood up. 'I want to make jollof rice. You are welcome to help, or you can sit in the kitchen and talk about anything else but your uncle.'

They worked side by side in the kitchen. Nnanna sliced the tomatoes and pepper and onions, while she parboiled the rice and prepared the fish broth. He made the sauce and mixed it with the rice before adding the fish broth and spice. He tasted the mixture, added some salt, before setting the pot on the stove. She smiled sadly. Ada was going to marry a good husband.

Later, they sat in the parlour, eating and talking. The rice was spicy, just like she wanted it. Tension had lifted from the air. They watched TV, and she could almost breathe well.

'Once we marry, the first thing is to make sure she does not get pregnant. No babies until, maybe, after two or three years,' he said out of the blue.

She turned to him. 'Why?'

'I want to enjoy my wife. Just the two of us and no one else.'

'That doesn't explain why you don't want children early. Isn't that why men marry women – to get their wives pregnant quickly and have children?'

'That's not what I want.' He shrugged. 'I want to enjoy my wife first without all those distractions.'

'You think children are a distraction?'

'I am not saying they are. But they do distract. A woman bears a child and it gets all the attention. The couple spend less time together. And over the years they have more children and they spend the best of their years raising them. Then, one day, eighteen or twenty years later, these children pack their things and leave for university or wherever – they just leave, and the couple become strangers. I don't want that. The memories we will make together in the first two years will ensure we don't end up as strangers after our children leave home.'

She pondered his words. 'What if Ada wants to get pregnant immediately?'

'I will make her understand why we need to understand ourselves first.'

'What if she insists?'

He shrugged. 'Then I will have no choice other than to cram all the memories into nine months, before the child comes.' He pushed his plate away. 'I know what you are thinking: she is older than me and shouldn't waste time. But, you know what I think? I just want to be happy with the person I have chosen to spend my life with.'

She shook her head. He didn't get it yet. 'You know what I was thinking? If Tobe were half the man you are, I would not have left.' She began to gather the plates. He stopped her.

'I will clean up later. Sit, please. There are things I must say to you.'

She sat.

He spoke slowly, as though testing the words for bluntness before rolling them off his tongue. 'I was trying to hold fast to the image I had of you and Uncle Tobe. I was trying to understand. I am sorry if I said the wrong things.'

'It is okay.'

'I see you are happier. And if ending your marriage with Tobe brought you peace, I support your decision.'

'Thank you.'

A pause. 'There is something you should know. Tobe has been sick for many months now.'

Something lurched to her chest. 'He is sick?'

'He is getting better now. But for many months, he was sick. His stomach started bloating. At a point, he looked like a heavily pregnant woman. His face was so swollen, all of his body was. He hurt when you touched him. They said it is a liver disease.'

Her heart thumped furiously, so much that when she spoke, she barely heard herself. 'How is he?'

'He is almost better. He has resumed going to work. He is doing well.'

'Am I supposed to feel sorry for him?'

'I haven't asked you to.'

'Okay, because I don't.' She wanted to believe it, and she said those words to herself over and over, although her insides wouldn't stop trembling, her hands wouldn't stop shaking. 'What about my son?' she asked.

'He is living with my mum. He looks just like you.'

She nodded. 'I knew he would,' she said. There was a hot tingling at the back of her eyes and she suppressed the desire to dissolve into a fit of hopeless tears.

He looks just like you. The words played over and over again in her mind, formed a loop, haunted her. She fell asleep thinking of his face, but she could no longer remember what he looked like. She woke after twelve, her body bathed with sweat, as she tried to remember him; the shade of his skin, how he smiled when he dreamed, how he cried when he was hungry. All of those important pieces had slipped away. She was devastated. Was this what it meant to lose someone? The room was closing in on her. She wept until her eyes hurt.

She called Kelechi in the morning, and when he picked up the phone, she tried to speak but cries surged up her throat. He could not comfort her, and this made things worse. She ended the call shortly after and didn't pick it up when he called back. She went to her flat and locked herself in and didn't answer the door when Oga Deji knocked to inform her that Kelechi had rung again.

She found Kelechi at her door the following morning. He did not ask why she couldn't say what had made her cry; he simply wrapped his arms around her and held her.

'I am here,' he said. 'I am not going anywhere until everything is all right.'

She pulled away, sniffed. 'Ah, I have cried too much,' she said. She tried to laugh. He laughed too.

'Tell me what happened.'

'I can't remember my son's face.'

'Come with me.' He led her into the flat.

Inside, he brought her a glass of water and gave her his kerchief. She blew hard, sniffed and gathered herself together. 'I am a terrible woman. Only a terrible mother would leave her baby behind.'

'You and "terrible" do not belong in the same sentence. You left because you wanted to survive, you wanted to be alive for him. And you haven't stopped thinking about him.'

'He has forgotten me. My aunt is the only mother he knows now.' She leaned against the sofa and gazed at the ceiling. She imagined, fleetingly, if she should steal her son. The idea was so silly, like something out of a movie, that a small wry smile appeared on her face.

'Why are you smiling?'

She sighed and shook away the ridiculous thought. 'I hear he looks just like me.'

22

Shopping at the supermarket two streets from hers, she found the large salon filled with hairdressers and makeup artists. Intrigued, she walked into the salon. The lady at the reception said it was a beauty school, that the hairdressers and makeup artists were students of the owner, Madam Vonne.

'Are you here to register or to braid your hair?' the woman asked as cheerily as she could, eyeing the bag of groceries in Ogadinma's hand.

'How much is your registration fee?' Ogadinma asked.

The receptionist told her the cost. 'When do you want to begin?'

'Is tomorrow too early?'

'Tomorrow is perfect.' The receptionist's smile had stretched from ear to ear as she brought out the registration pack.

Ogadinma fumbled with her purse. She had some change left, not enough for the registration fee but enough to show commitment.

As soon as she got home, she pulled out her bag and brought out the stash she had left at the bottom, underneath her clothes, and hurried off to make the payment. It would take six months to complete a training session, and though it felt like a lifetime, she was too excited to worry about the passage of time.

The salon was the size of a flat that must, from the positioning of the pillars and the bathroom, have been an apartment whose walls were knocked down and fitted with hairdryers, sinks, chairs, countertops and cubicles where young women worked on clients' faces, their boxful of make-up items propped on their tables.

Ogadinma stood in the middle of the organized chaos the following morning, staring as people walked up and down, getting their working tools ready, settling down on arranged seats. She had never thought she would go to school again, and now she was a student. Although this was far from her earlier dreams, she was glad she was finally in a classroom. She closed her eyes and smiled; she was contented, and this filled her belly with something warm, filled her mouth with something sweet. Someone touched her from behind, and a familiar voice spoke. 'I know you.'

Ogadinma whirled around. 'Oma!'

'You live in Aba?'

'I visited. I am Ogadinma.'

'*Ehen*, Ogadinma! I never forget a face!' Oma chuckled.

Oma said she had come to learn new tricks. Twice a year, she interned with skilful hairdressers and make-up artists whose work was shown in top magazines. 'Styles change every day, so I am always learning new things,' she said. 'I saw Madam Vonne's work in *Society People* and loved what she does with contours and shadows. Her hairstyles are better than those in *Vogue*.'

She introduced Ogadinma to Madam Vonne, a small churlish woman who spoke with a thick Anambra accent. The woman merely lifted her brows to acknowledge them before turning her attention to a new client.

'She has a shitty attitude,' Oma said afterwards. 'She recently married one small boy like that and now insists everyone must add "madam" to her name, as a sign of respect. You know, as a married woman.'

Ogadinma hissed. 'Does she really need to put her marital status in everyone's face?'

'I don't blame her o. People disrespected her because she was unmarried, even though she is the most successful hairdresser in Lagos. So, she got herself a small boy, married him and took his name, and now wants everyone to call her madam.'

The training at the salon began. Ogadinma and Oma had opted to learn the art of makeup and so they watched Madam Vonne work on a client, listened as she took them through every step, every trick. Oma's eyes followed Madam Vonne's hand as she traced the eyebrows, as she lined the brims and coated the lids. Madam Vonne explained why she used a certain shade of concealer, why she angled or softened the brow, why she chose a colour of lipstick, the brands she preferred to work with. As she spoke, Ogadinma's gaze kept drifting to Madam Vonne's face, the mouth thinned in concentration, the fingers toughened from labour.

Despite the terseness of Madam Vonne's words, despite what everyone thought about the woman and how they loathed her stiffness, despite the silence that fell in the salon whenever she walked in, the apprentices all respected her. They nodded when she gave instructions, they smiled when a flicker appeared by her lips, and spoke enthusiastically when she paused to chat with them. In the salon, everyone did as Madam Vonne wanted, and none rebelled against her will because they knew they would be the ones to lose out if the relationship went wrong; Madam Vonne was the best at this job.

The classes ended on Fridays and Madam Vonne ran a normal business over the weekend, but Ogadinma always showed up. On her first Saturday, she hovered by as Madam Vonne worked on clients, and presented her with every makeup item she reached for. Why had she taken on this job? Because she was bored at home? That was true, for she had woken that morning feeling the need to leave the apartment. But as they worked on client after client, she admitted that it was because she liked the woman and the authority she wielded. And Madam Vonne was not repulsed by her presence.

Madam Vonne offered her a bottle of Coke and meat pie afterwards and asked if she was free the following Sunday to work on a big client who was getting married.

Ogadinma said yes.

Ogadinma had been working with Madam Vonne for three months when she decided she would no longer hide her marital status. She had always steered clear of her colleagues who asked intrusive questions. Some invited her to their church for programmes designed for single women searching for husbands.

'I met my fiancé the weekend after I attended one of them,' said Ifunanya, the Anambra woman who spoke with a deep Nnewi accent that reversed her *r* for *l*, such that 'road' became 'load', and 'lawyer' rolled out of her tongue thick and slow, as 'rawyer'. 'I knew Chinedu was my husband when he *reft* his table at the *lestaulant* in *Rekki* and offered to sit with me. He is *vely lich*!'

Ifunanya laughed a lot too, even over inane things, but it was always a genuine chortle that seemed to start from the pit of her stomach and spread over her body in swift waves. And this made it impossible, no matter what a nuisance she had become, for Ogadinma to rebuke her.

So, she tolerated Ifunanya. She would nod when the woman went on and on about her church, about her fiancé, about her upcoming wedding, and then Ogadinma would smile and quickly change the conversation to makeup and hairstyles, because if there was something Ifunanya loved second, it was makeup and hair. But that day in June, when she resolved to stop hiding her status, she wanted to slap Ifunanya.

She had just walked into the salon when Ifunanya came over and thrust a wedding invitation card into her hand. She wanted Ogadinma to be her bridesmaid because she was so sure Ogadinma would find a husband at the wedding.

'There is no man that will meet you that won't want you as his wife.' Ifunanya was smiling.

'I used to be married and I have a son, too,' Ogadinma said.

Ifunanya's smile disappeared. 'And you have been hiding this?'

'Hiding what? There was no need to come here every day and announce that I used to be a married woman, just as there wasn't any need for you to keep hassling me about marriage.'

Ifunanya lowered her eyes in remorse but she still wanted Ogadinma to attend the wedding, and when Ogadinma agreed, the light returned to her eyes and she hurried off to distribute the cards to their other colleagues.

Without warning, the image of Ogadinma's father came back and she pictured herself telling him how he had hurt her. She had never considered the possibility that he would one day not want anything to do with her. He had always been set in his ways. Disciplined and stubborn. Still, he made her bed when she went to Lagos, swept the floor and dusted the windows. She wondered how he was faring now, if he still cleaned her room, if he thought about her. But then a light shudder ran through her; she remembered the whips, how firm his voice was when they last spoke. He would not change his ways and she would never return to Tobe, which she knew was all it would take to win back her father's good graces. She could not afford to put herself in a violent situation ever again just to please him.

That evening, after class had ended, she trekked to the eatery in Ikoyi, where she met Karim for the first time.

The hall was crowded. People stood in long queues. The two women in the front were chuckling over a joke. Karim stood well away from them, looking through the *Newswatch* magazine spread open in his hands. The women would not stop talking and laughing, and from the way he twisted his face, she could tell that they were interrupting his concentration. And then, he whipped round and lashed out at them.

'Please, can you stop making noise,' he said. 'Some of us are trying to concentrate here.'

The women began to mutter apologies until Ogadinma spoke up.

'You don't have to apologize to him,' she said.

They looked at her, and then at him.

'This is a public place, a noisy eatery for God's sake, not a library.'

Karim put away the magazine. 'How is this any of your business, please?' He was clearly embarrassed, more so because the women seemed to be agreeing with her; they glared at him and turned away to resume their small talk.

'It is my business when you feel you can intimidate women because you are what – a man?'

'I would have said the same thing if they were men.'

'You would not dare. Or you would have gone over there, where those loud men are, and demanded that they keep their voices low, too.'

He glanced over at the other side of the hall, saw the snickering men and turned back to her. 'I didn't mean to shout,' he said finally.

'You should be telling the women, not me.'

He looked around, but the women were already placing their orders, had already forgotten about him. He turned to Ogadinma. 'So, do you do this all the time: you go about rescuing women from men?'

'I wish I could.'

He smiled. She stared at him, at the broadness of his shoulders, the evenness of his skin that was the colour of new yam, wondering how smooth it would feel if she ran her fingers over the length of his arms, and why such a rude man should have such fine skin. Embarrassed by her silly thoughts, she walked over to place her order. She did not turn to look at him again.

After she found a table to sit and eat her moin-moin, Karim showed up, carrying a plate of jollof rice.

'May I sit with you?' He pointed to the empty chair before her.

She began to say no but her old manners, which constantly crept into her daily relations with people, begged her to be nice.

She waved him over and he sat, settling right in front of her. The table was short and square and there wasn't enough space, meaning that their hands would touch once they began to eat, and that was the least unsettling part: he would be looking directly in her eyes, watching her every move, from the lift of her fork to how she chewed her food, even how she drank her water. The unexpected intimacy made her self-conscious; she, who had only that morning sworn to be a strong, unbending woman. And so, she stared at her moin-moin, watching it turn cold.

'I am Ogadinma,' she offered.

'My name is Karim,' he said.

He didn't extend his hand and she flushed with relief. She was not ready for the touch of skin; her mind was running in circles as her gaze hovered over him. He carried himself well without effort. He started to talk, and she watched his lips move. It had been a while since she observed a man like this, since her head got filled with silly thoughts. And this amused and irritated her.

Karim talked on and on, and she listened; he could not read her mind anyway, and this comforted her. Then he said he visited the eatery often and had never seen her before; he would have noticed her because she could never hide in a crowd. He grinned as he said this, his eyes crinkling at the corners. He was flirting but he was careful, too, not to appear too forward.

'This is my first time here,' she said. 'It appears you watch everyone, or should I say every woman, who comes in here.'

He seemed taken aback, only for an instant. And then he smiled, two dimples sinking deep in his cheeks. And Ogadinma would later remember it as the moment they bonded. She liked his smile, the flash of his coconut-white teeth as he said, 'No. No, I run a business place next door. How is it even possible not to watch women who come here? Come on. I noticed you because of the little drama,' he said with pious emphasis.

He dug into his jollof rice, and then glanced at her plate, which still sat untouched, his eyes asking if she didn't want to eat any more.

She wiped her fork with a napkin and began to eat.

'So, what do you do next door?' she asked, picking through her moin-moin, forking tiny pieces so she could chew without opening her mouth too wide.

'I run an art studio. I am a visual artist and a photographer.'

'Nice.'

He shrugged.

'I could never draw a straight line,' she said, and immediately felt she sounded stupid, uninteresting. 'I am a makeup artist,' she added quickly.

He lifted a brow. 'Awesome. Do you have a studio yet?'

'Not yet. I still work under my boss. You could be my next client *sef.*'
'I don't wear makeup.' He laughed.
'But you have a girlfriend, a wife?' She glanced at his ring finger;
he was not wearing any, and she was surprisingly filled with relief.
'I don't have a girlfriend or a wife.'

They watched each other, contemplated his declaration which
sank heavily between them, taunting. He had put the first foot forward, and his eyes urged her to declare her status too.

'I am divorced, and I have a son, but he lives with his father,'
she said, then held his eyes, examined his face to see how he took
her declaration. Nnanna had informed her the week before that her
father had finally returned the bride price Tobe paid, nullifying their
marriage. The news had brought her relief; she was no longer tethered to Tobe. But now, as she watched Karim lean back in his seat,
his face seemingly folding in, she remembered her father's long talk
about second-hand women and how men want nothing to do with
them. 'You have a problem with divorced women?' she asked Karim.

'No, not at all. I don't.'

He had finished eating his rice and had begun to gather his things.
And for a moment, she was worried that he was in a haste to leave,
that she had scared him with her truth. Something heavy sank in
her stomach. She bent over to finish off the last of her moin-moin.

'Would you like to share a drink with me? I know a bar near
here,' he said.

She looked up. Blood was thudding in her ears. 'I wouldn't want
to be a bother.'

'Please.'

She considered this; there was an earnestness in his eyes that
tugged at her, that warmed her heart. So, she gathered her bag and
followed him.

The bar was right across the road and crowded with people even
though it was only seven in the evening. Perhaps it was so because it
was a weekend and workers, many of them dressed in business suits,
most probably bankers, finally found the time to mingle. Karim led

them to a table at the far end of the bar, a booth which opened directly into a large space lit with disco lights and occupied by couples who wanted to stay away from the glare of roving eyes.

'This doubles as a nightclub,' Ogadinma said after she sat.

'Yes.' He raised his voice because the music and the chattering from other booths were too loud, so that people huddled close, faces almost meeting at the middle of the tables, in order to hear each other. 'Do you club?'

'No, never. When I was a small girl, we were told only bad girls go to clubs. I feel like a bad girl now. I like this feeling.' She leaned close. She could smell his cologne. Her heart was racing with something new, a feeling that was so fresh, so strange. She wanted to kiss him. It felt like a reckless but right thing to do. She thought back to two years ago when she had sat demurely in a bar with Tobe and his friends, listening to them talk politics and about their childhoods; how she blended with the background rather than shone. Now, she didn't need to lurk in the shadows or seek anyone's permission before she spoke. Now, she could dictate the tone and flow of her conversation with a man.

'This place will fill up in a few hours.' He was leaning close, too, so that their faces were inches apart. 'I haven't been in a club in ages. I mean, I come here to drink sometimes, but I never stay long enough for the music and dance. Do you want to stay?'

She reached across the table and touched his hand and realized what she felt with him: confidence. With him, she was comfortable in her own body; she was not ashamed of being silly or doing whatever she wanted.

A waiter arrived, and they ordered drinks. Jack Daniel's with a dash of lime for him. She had never liked alcohol, but she asked for what he ordered. He waited until she took a sip of her mixture and then he began to laugh as her face crumbled.

'I like it,' she protested. 'It is a little strong, but I like it.' She had never understood why anyone would like alcohol. Once when she was younger, she had uncorked the bottle of brandy her father hid behind the TV shelf, the one he brought out only when his friends visited, and took a long swig. The dry spirit burned her tongue and she spat it out, but some had already travelled down her throat, sending a burst of fire into her stomach. For many hours, her head reeled, her legs were unsteady. But she came to hate alcohol after she saw how it transformed Tobe into a violent stranger. She stared down at her glass, took a long sip this time. This wasn't as bad as she had expected. 'I like it,' she said again.

She was already feeling the buzz of the alcohol as he talked about his studio, the works he had created and his inspiration. She was flying as he listed his solo exhibitions at the National Theatre in Lagos, his works that had also been shown in Venice and Taipei and Beijing and London and Dakar. He was studying Law at the University of Benin, but dumped it for Painting and Photography.

'I couldn't stay in school. I just don't understand how people can sit in one place and listen to others talk for hours. I almost went mad,' he said.

'You are doing what gives you joy, that's the most important thing.' She was happy, inexplicably excited. She finished her glass and requested another shot.

'And you, are you doing what makes you happy?'

'I finally am.' She reached out and ran a finger along the bridge of his nose. Although she was drowsy and silly, there was a certain warmth that came with knowing that she was living on her own terms and no one was dictating to her. 'I want to kiss you.' She leaned forward and prodded his lips open with her tongue, kissed him. She pulled back. His eyes were drifting shut. She kissed him again.

The music grew louder. She didn't know what the time was and didn't bother to check. She led him to the dance floor, which had filled up. She danced up close to his body. She was floating, her body rising with his, until he was the only person she could see.

When they came outside later, the car park was filled with couples clumped together and whispering drowsily into each other's ears. The faint sound of music came from the open doors of the club.

'I should get a taxi. Can I get a taxi here?' she asked him. He was leaning too close, his eyes hooded under the thick brows.

'Let me drop you off,' he said.

'I will take a taxi.'

'Please.'

'No.' She backed away from him. Her cautious self had taken over her mind. She needed time away from him, to think. She had acted too wildly, and now she needed to think her actions through. She flagged down a taxi.

He brought out his business card. 'Please, take this. Do you have yours?'

She took his card and did not look at it as she shoved it into her pocket. 'No, no, I don't have a business card.'

He brought out a second card and a pen. 'Could you tell me your number? Please?'

She called out Oga Deji's telephone number as she headed to the taxi and didn't wait long enough for him to reconfirm. Then she entered the car and told the driver her direction.

'I will call you,' Karim said. He was peeping in from the window. 'Good night, Ogadinma.'

She waved and then sank back in the car as they eased away from the park, and she could finally breathe.

ACKNOWLEDGEMENTS

Because I could never have done this without the help of my community, my family, my friends – all those keep giving me the reason to continue on this path:

Cate DiCharry, Noni Salma, Rebecca Jamieson, Tracy Haught and Kelsi Long, Amara Nicole Okolo – friends who became my sisters and support system; Erin Stalcup, Justin Bigos, Rita Banerjee, Miciah Bay Gault – all my heroes at the VCFA, for giving me a safe place to create, to breathe. Julianna Baggot for lifting her voice and singing my praises whenever that song is needed. Othuke Ominiabohs, for showing up at the perfect time. My parents Fred and Nkiruka Okoye, and my siblings who anchor me to this world – Ijeoma, Chimezie, Tochukwu and Nonso, for having my back, always.

Nwanosike, for believing in me and my dreams.

Christopher Merrill and everyone at the University of Iowa's International Writing Program, for giving me a home when I needed it and keeping those doors open for me.

Claire Anderson-Wheeler, my agent who saw the promise in the manuscript and believed in it.

And everyone who understood that this is all I have always wanted to do.

Ka odili unu na mma!

ABOUT THE AUTHOR

UKAMAKA OLISAKWE is a Nigerian novelist, short story writer and screenwriter. In 2014 she was chosen as one of Sub-Saharan Africa's most promising writers under the age of 40. She was born in Kano, Nigeria, and in 2016 was a resident at the University of Iowa's International Writing Program. Her writing has appeared in *Catapult*, the *New York Times* and *The Rumpus*. She wrote the screenplay for *The Calabash*, a Nigerian television series that premiered in 2015 on Africa Magic Showcase.

INDIGO
PRESS

Sign up for our newsletter and receive exclusive updates, including extracts, podcasts, event notifications, competitions and more.

www.theindigopress.com/newsletter

Follow The Indigo Press:

@PressIndigoThe
@TheIndigoPress
@TheIndigoPress